Sunny
Book One of The Weather Girls

Jennifer Lynn Cary

Tandem Services Press

What Readers Are Saying

The Crockett Chronicles

"I love historical novels and this one did not disappoint. I was caught up from the first sentence and completely in love with the Crocketts by the end. Can't wait to follow along their next journey. Well done!" –Virginia Denise

"I love this book! The story is soooooo engaging! I can hardly put it down!"—DeNage

Tales of the Hob Nob Annex Café

"This is a well written book that hooks you on the first page. It's a very enjoyable read that makes you forget about all your troubles and step back in time. I loved this book and look forward to what this author writes next." –Ann Ferri

"I loved reading this book! It had me intrigued from the first page, and as the stories began, I could hardly wait to turn the page to see what happened next! Love the mix of true facts mixed with some good, clean, fun fiction! Easy, quick read. I highly recommend this book!" –CatSmit

The Relentless Series

"I lost my heart in this book, caught up in the lives of each character. I remember these times, which made it more real to me. I had tears of joy, tears of sorrow, grief, and smiles in the unexpected. Great story and hard to put down. Keep reading.... You won't regret it."—Novabelle

"I enjoyed another book by Jennifer Cary! As with all her books the story held your attention from the beginning to the end and I look forward to reading all her future books!"—Mary Rima

"I live in Indiana so I know of the places this book talks about. I so absolutely LOVED this story. It's the first one in this series I've read. I'm glad because I feel it should be the first book as it tells of the 2 families & how they connect. It so touched my heart that at times I cried. I couldn't put it down after starting it so anxious to know how things would turn out with all the difficulties Val & Jimmy had. I'm sure the other books in this series are equally as great."—Pat

The Traveling Prayer Shawl

"When her sister's inheritance depends on it, Cami must do the thing she resolved she'd never do, the thing which will break her heart as well as add one more tough task to her already overstuffed calendar. She must fulfill her grandmother's last request - and what's more, there's a deadline that puts in jeopardy her major project at work. As she begins working on the request, she finds even more complications. The inheritance may raise a conflict of interests. How Cami negotiates these and other potential pitfalls made for an interesting and warmhearted story.

Recommended to those who enjoy Christian Women's Fiction and readers who enjoy Debbie Macomber's stories."—Dana McNeely

"I loved this book so much I hated for it to end!"—Cindy

Also By Jennifer Lynn Cary

The Crockett Chronicles Series:

The Patriarch: : Book 1

The Sojourners: Book 2

The Prodigal: Book 3

Tales of the Hob Nob Annex Café
The Relentless Series:

Relentless Heart: Book 1

Wedding Bell Blues: Book 2

Relentless Joy: Book 3

Silver Bell Christmas: Book 4

The Traveling Prayer Shawl
The Weather Girls Trilogy:

Sunny

Stormy (releasing October 2021)

Windy (releasing November 2021)

Dedicated to my hometown, Kokomo.

I love that I got to grow up surrounded by your uniqueness, your history and most of all, your citizens.

A wonderful place to call home.

Trust in the Lord with all your heart and lean not on your own understanding; in all your ways submit to him, and he will make your paths straight. ~ Proverbs 3: 5-6 NIV

Contents

1. Prologue   1

2. Chapter One   3

3. Chapter Two   17

4. Chapter Three   31

5. Chapter Four   45

6. Chapter Five   59

7. Chapter Six   75

8. Chapter Seven   91

9. Chapter Eight   105

10. Chapter Nine   119

11. Chapter Ten   133

12. Chapter Eleven   147

13. Chapter Twelve   161

14. Chapter Thirteen   175

15. Chapter Fourteen   191

16. Chapter Fifteen   205

Epilogue   217

Acknowledgments   221

Author's Note   222

About Author   224

Sneak Preview of Stormy   225

Prologue

May 20, 1947 Los Angeles, California

Aaron Day scooped up the pink bundle and cooed at the scrunched face staring back while he bounce-stepped to the window. A glance at Cheryl, his wife, told him she followed his every move.

This was their first child. A tiny, exquisite little girl. But she needed a name.

Then, as he turned to gaze out on the magnificent Southern California spring morning, the perfect name for their perfect baby bloomed in his head. Inspired by the azure sky, he knew exactly what he'd christen his firstborn.

Aaron drew the receiving blanket back more and pointed the vista out to his daughter. "See the beautiful cloudless horizon, sweetie? You don't understand yet about the glorious weather and golden rays shining in through this glass. But you will. One day you're going to embody all the promise today holds." His fingertips skimmed over her feathery blonde hair before he leaned in and kissed her wrinkled forehead, her eyes continuing to bore into him all the while. "I name you after this day of your birth. You are Sunny May. You'll be a light in our house, filling each room with laughter and joy."

"Aaron, her last name is Day. Must you do that to her? Sunny May Day? Even Sunny Day's gonna get some cracks." Cheryl rolled to her side in her hospital bed and leaned on her elbow.

"People will remember her. If she goes into the entertainment business with us someday, she's got a ready-made name. She'll be recognizable."

"True. But she'll hate us for doing this to her."

Aaron shook his head. "Not if we tell her the story. From day one, she'll understand that her name is perfect for her. She is Sunny May Day. Yeah," He sighed. "She's going to do big things with that name."

Cheryl chuckled and laid back on her pillow. "You might be right. It would be a great ingenue name. Maybe she can follow in my footsteps with the movies."

Aaron brought the baby to her mother and cradled her in the crook of Cheryl's arm. "She can do whatever she wants—music, acting, designing skyscrapers for all I care. I just want her to stay our happy little sunshine girl. She'll be a success. I have no doubt."

Chapter One

February 16, 1970 Governor's Office, State Capitol, Indianapolis, Indiana

"Are you Sunny Day?"

Sunny glanced at the delivery guy who interrupted her concentration. These figures needed to be collated and organized before the governor's meeting in an hour. "Yes, that's me." She waited for the snicker or not-so-funny quip.

"These are for you." He handed her a vase overflowing with two dozen long-stemmed roses.

She'd been so intent on nailing the poor kid for making fun of her name, she'd missed the giant bouquet in his hands. "They're gorgeous." After clearing a corner of her desk, she took the delivery from him and adjusted the flowers. "Oh, a tip. She tugged her purse from the bottom drawer and dug out a couple quarters. "Thank you."

He nodded and moved to leave before halting. "Your name is Sunny Day?"

She fisted her hands, holding her temper in check. "Yes, I was born on a delightful Southern California day, full of sunshine and promise, so my parents deemed me Sunny." No need to get her middle name involved. "Born on a sunny day, named Sunny Day. There you go." She turned her back on him, resisting the urge to ask for her quarters back, and swiped the card from the arrangement. Who sent her these beautiful...?

No. Nope. No way. She tore the little card to pieces before pulling the roses from their holder and shoving them into the trash can. Then, after swiping the vase from her desk, she trotted off to the Ladies Room to dump the water before chucking the cut crystal in her wastepaper basket after the blooms.

Teresa Knept strolled past. "Saw someone got flowers—" Her gaze fell on the stuffed receptacle. "What did you do that for?"

"They wilted." Sunny returned to her figures.

"What do you mean? I gasped when he brought them up."

"Yeah, me too. Until I read the card. There aren't enough roses to fix last weekend. Some Valentine's day."

Teresa leaned a hip against the corner of Sunny's desk. "What did he do?"

In truth, she'd rather just forget about it. And him. If he couldn't be bothered to call, explain he'd be late, or that he had an emergency, or anything...After all, she'd given him Saturday and Sunday to contact her. But this? Flowers and only a "love, Brock" scrawled on the card? Did he imagine that's all it took?

She shook her head. "Not now. I've too much work, anyway. Maybe when I cool off, okay, Teresa?"

"Okay, Sunny. Let's meet at lunch." She pushed away from the desk, but after a step she bent to whisper in Sunny's ear.

"Looks like someone's about to get blindsided."

Sunny laid aside her pencil and glanced where her friend indicated.

Brock.

A big grin on his too handsome face while he waved at her coworkers as if he were a campaign hopeful, working the crowd.

Where did he mislay his brain?

He arrived at her desk and planted one on her cheek. Clueless.

"Hey beautiful. Did you…" Brock caught sight of the wastepaper basket. "Um, I guess you did. What's the matter? Didn't you like them?"

Sunny stood, fists clenched at her side. Her temper would take charge if she didn't gain control. She held her breath, starting her silent count while she rubbed her earlobe. She would not explode in her workspace. But this egomaniac tempted her to break that rule.

It took to number thirty to pour enough calm over her where she spoke without raising her voice. "Brock, I think you have mistaken me for someone you can manipulate. I do not want to see your big dopey grin or your thorn-filled flowers or your one-syllable name ever again. I hope I've made myself clear."

"But Sunshine Girl. I sent the roses to say I'm sorry." He flashed his little boy pout that was hard to resist. But this time his charm act failed.

"How did I know that Brock? You only signed your name. Nothing about what happened. Were you stranded on the highway? Bleeding in some hospital? You might've run off with a rock band for all I knew." She pushed his face away from her. "If this relationship had a chance, you destroyed it by standing me up on Valentine's Day. I am done. Goodbye, Brock."

"Sunny, baby, you can't mean that."

Before Sunny answered, she spotted another visitor headed her way. How did she get so popular? No one wanted her to finish this report. "May I help you?"

"Are you Sunny Day?"

Brock spun at the voice and his LA worthy tan drained from his face. "Venita."

Sunny watched the exchange between "Venita" and Brock, a spidy-tingle racing her spine. "Yes, I'm Sunny Day."

"Really." The woman shook her head. "You couldn't even find someone with a normal name." She snorted and then turned her full attention on Sunny. "And you, stupid name girl. Women capable of landing positions with the governor's office should be intelligent enough to avoid entanglements with married men. But let's be clear. He is married. To me. This is your last mistake. And I will have your job for it." She spun on her heel, all one hundred pounds of her, and thundered toward the executive offices as if she towered seven feet tall.

"Brock, what did she mean?"

"Sorry, Sunny." He followed the woman.

"Brock? You're married?"

He stared at the floor but nodded before taking the same route as his wife.

Married? She'd been dating a married man? Ever since New Year's? Well, another reason for good riddance. She held marriage as sacred and would not cause one to fall apart.

She glanced about the room, noticing her coworkers—some stared while others merely stole peeks. Her cheeks bloomed with heat and she brushed her bangs from her brow before sitting at her desk and picking up her pencil. With a swivel so no one saw her shame, she pulled her focus onto her job.

But the numbers wouldn't add. They danced around, the ones pointing at her, sharp little digits morphing into accusing arrows of condemnation as she tried to key them into the adding machine. She began the column again when her phone rang.

"Treasurer's Office. Miss Day speaking. How may I help you?"

"Sunny, it's Belinda. Can you come to HR, please?" Human Resources?

"Sure. I'll be right there." She hung up, grabbed a stenographer's pad and pencil, and headed for the next floor. After the drama in her public office area, stepping away from prying eyes proved a welcomed respite. She didn't wait for the elevator, not when taking the stairs beat it by minutes. A moment later she tapped at the jamb, then entered. Only Belinda. Seated behind her desk.

"Close the door, please, Sunny."

A chill went up her spine. Not good. "What's going on?"

Belinda stood and walked around to her. "Somewhere you've upset someone. I'm to let you go. Now."

Sunny sank into the chair, her legs giving way. "Fired? Now?" What? Even if that woman followed up on her threat, her boss called Sunny's work flawless. Her boss told her so many times. There'd been talk of being groomed for promotion in a couple months. "Why?"

Belinda shrugged. "It makes no sense to me, but the complaint comes from the governor's office. Like I said, you've upset someone. I need you to sign this paper and I'll cut you your final check. They want me to send a guard with you to get your things, but you won't cause a fuss, right?"

A guard? "I'm too confused to be a problem. What do I do?"

The sooner she complied, the sooner she'd skedaddle from this nightmare.

"Just sign here. I pointed out that you've been a model employee and deserved a severance besides what you are owed. They agreed." A moment later Belinda handed her a check, showing triple what she normally took home. Two weeks' severance then.

"I'm allowed to pick up my things?" Sunny tucked the check inside her steno pad, unable to meet Belinda's gaze.

"How about I walk up with you? That way it won't look so bad and I'm covered."

Sunny nodded. She'd never been this humiliated in her life. But she wasn't about to cry or cause a scene. Just get out of there. That's all she wanted to do. Get out.

She stood and Belinda followed her into the hall. "Can we take the stairs? Fewer people that way."

"Sure." Belinda opened the stairwell door.

They climbed the steps in silence. Why talk? Normal sounds fell muted. Even their footfalls on the cement treads echoed as if from far away. Sunny felt encased in a bubble that hushed the surrounding world.

At the top, Belinda let her hand rest on Sunny's shoulder a moment before entering the corridor. She offered kindness despite being forced to do a hatchet job. It wasn't Belinda's fault.

It was Brock's.

If he'd been a faithful husband, none of this would've happened.

Or did she own part of the blame?

Had she taken the time to look for telltale signs? Had she overlooked a signal that shouted "married?" What wrong did she commit that they must fire her?

At her desk, Sunny noticed the adding machine and financial books now sat elsewhere. Guess word leaked back and someone else got put onto her task. Well, considering the governor needed the figures, that made sense. Just another slap.

She gathered her purse, tucking in the small family photo she displayed to anyone who stopped by her desk. An extra tube of lipstick, a hairbrush, a brown bag lunch, and her latest book purchases—*Jonathan Livingston Seagull* and *Love Story*. Neither of which she'd started, seeing she hadn't made up her mind which to read first and had saved the decision for lunchtime.

Then she remembered her steno pad. She was too embarrassed to think.

Books and lunch in hand, her tooled-leather purse strap over her shoulder, she finally glanced up and caught Teresa's sympathetic gaze. With a forced smile, she wiggled her fingers in goodbye at the one friend she'd made in the office and walked with Belinda back to the stairs.

This time she heard the creak of the metal door as it swung on its hinge—like a cell door opening. Only she wasn't being locked in. They were about to lock her out.

At the next floor down, Belinda offered a handshake. "You're going to bounce back from this, Sunny. You have too much intelligence and talent. People who do things like this always end up getting theirs in the end. It was nice knowing you and if you need a reference, ask for me. I'll give you a good one."

That was more than Sunny could take. A tear forced its way down her cheek. She swiped it away from her jaw before it dripped and cleared her throat. "Thanks. I appreciate that. Goodbye." Because if she didn't get out of there now, she wouldn't be able to see to do it. Tears were going to fall. If only she could hold them off until she got to her car.

Belinda headed to her office and Sunny continued to the first floor.

Just as her hand grasped the handle, the stairwell door pulled away and someone bowled her over.

The next thing Sunny knew, she sat on her bottom at the base of the stairs glancing away from most chocolate eyes she'd ever seen.

"Are you all right?" Pat held out his palm to ease the lady to her feet. A petite blonde with big blue eyes swimming with a sheen of moisture. He must have hurt her. "Let me help you."

She took his hand but glanced away. "Thanks, I should've been paying better attention."

The tingles racing up his arm thickened his voice. "No." Pat shook his head. "My fault. I stormed the stairs, trying to beat that behemoth of an elevator." He reached for her bag, whose contents lay scattered on the concrete floor.

"I'll get it. I don't want to hold you up. You're in a hurry."

She stooped and reloaded her purse, flung the strap over her shoulder and grabbed at her other items.

He picked up *Love Story*. She's a reader. Of course, every woman over fifteen inhaled that book. He glanced at her other title. "Have you read *Jonathan Livingston Seagull*?"

She shook her head and accepted the paperback from him.

"No. If you'll excuse me. I'm sorry." Her face twitched as if she tried to control something, but she had yet to meet his gaze when she spoke. Instead, she shoved out the door. Out of his life.

The words "what a shame" bounced through his brain. But he brushed them away and with one more glance at the now closed door, he resumed his trek up the stairs, sure he'd still beat the elevator to the third floor.

Childhood friend Trey Haynes worked in finances. As long as he had a lunch break today, he might as well check if Trey would join him. Both manned jobs which placed them downtown, but somehow being able to catch up didn't happen often.

Pat decided to make an effort. He exited and found Trey's office, or open shared space. The guy sat bent and focused over a column of numbers, punching keys on an adding machine.

"Hey, did you forget about lunch?"

Trey looked up, a blank stare at Pat. Then a light glowed in his eyes and his face showed recognition. "Oh, man, I'm not going to get a lunch break today. It's been crazy around here, and I just had an urgent report dumped on me. Someone got canned. Now I gotta figure where he left off and finish this data form in the next ten minutes."

Pat glanced at his watch, gauging how much time he had. "Want me to wait?"

"Nah. We can try again another day. Thanks, anyway. I'm sorry."

"Hey, don't worry about it. I'll call you."

Trey waved, but his attention returned to the figures before him.

Pat started back to the hall. He still had time. Plus, a little company for lunch would've been nice. But his other friends worked farther away. No chance to meet them with the minutes remaining. He decided to go back to his office.

Just as he rounded the corner toward the exit, he spotted a familiar someone. He caught himself ducking on instinct and sighed. If he was ever going to smooth out their relationship, he first needed to stop avoiding her.

Did he want a relationship with her?

Yes, he had to admit he did. She was his big sister, after all. Though these days she stood about half his size. In stature. In measured personality, she loomed gigantic.

"Hey sis, how about lunch?"

The woman with the trademark Whitcomb raven hair glanced over her shoulder. Her face pinched for a moment, then she sighed. "Yeah, I could do with a nibble. Where do you want to take me?"

He chuckled. Well, he had invited her.

She clicked over in her heels, which gave her a couple added inches in height and took his arm. "I need to talk to you, anyway. Let's go to Mario's. Not far and I'm in the mood for Italian."

Pat covered her hand with his. So far, things were pleasant. A tasty lunch with pleasant conversation might help. "Sounds great."

Rather than make her take the stairs in those shoes, he resigned to riding the elevator with her. With others in the car, she didn't start a discussion, and he felt gun shy enough about what might trigger an explosion, so he enjoyed the quiet. Which lasted the couple of blocks to the restaurant. Then once seated, her expression revealed she was about to launch into something big.

"I'm glad to see you. I've been meaning to call. I need a favor."

A favor? Hm. At least she didn't yammer calling him the crowned prince and her a mere peasant struggling for notice.

"What kind of favor, sis?"

"I found this parcel up in Kokomo. A beautiful setting for a new high rise. If I can acquire the land, I expect I can push this project through. I'm having trouble, though, getting the owner to give me a definite deal. She keeps needing to think on it and other questions. Fairly sure she's stalling, and I don't want someone else to get that property."

The server stopped by with water and bread sticks. "Are you ready to order or shall I come back?"

"I'll have the pasta primavera." She ordered the same thing like clockwork.

Pat gave his usual choice—spaghetti and meatballs. He had no other conferences today. If he spilled on his tie, he had others in his office. He considered ordering for them both, but she would've taken that as him insinuating she lacked ability. Which floored him. She was more than capable.

Part of him understood why she struggled so to prove herself. But the other part wished she'd relax and not paint him with the same brush as their parents. He wasn't the problem.

However, the way their mother and father showed preferential treatment, it made him out the bad guy. And he hated that. He loved his older sister and wanted them to get along.

"So, tell me more about this parcel."

"I've got a chance, Pat. A real chance. This deal's loaded with potential and will bring a steady income to Whitcomb. I should be able to buy the land for a steal. With the economy as it is, I could negotiate something to be built quick and then offer midlevel housing netting a constant source of capital. Dad will have to admit I pulled off a major coupe and consider me for more than this token position."

"Sounds wonderful, kiddo. I'm proud of you." And he was.

"But..."

There's a but, and somehow she'd put his on the line. He knew it. "But?"

"I'm pretty sure the owner doesn't like me. I realize I come off too gung-ho, but I need this deal. Would you drive up to Kokomo and talk with her?" Man, she gave him the puppy dog look.

"Sis, I can't today. Got a brief to finish. Followed by two weeks of negotiation with Judge Maupin overseeing. Tell you what. I'm available after that. Two weeks is the soonest. Then my calendar is clear enough to leave the city."

She pouted. "All right. If that's your best. I feel it in my bones, someone's going to snap that property up."

"Is the location on the market or are you talking her into selling?"

"No, not yet. But she might get an idea. Oh, I hate to wait that long."

Pat sighed. "If I had time, I'd go. As it is, I carved out this lunchtime to meet with Trey, but he got stuck on an emergency project. I'd planned on heading back to the office to skip lunch before I saw you."

She smiled. "I'm glad you did. This is the nicest thing that's happened to me today. It's been pretty bleak."

He covered her hand. "I'm sorry. Want to talk about it?"

Perhaps she'd realize he cared.

She shook her head. "No, not really. I've already taken care of it. Just more fuel to add to Mom and Dad's fire. I'm incapable in their eyes."

"They don't believe that." Well, maybe. Not because she'd done anything, though.

"Yeah, they do. That's why this deal's so vital. If I land it, all by myself—and don't you dare mention that you sweet-talked that old woman into selling to me—they must admit I've got worth." She blinked fast, and he spotted her tears welling close to the surface.

If he could just help. But anything he did for her only made her appear weak.

No, he'd never reveal to his folks he'd gone to Kokomo for her. But were there other means to point his parents at her outstanding qualities?

Not that they doted on him and fed her the crumbs. They also wanted to control his choices, including where he worked.

Family first. Family is important. Whitcombs took those adages to a whole new level.

The Whitcombs were a first family in Indiana, with parts of their giant business holdings in all sorts of Hoosier endeavors, from politics to construction to marketing to farming. Darned near impossible to find a field where they didn't have input. And income. Which was why they insisted on Pat bringing his legal credentials into the corporation. All in the family. That was their motto.

"They recognize you have worth. They're fighting generations of tradition where men do the business and women raise the kids. It's messing with what they understand. That's all. Give them time. I mean, look around. The women's movement is opposing this all over. You get to battle it at home." He smiled and hoped she saw him as an ally.

"You're right. But I need you. Please, if you can do it sooner, tell me. I'm not sure my presence would help. That old gal doesn't seem to like me." She dabbed at her lips and pushed her less than half eaten plate away.

"Not hungry?"

"Don't need the added weight. Tastes good, but a taste is enough. No desire to give my husband more reasons to not be attentive."

Her husband was a slimeball, but he'd never tell her that. He was the one thing her parents cheered. She'd married a pretty-looking charmer. The problem was, he didn't always remember he was married.

"You look great. Brock's an idiot if he's not paying attention to you."

She smiled, though it radiated sadness. "Thanks. After this morning, I needed to hear that. I'm glad you asked me to lunch. Pat, I wish we had more times like this."

"Me too." And if she felt that way, maybe they would. He checked his watch. "I'd better pay the tab. Need to get back to the office and finish that brief." He raised his hand, and the server brought them the bill. After leaving a tip under the ashtray, he stood and helped his sister with her chair.

"Thanks." She stood on tiptoe and kissed his cheek.

"What was that for?"

"For improving my day."

He wrapped her in a quick hug. "You are welcome. Let's make this a regular thing. I miss just talking with you."

She nodded.

"And Venita, I promise to get to Kokomo first chance I get. I'll let you know."

"Thanks, Pat."

He paid the tab and walked her to her car before going back to his office. Now to finish that brief.

Chapter Two
Tuesday, February 17, 1970, Indianapolis, Indiana

S unny waited her turn in line at the bank. After she closed her account, she'd pay off her landlady and load up her car. No more staying in this town. She needed a safe place to pull herself together.

She wasn't the big-girl adult she wanted her family to see. And running home to her grandmother's would only prove that in spades.

The line moved, and she stepped forward, putting herself next for the cashier. A long liner mat they stood on squished from the melted snow puddles tracked in by customers.

It'd be almost as humiliating as yesterday, explaining her downfall to Gramma. However, in Kokomo she'd be loved, not gawked at as an award-winning idiot. Plus, with her sisters out of the house and Dad still working in California, this debacle would stay private a short while longer. Until some of the sting faded.

Her turn. She stepped to the window, handing the teller her bankbook. "I need to close my account. I'm moving out of town."

"We're sorry to lose your business, Miss Day. How much will you withdraw in cash? Do you want part on a bank draft?"

Sunny figured the math in her brain and answered the clerk.

Ten minutes later she exited the building, her life savings tucked in her purse and the strap across her body inside her coat for added protection as she bent her head against the wind. She crossed her fingers that the day would warm up and the highway wouldn't turn into an ice rink.

She'd notified the phone company. Utilities were included with her rent. Once she settled with Mrs. Fortner, her landlady, she had only to carry her things to the car. And get Frazier installed for the trip. Her tabby. He wouldn't appreciate the drive. But it only took an hour. On a good day. Then they'd be at Gramma's.

By noon, Sunny cruised the road, driving north on Meridian Street until it morphed into US 31. Fifty-one miles further she'd turn onto LaFountain Boulevard and follow that road into town, finding Gramma's house in the historic Silk Stocking Neighborhood district.

Kokomo, her real hometown.

As she pulled up at the curb, dread and relief poured over her. Dread that she must admit failure to her biggest cheerleader, and relief that someone loved her even when she failed. She put her three-year-old Camaro into park—a gift from her dad for graduating summa cum laud from Ball State. A lot that Herculean effort did for her now. After turning off the ignition, she gathered her purse and Frazier's crate and started for the top stoop. "Here we go, Buddy. This is home."

Frazier stared from between the wires of his cage, not looking all that excited at the slushy weather that awaited outside the vehicle.

The big-windowed door on the porch flew open and Gramma stood with arms opened wide. "Sunny girl, oh my, get up here. Let me look at you." Despite her words, Gramma pulled her into a mama bear hug before drawing back to peer into her face. "Something's wrong. Well, let's go inside and warm up where we can talk." She glanced at the car, noting the rear seat stuffed with boxes, *tsk*ed, but said nothing more as she guided Sunny and Frasier into the house.

At the dining room table, Gramma pulled out a chair and gently shoved Sunny into the seat. "You rest here. I'll brew some tea and we'll chat." She spun to leave, but stopped, plopping a box of Puffs on the quilted placemat in front of her. "Just in case."

Sunny didn't know whether to laugh or cry. So, she did both.

When Gramma returned with a teapot, two cups, and a plate of coconut macaroons, she was prepared to talk. "How do you do it, Gramma? How do you find the perfect thing even before I give you the details?"

"Oh, my Sunny girl. I can read your face like my favorite Harlequin Romance. I might not be privy to all the details, but you'll share when you're ready. But something's wrong and you need a soft place to land. That's what my house is. Your soft place." She gave Sunny one more hug before dropping into her chair.

"Yeah. Always has been. Think it can be indefinitely?" The tears forced their way past her lids, no matter how much she blinked. She dabbed with her wad of tissues.

"Of course. This is your home. Want to tell me what happened?"

Sunny nodded and recounted her weekend of waiting without news, the flowers, the breakup, the wife, the termination—she couldn't say the word fired one more time.

Gramma only listened. Never said, "I raised you better," or "You should've known." She patted her hand a few times, but when Sunny finished, she only saw love shining in her grandmother's eyes.

That made her cry harder.

"Let's finish our tea and then I'll help you put your things in your bedroom." Yeah, Gramma's was her soft-landing place.

In less than fifteen minutes, they'd carried her meager possessions up the stairs to the large bedroom she used to share with her sisters. Now the space belonged to her. She'd spread out.

Gramma left her to unpack.

Frazier wandered the area, exploring the nooks and crannies of the comfy Victorian.

When her suitcases and boxes lay emptied, Sunny plopped across her bed, hugging her childhood teddy bear, Mr. Murphy. The well-loved toy kept many a secret whispered into his worn ear. But this time his coat only collected her tears. She'd come home. A failure. Seeing beyond this moment proved too much to handle.

Frazier jumped up with her, which made her heart pound. Deep shadows and a dimming light through the lace-curtained window told her she'd fallen asleep. Twilight now held the day.

Sunny set Mr. Murphy aside and stretched. The nap helped. She should check about helping with dinner.

On the stairs, voices carried. Gramma hosted company. *Great.* She hustled back up to check her face in the bathroom mirror. No tear streaks, sleep scars, or smeared mascara—at least not after she ran a tissue under her eyes. With a gigantic sigh, she geared herself and went downstairs, slapping on a smile for her grandmother's guest.

"Sunny, you remember my friend, Chloe."

She did and gave Chloe a quick peck on the cheek. The tiny woman smiled before returning to her topic. Sunny half listened while she studied the two old friends.

They were as different as night and day. Where Gramma wore a matronly air about her—you best be doing as she said—Chloe seemed more fairy god-mother-ly. Her hair wisped framing her face in the softest of white curls, and her little bow mouth appeared sculpted in bright pink lipstick that matched her bulky cable-knit V-neck sweater. With twinkling cerulean eyes flashing recognizable color for yards, the woman's every movement rivaled that of a flitting hummingbird. That was Chloe.

And her speech fit the pattern as well. "She won't take no for an answer, Hazel. I just can't see my family home razed for some modern apartment complex monstrosity. Living alone in that big ol' house much longer isn't an option, but Ferguson House is too historic to destroy. What should I do?"

Sunny pulled up a chair and swiped one of Gramma's cookies. "Someone's trying to take your house?"

"No, sweetheart, they want to buy her home. But they're pressing Chloe to sell to them." Gramma put another cookie on a plate and handed it over with a napkin. Nice way to remind Sunny to use her manners.

"It's all that pressure. I need to do something. They plan to tear down the 'structure'." Chloe made air quotes as she spoke the word "structure." "This is criminal. If I could figure how to keep the house safe, I'd sell, and move in with my niece. Then the family legacy would be protected." She pushed away a rogue curl that slipped free of her hairnet. "Hazel, do you have some Bromo Seltzer? This is making my stomach churn."

Sunny remembered the old place. A mansion in its day, complete with a carriage house and three floors of stained-glass windows and Romanesque revival architecture with a touch of Queen Anne and Moroccan thrown in for added attraction. The "structure" held the power to still one's breath.

Once when Chloe invited Gramma over she'd brought the girls along. Sunny'd suffered keeping her hands to herself. The impressive woodwork; the colors gleaming through the windows; the view excited. Then her youngest sister slid down the banister into the newel post lamp. They cut the visit short.

Though past the dressing-up-for-Halloween stage when they moved in with Gramma, Sunny's sisters still enjoyed the holiday activity. Chloe's Ferguson House mansion demanded a stop. Gramma's friend offered the best goodies. Knowledgeable trick-or-treaters put her house first on their list of stops before things ran out.

Chloe had lived nowhere else, rattling around the mansion alone since her parents passed on. She'd never married, but took care of the family home, which her grandfather built during the local gas boom at the turn of the century. A few rooms she'd sealed up, but she occasionally offered tours to offset financial burdens. The historical society liked to host shindigs there as well, all helping to keep the mansion afloat. But Chloe was getting up there in age. It had to be hard to maintain.

"Have you thought of turning it into a business?"

Chloe shook her head. "I'm too old for that."

But Gramma patted her friend's hand and nodded at Sunny. "What do you have in mind?"

What *did* she have in mind? As an idea came to her, Sunny let it race out her mouth. "You could give your occasional tours and make it an added draw. Ask the historical society to put up displays. You could start a tearoom using the downstairs as a brunch and luncheon place. Hm, let's see. Oh, you could start a bridal venue business. Maybe even do an all-in-one place thing. Have certain rooms to show a particular theme or style with examples of gowns and suits for the whole bridal party that matched. The dining room could be used for sampling cakes and *hor d'oeuvres*. Upstairs could be try on rooms. You could even have venues set by size—one room in the house for a small intimate ceremony, the carriage house for a medium one, and the outdoor garden for a larger one." Sunny glanced up from her thinking aloud to see both women staring at her.

"Sunny, that's brilliant. The house would stay intact, more people could enjoy it, and have a special memory. How did you come up with that?" Gramma beamed at her.

She shrugged. "I don't know. I just said what popped into my head. I'm sure there's a lot of other things."

Chloe shook her head. "No, no, you said it perfect. I love that idea."

Sunny smiled and sighed, happy to finally do something right. "Good, now you won't need to sell it."

"Oh, but I do. I need to sell to you so you can do all that."

"What?"

"Chloe, that's exactly what I was thinking. If Sunny bought it, you'd rest easy knowing the place would be well cared for."

Oh, no, Gramma had that look in her eye. The one where she would tell you what to do and you'd better do it. "I don't even have a job. I wouldn't be able to qualify for the loan. I only have my savings and what was left of my checking account and I doubt it is enough." She ran the figures through her head. It wasn't enough.

Chloe squeezed her hand. "Sunny, it's not a matter of needing a lot of money. Moving in with my niece will save me a lot. I still have my trust payments from my inheritance. So, name your price. Make it something you can pay me now, no loans or anything. We'll draw up the papers and the mansion is yours."

Sunny glanced from Gramma, to Chloe, to her hand encased by her fairy godmother's. A business of her own. No one could fire her ever again. It would be hers and if anyone did any firing, it would be her job to do it. "Yes. Let's."

A bolt of electricity shot through her. What had she just agreed to?

Wednesday, February 18, 1970

Indianapolis, Indiana

PAT LOOSENED HIS TIE and kicked off his shoes as he closed his apartment door with his elbow. Home. At last. This negotiation turned out far more complex than the original estimate. Plus, the space between desired outcomes seemed to have widened the more they talked. The worst part? His father would not budge one iota, leaving him zero wiggle room for compromise.

Yet walking away wasn't a choice. His old man, the almighty Virgil Alexander Whitcomb, expected to get his way. No matter what. Not the easiest of challenges to foist on your lawyer. Or your son.

Hence, the main reason Pat didn't live at the family home. He needed a break, but under his father's roof the job never ended. He chuckled as an image of his father sleepwalking into his bedroom to deliver another business ultimatum flitted through his brain before twisting his chuckle with trepidation. A strong possibility with his dad.

He flipped on his stereo and *Blood, Sweat, and Tears* dropped down the spindle into place, allowing the needle to send out the throaty notes of David Clayton-Thomas singing "Spinning Wheel."

The vocalist sang a musical portrait of Pat's life. A spinning wheel going round and around. He longed to stop this hamster impersonation, but as long as he worked for his father, that was his reality. If he stood on his own feet, did the less prestigious work he longed to do, Father would rip him a sparkling new reality. Somehow reminiscent of that play he read in college, *No Exit* by Jean-Paul Sartre.

Not quite hell. But he remained trapped. For now. At least he held onto the hope of someday.

The phone rang, slicing through his thoughts, and he snagged the receiver.

"Pat, I thought you'd be coming to dinner tonight."

He'd forgotten his mother's invitation. "I'm sorry, Mother. Been a brutal day. Out of habit I drove home."

"That apartment is not home. This is your home. That's just a convenient place to drop when needed." Her whine grated.

Rather than argue, he changed the subject. "Who all's there?"

"Only family tonight. Venita and Brock arrived a few minutes ago. Your father's in the den on his business line. I'll hold supper if you hurry."

He glanced at the outside darkness while sleety-rain peppered the window and the wind caused the tiny bare branches of a nearby willow to scrape against the pane. A shiver ran up his back to even consider dressing for dinner and driving in that wintery mess. "Not tonight. The roads are awful, what with commuters trying to get home in this weather. I'm sorry I forgot. I'll see if I can make it Sunday afternoon." He didn't care to go then either. But his mother would be hurt if she read his mind.

"If that's your best. I miss you, Patrick. It's simply hard on a mother when her babies grow up."

He'd heard that before. Like he's to blame for becoming an adult? That's the point of maturing, right? But he held some sympathy for her. Without her children, life morphed into a cycle of women's meetings, charity functions and keeping the Whitcomb name prominent in social circles. Sans scandal, of course. No wonder Venita wanted no part of that circus.

"Then I will let you go. Please remember about Sunday, Pat. Don't disappoint me."

Man! Mother's mad guilt skills. He started to remind her he'd just been there but changed his mind. "I won't forget. Have a nice dinner, Mother."

"You too. Bye."

He almost said "I love you" but what would she do if he did —burst into tears, keep him on the line another hour, or make him repeat ad nauseam out of

disbelief? Not something one voiced in the Whitcomb family. Not that Whitcombs didn't love each other. They understood without fanfare or verbalizing.
Funny, but a significant part of his childhood memories concerned visiting
his buddy Trey and centered that sentiment. His clan expressed themselves with
no trouble saying those three little words. Trey even said them at the end of their
conversations, sort of. "Luvyaman." All rolled into one word. Pat never doubted
the sincerity.

Someday, with a family of his own, they'd speak those words. Often. Out
loud. And hug. He liked hugs. His wife and kids would know he loved them;
they'd never harbor a doubt. A promise he made himself that he intended to
keep.

He wandered to his kitchenette and checked the fridge. Not a ton of choices.
So, he tugged open his canned goods cabinet. Crazy to fix a full meal for one
person. He sighed. After grabbing the loaf of Holsum's, he settled on a bologna
and cheese sandwich. Due to the weather, he took time to toast the bread in
a skillet—another skill he picked up from Trey's family. Made it more home
cooked. He added a handful of Bugles to his plate and popped a Dr Pepper. Not
the cuisine Mother served, but the company proved better. If he counted David
Clayton-Thomas on his stereo.

After getting comfortable on the sofa, he went through his mail. Bills. Bills.
Bills. Oh, a letter from his college roommate, Eric Waldon, with a belated
Christmas card.

Pat glanced through the group photos enclosed before unfolding the hand-
written message. Eric followed his dream and married his college sweetheart.
Now blessed with two children, a boy and a girl, they lived in Arizona where
her family resided. As a defense attorney, Eric helped people, fought against
injustice, and lived the life of Pat's dreams. But his buddy hadn't been born a

Whitcomb. Eric possessed choice in how he wanted to utilize his degree. Their smiling faces shouted they'd found the better decision.

He tossed the mail on the coffee table. Perhaps one day he'd take a vacation. Visit Eric. He'd tell him if it was worth it.

The album stopped, the needle arm moving back to the rest, and the turntable's spin ended. Instead of flipping the vinyl over, he snagged his new Commander remote control and turned on the TV. The news started, and the anchorman gave a replay of the latest court case involving a black youth accused of attacking an elderly couple in the park. The young man got arrested two blocks over from the scene, exiting a drugstore.

As Pat listened, something didn't set right. Did this kid get the right defense? Who's his attorney? A court-appointed one? Those legal eagles got overworked. Often, they tossed in just enough effort to get by. Not because of laziness, but sheer survival. An overwhelmed system with little regard for excuses.

The type of thing he'd help with. If only his father would listen. He wouldn't. That's why he remained stuck in the hardening cement of Whitcomb Enterprises. Or was it?

Honestly? So easy to blame his dad, but in the end, Pat held in his desires and performed as told, never risking the pain of getting his hopes shot down with his father's pointed barbs.

If he were ever to do what he desired, turn this dream inside him alive, he must take a risk. But how? Where did he start?

His gaze fell on the letter. He picked it up and reread the note.

Pat,

Realize this is tardy. We spent Christmas at the maternity ward welcoming baby girl Julie. Figured better late than never. Ha! So, how's life treating you? Building a name in the corporate world? I've been keeping busy with my new practice. Leaped out on my own and surprise, surprise, the clients appeared. Most are discrimination cases, but that's what we dreamed of, right? Correcting injustice, maybe arguing before the Supreme Court on a life-altering case. I'm not there yet, but with this clientele, I'm closer.

Sure miss our late-night discussions on old classic suits and Perry Mason reruns. Ha! If you're ever in the neighborhood, you better stop by. Marti is the best cook, and we'll throw a barbecue in your honor.

She sends her love, by the way. Take care.

Your buddy,
Eric

Pat grabbed his calendar and flipped some pages before gathering a pen and paper. He would do it.

Eric,

Got your card and letter. The family looks great. Congratulations on the new little princess. Bet she has you twisted every which way but loose, all around that tiny little pinkie.

I have a surprise for you. I've pulled out my calendar and am prepared to circle a date in red. I'm smart enough to know better than to visit the desert in the middle of the summer. But based on what's already scheduled, I have some free time come November.

How would you feel about a guest around the first of the month? Let me know if that works for you. I think I can carve out a week. Should be enough time for us to get into plenty of trouble. Marti knows who to call to get us out, right? I'm ready, man. So ready.

It's been sleety and cold here. If I weren't already committed for the next couple of weeks, I'd drop everything now. But, hey, this gives me something to look forward to. Again, let me know if the dates work on your end. If they do, I'll purchase the airfare.

Keep out of trouble until I can join you. Take care.

Your buddy,

Pat

He read through the letter once more and paused when his father's face scowled through his mind. No, it was now or never. He shoved the page in an envelope, addressed, sealed and stamped it, and set it aside to mail first thing on the way to work in the morning.

This he could do. A taste of freedom. It almost made him giddy. Then he remembered just how far off November really was.

Chapter Three

Thursday, February 19, 1970, Kokomo, Indiana

"What am I doing?" Sunny's insides quivered as she waited for the teller to finish drawing up the bank draft. This would leave a hundred dollars in her account. And she still had no job.

Sure, living at Gramma's helped with expenses. Tons. No rent, no grocery bill. Did she want to sponge off the one person she could depend on?

As the clerk passed the check across the counter to her, her heart froze. She'd never spent so much money in her life.

A queue formed behind her. She toyed with having the teller put every penny back in her account while she escaped, but the exasperation on the face of the guy next in line pushed her to complete her transaction. She squeaked out a thanks, shoved the check into her purse, and pulled out her keys before zipping her coat up over the shoulder bag. Now if only her legs wouldn't turn to Jell-O before she reached her car.

But once inside, she locked her doors. This much money, even in draft form, terrified her. It was one thing to bring her savings to Kokomo when she moved. She knew she'd put that hard earned capital in the local bank. Another safe place. This, this was different. She proposed to sign away most of her life savings. And on what? Some words that fell out of her mouth before she clamped the fool thing closed.

Sunny needed to tell Chloe she'd changed her mind. And then march back into line and redeposit the money.

That idea calmed her shaking. A little. At least she'd formed a sensible plan.

Poor Chloe would be stuck again, and Gramma wouldn't be impressed with her vacillating and reneging. But perhaps she might figure another way. She didn't have to buy a twenty-six room, three-story Romanesque revival mansion to prove a willingness to give aid.

Her breathing returned to a semblance of normal as she headed west toward the heart of the historic Silk Stocking district. This entire area sprang up overnight when natural gas turned up on the western edge of Kokomo. Founding fathers wooed entrepreneurs to come start businesses, moving the sleepy farm community into the industrial twentieth century.

They built Gramma's old Victorian three years later.

The grandest structure to emerge belonged to the Seiberling family, a couple blocks from Chloe's home. Arguably the loveliest section in town. A drive along the tree-lined streets, peering at the houses and imagining the insides, had been a high school pastime for Sunny.

Now she might own one of these majestic structures.

No, she'd not talk herself back into this fiasco. This would not work.

She pulled up in front of Chloe's. Seasonal flower beds once lined the brick paver walk to the porch steps, but the piles of melting snow tried to hide the rotting leaves and dead stems. Before long someone would plant those tulip bulbs. When they pushed their delicate blooms toward the sun, with the crocuses, the walkway to the steps would look stunning.

Stop noticing.

No more imagining.

Sunny stepped onto the wide porch and used the brass knocker to announce herself.

Chloe opened as if she'd been watching. "Come in, child. No need to stand in the cold."

Sunny followed as the fairy-like woman seemed to float further inside the mansion. That amazing staircase loomed, beckoning her to run a finger over the hand-tooled workmanship and inlay.

Sunny's heart thundered in her chest.

The brass newel lamp with the round globes gleamed with light, even in the daytime, bringing an atmosphere of yesterday. And the mahogany wood panels lining the wall side of the stairs framing carved floral designs whispered for Sunny's touch. Every doorway stood framed with patterns crafted into the pillars and lintels, capped off with cornices of geometric design. Her involuntary sigh escaped.

The value of this home more than exceeded Chloe's agreed to price. They weren't talking a mere bargain. She stared at an investment. By utilizing Ferguson House to build a business, her investment would grow. Like the tulips leading to the door.

One day.

And Gramma would let her stay until she started making money.

Besides, she might live in one wing. Keep a private bedroom from the rest of the residence. If she wanted.

Her brain tapped her shoulder, reminding her to stop planning with her heart and to use the commonsense God gave her.

"Let me show you around." Chloe linked arms with her.

What would it hurt to look?

They wandered through the downstairs rooms while Chloe relived the history and shared childhood anecdotes.

Unlike the Seiberling Mansion, Ferguson House remained in the original family, built by Chloe's grandparents, and inherited by her father. Her mother gave birth to Chloe in one of the second-floor bedrooms.

"As a rule, I keep the special areas covered to keep out dust but ready for the historical society if they want. I eat in the kitchen. Before the wars, servants ate their meals in that space. That's good enough for me." As they crossed through the 1950s style kitchen with its pink Kenmore appliances—of course, a gas stove with an oven—and turquoise cabinets, the nostalgia overwhelmed. "I guess I should've updated, but when everything works just fine, why? I picked this all out new when I inherited the place from my parents. Even installed this checkered linoleum flooring over the old hardwoods. They get so noisy, but this flooring brightens things, right?"

In truth, despite the fifties style fun, this room appeared more dated than the rest of the house. Which breathed classic.

Sunny wouldn't mention that, though.

Chloe opened the rear door to another porch. "Let me show you something. This is why I believe your suggestion of a wedding business is wonderful." Still linked arm-in-arm, Chloe led her outside to a giant old sycamore with hundreds of branches fanning off in various directions, a few even draping to where Sunny with her short stature might reach up and touch. A couple V-ed off early as if Siamese twins, leaving a place where someone could sit. And one branch in particular appeared to create a loveseat before spreading out into multiples.

"This is gorgeous. I'd no idea this was here."

Chloe grinned and patted the trunk. "There's an old legend. My mother told me the story. She learned the tale from an elderly man who lived in the area before they established the town. He'd heard tell of this tree from Indians he knew as a kid. They call it the Sweetheart tree. The story goes that if you kiss your intended in its shade when a cardinal is sitting on that branch right there," she pointed to the place that looked like a love seat. "Then it is true love, and you are destined to be together."

"I love that story. Did you ever try it, Chloe?" The words were out before she thought. If Chloe never married, what happened?

The old woman seemed less hummingbird like. "I wanted to. My beau enlisted. I wanted to kiss him goodbye here, but he said it would be more fun to kiss hello when he came back. Instead, I read the telegram that he'd died in France and his last letter to me. There never was another man. Didn't even want to look. So maybe I tried it. He signed his letter with XXX and a cardinal sat on that branch while I read it."

Sunny didn't know what to say. But she knew what she wanted. This house. This very special house.

As if reading her mind, Chloe patted her arm. "Let's go in and take care of this. I have the deed inside."

"Sure." There'd be time for more exploring later.

As they got into the kitchen, there was a knock at the front. "Bet that's my lawyer. Thought he could check everything out for you."

Sunny was glad Chloe thought of that. It felt like a safety net.

A forty-something man with a receding hairline and budging briefcase stood at the door as Chloe opened it. "Come in, Alden. Want you to meet my friend, Sunny. Sunny Day, this is Alden Hingst, my lawyer. Let's go into the kitchen and sit at the table." The cracked pink motif table with the chrome edging and matching padded chairs.

Mr. Hingst nodded and mumbled, "Nice to meet you" before following Sunny, who followed Chloe to the kitchen.

An hour later, all the Ts were crossed, Is dotted, and the draft handed over. Sunny was now the proud owner of Ferguson House.

There was no time for regrets, she needed to craft a business plan. First, she did a thorough tour through the whole building and carriage house, noting ideas and possible needed renovations.

She even took measurements and sketched a floor plan that she took home to redo into something of scale. Once she had that, the real work began.

Though it was only Gramma and her at the house, one would think it was Grand Central Station with a revolving door. Neighbors popped in, Gramma's friends from church, even a guy Sunny was surprised to learn had asked Gramma out on dates. And she'd accepted. Gene Norman was kind of cute for an older guy. Even cuter was seeing Gramma and him together. But none of that gave her the peace and quiet she needed to get this figured out.

Therefore, noon Friday, Sunny had locked herself in her room with her sketches and idea doodles to put together a cost analysis and business plan. By that evening, she couldn't deny what the figures proved: there wasn't enough money to get her started.

So now what did she do?

At eight she slipped downstairs to see if Gramma had saved her any dinner. She was pretty sure there'd be some sugar cookies in the little pig cookie jar, and she was right. A nice dessert after a leftover roast beef sandwich. Just as she sliced the meat for her meal, she heard a shuffle behind her and spun. "Oh, you scared me."

Gramma covered a yawn. "Let me fix that for you, honey."

"I'm sorry, didn't want to disturb you."

Gramma shook her curler covered head. "That's not a problem, sweetie. I was drawn to come in here. Got an inkling we need to talk."

"Gramma, you are the best." Sunny gave her a quick hug. "You want a sandwich?"

"No thanks, I'll just fix a cup of tea. Shall I fix two?"

Sunny nodded and finished making her sandwich before putting the meat and bread away and adding two cookies to her plate. She sat at the kitchen table and waited for her grandmother to join her.

"So, what is bothering you, Sunny, as if I don't know."

With a sigh, Sunny shared her dreams and visions and then the bottom line. "I don't have the money to do any of that. I don't have the money to get any type of product I could sell out of there. I don't even have the money to pay for my share of the groceries after another month, let alone give you anything towards rent. Guess I could sleep in my new house. But I'd have to pay the utilities by selling off Chloe's antique furniture. I don't know what I'm gonna do, Gramma. I let my dreams overcome my good sense."

"Dreams are made to be stronger than our good sense, so we'll get off our duffs and take a risk. Don't give up dearheart. It's time to step it up with what we should have started with—prayer." Gramma covered Sunny's hand.

"Okay, you do it, I'll agree." Praying aloud wasn't her thing, but it was Gramma's.

They bowed heads and Sunny closed her eyes.

"Lord, You put this dream in Sunny's heart and provided the means to get started. Even put her in a place for it all to happen. I've got a feeling there's more to this story so we're looking to You to provide the money to make this work. We know it's in Your timing but if You could make it sooner, there'd be a lot less worry here. Thanks for all You've done and all You're about to do. In Jesus' Name, Amen."

Before Sunny could open her eyes and lift her head, a slam sounded from the front room.

"I swear, I'm going to wring Dad's neck. Why did he have to inspire someone to write that stupid song?"

Her sister Stormy just blew home.

Tuesday March 3, 1970

PAT PULLED TO THE CURB and shoved the gear shifter into park. More than the last of a winter's dying blast made him shiver. This had to be the wrong address. He glanced at the note again.

How could Venita want to destroy this beautiful old building? The way the turrets reached for the sky and the octagon roof shingles glinted when the sun peaked through the March clouds alone brought an air of nostalgia, like stepping into the beginning of the century.

Yet, this was the place. He shook his head. As he climbed from his Mustang, angry for agreeing without more facts, he struggled to find a clever opening to win the old lady to his side.

Venita's side, he amended. To tear down this piece of history was not his idea. He wouldn't lay claim to any part of that.

But as he approached the porch, voices carried from inside and he noticed the front door wasn't properly closed. Not that he sneaked, but why announce oneself with noise?

"Stormy, I have to try. Of course, this isn't ideal, but I've gotta make this work."

"I get that, but I can help. If you'd just listen to me, we could do this together. Please trust me."

Pat hated to eavesdrop, but the temptation proved irresistible.

"There's no other way. End of discussion."

"There would be, Sunny. If you let me in. I have the money."

"What about Rob? Doesn't he have a say? Hey, someone's on the porch."

That was his cue to knock. He raised his fist to do so as the door flew wide.

"Can I help you?" The speaker had that frustrated, you-interrupted-me tone, though it also seemed she was trying to amend it with a forced smile. And those eyes. They flashed as if tossing out a challenge. His mission had better be important.

He cleared his throat, grasping one more second to think. "Hi, my name is Pat Whitcomb." He pulled a business card from his pocket and held it out. "May I speak with Chloe Ferguson?"

"She doesn't live here anymore." At least she was calmer, a tad. She'd rubbed her earlobe through his entire speech, but now extended her hand to accept the card.

"Did she pass away?" If she died, there'd be an estate sale. Maybe. He could deliver the full mess back to Venita and be done with it.

The speaker shook her head. "No, nothing like that. She sold the place to me and moved to Greentown with her niece. I'm sorry, but you might find her there. Come on in. I should have her new address and phone contact information here somewhere."

He stepped through as she held the door, knowing he should explain himself. But the view inside left him speechless. Aside from the furniture in awry, the architecture stunned with a sweeping staircase crowning the focal point of entry. Somehow, as the petite blonde with flashing hazel eyes and a feisty ponytail sorted a stack of papers on a parson's table, he found his voice.

"Actually, if you're the owner, I came to see you. I didn't realize the place had sold."

She stopped and glanced up. "Yeah, I'm the new owner. Guess we're back to my first question. How can I help you?" It sounded friendlier this time.

He chuckled. "I think you've beat me to the punch. I was hoping to negotiate with Miss Ferguson. I'd like to purchase the house."

"You want to tear it down?" Her friendliness morphed into something akin to a mama bear protecting her cub. Did she just grow a couple inches?

"No! I don't want to tear it down. I'm stunned by this beauty." True. All true. He wasn't the one talking demolition.

However, no need to mention he was on a mission for his sister and destruction was her game plan. This woman's smile was a ray of sunshine when amenable. A mood he preferred.

She relaxed and stuck out her hand. "I'm Miss Day. Sorry I can't help you. I've no intention of selling this place. Chloe picked me to buy it, and from the bargain I got, it's more like an inheritance. I hope you understand."

He nodded. "I get that. So, what are your plans?" His gaze insisted on another scan of the room, taking in the hand-carved wood beams crisscrossing the ceiling and the panels lining the stairway wall. It made his heart beat faster. Or was it this spunky woman/girl with her ponytail/fresh-faced professional manner?

"I want to start a business. A bridal business. Turn Ferguson House into a venue, like a one-stop place where a couple can choose the bridal wear, have the event and photographs. We'll provide for several sized weddings or will be able to. I'm just getting started and need to complete my inventory. Chloe even left me her china and crystal." She shook her head. From her expression, that last bit of news surprised her.

"That sounds like a wonderful idea. I wish you luck."

"Sunny, if you're going to tell him about it, really tell him." Another woman, close in age and with obvious family resemblance, popped into view. She stood a tad taller with more angular features and her hand outstretched. "I'm Stormy Crawford, Sunny's sister. Let me show you around."

Before Pat could utter a sound, the sister slipped her arm through his, guiding him further into the room. A peek over his shoulder caught a scowl on pretty Miss Day's face.

"This, of course, is where we will greet customers. We've plans to keep the charm of the age yet make it seem homier than business. So fewer counters and more seating for discussion."

She led him to a hall. "We've several rooms on this floor that we can stage according to wedding themes. In these we'll display complete wedding party dress to help clientele see a more finished tableau and find the look they desire."

She opened a door, revealing what appeared to be a parlor. He noted an antique piano in the corner before she continued the tour. "In the dining room we'll host tastings, intimate parties, the wedding supper, and rehearsal dinners. Can't you just picture how beautiful a ceremony would be in candlelight reflecting off the chandeliers—Tiffany designed, I might add. Imagine with the flickers from the fireplace for a fall or winter venue. Stunning, right?"

"Right." And she was. But he glanced over his shoulder again. Sunny, as her sister called her, had her arms crossed over her chest and at that point he wondered if they misnamed the girls. Sunny sure appeared stormy to him.

"Of course, we'll be updating the kitchen here to accommodate our needs, but if you step out to the porch, I think you will appreciate the view where we can host garden weddings in the late spring through Indian summer months. I envision a winter event might be lovely. Done right, of course. It must be brief and well planned to keep guests from getting too cold. I'm doubtful the bridesmaids would go without coats in freezing temperatures." She chuckled at that, and he could view what she described. "Can't you just picture wedding party shots around that gorgeous sycamore? Even engagement photos would be perfect there. This is so picturesque. Just imagine it in the spring and summer when everything's in bloom. The setting's perfect for almost any theme."

They came back in where Sunny waited in the kitchen. "Thank you, Stormy. But I'm sure Mr. Whitcomb has other things on his mind. Unless he's engaged..." She cocked her head to the side and peered at him. Yet, for a second, he could've sworn she glanced at his left hand.

His neck warmed. Well, that was unnerving. "Um, no, not engaged, nor attached."

That news seemed to relax Sunny. And for some crazy reason, he was glad that it did.

Sunny continued to gaze at him with a bit more intensity. "Then, I doubt you are interested in all the plans we've...*I've* put together." She cast a sharp glance toward Stormy, who smiled, shrugged, and left the room.

"You've given great thought to this. It's easy to visualize what your sister shared. Just wondering, though, have you spoken to a lawyer?"

She stiffened. "Yes, the sale is all legal, Mr. Whitcomb."

"Oh, no, I wasn't implying...I mean, if you are going to turn a residence into a business, you must check zoning ordinances and apply for your business license. I wondered since I'm a lawyer. Not soliciting work, just expressing a thought." He'd better be careful.

Sunny slowed to a stop. "No, I, well, I've got a lawyer. However, my plans never entered our discussion." She sighed. "Another thing for my to-do list. Thank you, Mr. Whitcomb. I would've figured that out too late if you hadn't mentioned it."

"Call me Pat. It's fine. I tend to wonder aloud at times." He grinned. "Would you mind if I stop by to check on your progress? You have a unique idea. I'd like to learn what you do with it." *And I'd like to see you more often, too.* Oh-oh, his mouth was saying things before checking with his brain.

Her smile lit the room with sunshine. "Sure, if you want. My name is Sunny. Yes, I'm Sunny Day. I blame my father. But you don't need my sad story now." She was aptly named, at least when she beamed that grin.

"Then I'll see you another time, Sunny. You've got my card. Call me if you wish." *Please wish.*

They shook hands, and he resisted the urge to hang onto her fingers longer than necessary, the tingles giving a pleasant thrill.

The soft yet firm grip told him she was genuine but not big into manual labor. At the base of the porch steps, he glanced back.

She watched from the door.

He waved, sucked in a breath, and headed for his car.

Once enclosed, it was as if his brain activated as he turned the ignition key. This was bad. Very bad. Venita would cut him in half like her favorite lunch if she knew he didn't push the sale. More than that, the fact he offered aid to the enemy, as she'd frame it, would only confirm her lack of trust in him.

Yet there was no denying it. Sunny beamed as beautiful as the most gorgeous summer day in Bermuda. Intelligent, gutsy—he could tell by her determination to hold on. Plus, he figured it was difficult because of what he'd heard from the porch. Money was in short supply.

As much as he craved to build a relationship with his sister, demolishing that mansion was wrong. So wrong. No way Venita would approve if she'd seen the house in person. Knowing that eased his guilt. Some. But convincing her to come see it wouldn't be a simple task. He'd need a plan.

But let's say he did. If he could get Venita to Kokomo, set her preconceived plans aside to really view the place, would he ruin it by revealing he was a little attracted to the new owner?

Fruitless to avoid that fact. Besides, there was something familiar, something he couldn't quite pin down. Like he'd seen her some place before. But where? He hadn't been to Kokomo in eighteen months. Where might they have met?

Chapter Four
Wednesday, March 4, 1970

Sunny closed the door on her Camaro and stared at Gramma's house. Her new home. Her old home. She was back where she started, only deeper in debt and more hopeless. The rezoning could be done, but it would cost. The license part was easy, but another cost.

To sell Chloe's antiques was the only choice. However, even considering it felt like she was letting the sweet old lady down. If she didn't sell off some things, though, she'd lose the house. And that would be a worse fail.

She trudged the steps to the porch. Voices in deep discussion poured out as she opened the door.

"—listen to me. I keep trying to tell her I can help but she's so all-fired determined to do this on her own. Gramma, why won't she take a chance on me?"

"Stormy, love, there's something personal going on with your sister. Let her work her way through this. Speaking of working one's way, have you spoken to Rob? He called again today. You need to talk to him."

"No, I don't."

"What happened, sweetie?"

Yeah, what happened? That's what Sunny wanted to know. But asking for explanations might force her into telling Stormy about Brock. Though Gramma might've hinted to make Stormy quit nagging her to death.

"Let's just say he didn't talk to me, so now I'm done talking."

Sunny coughed, and the women glanced up.

"How much did you overhear?" Leave it to Stormy to charge to the core. She always could read everyone in the family.

"Enough. Apparently, you're trying to get Gramma to plead your case." Sunny dropped her purse on the stairs to take up in a few minutes.

"Well, you won't even hear me out. What else am I to do?"

Sunny plopped on the sofa and slumped. "Fine. I'm listening. Give it your best shot."

Stormy's eyes got rounder, but she only hesitated a second. "You are amazing with numbers. You can handle business and keep books. You began with this dream, but you've never been the extrovert. Mother hen? Yes. However, I am an extrovert. I not only am energized by people, but I can also read them. I understand where their ideas are going, sometimes even before they do.

"Remember Jack Cullings? He was all set to buy a car in high school and I was able to help him pick out what he wanted when he didn't realize it himself when he started."

Sunny had to nod at that. But it was one time. And it was Jack Cullings, for goodness' sake.

"I see where you're headed with this. I understand your dream. I also know how to talk to customers. If I can handle third graders, I can handle brides and their moms." Stormy smiled, punctuating the end of her opening argument.

"Yeah, what about those third graders? Why aren't you with them now?"

Stormy's face got pink, then red.

Sunny regretted her words, knowing she might have started a new hurricane.

"I quit. It's a long story and has no bearing here. All you need to know is I'm available. And, I have the cash to help you."

Sunny sat straighter. "Not if you're unemployed. you'll need your money. Besides, hadn't you better check with Rob?"

"I won't be unemployed if we work together to build this business. Come on, Sunny. I can help. All you have to do is share. I'm not your little sister who's going to take all your prized possessions. I want to work with you. You've inspired me. Besides, I look up to you." She gave a slow grin.

Her sister was skilled at pushing the right buttons when she wanted something. "How much do you have?"

"How much do you need?" Stormy stood there, hands on her hips, knowing she was close to winning. She wasn't the only person in the family who could read body language.

Yet everything she'd said was true. Could they work together? Respect each other's abilities? "I spoke with my lawyer, like Mr. Whitcomb—"

"Pat."

"*Pat* suggested. I found out how much will it cost for the rezoning and business license. Add in getting the supplies, running ads, we'll have to put renovations further down the list. We need to make some money before we can spend it." Sunny sighed. "I'll show you the figures. But we need an agreement. I'm in charge of the finances, with input from you. You'll be the face of the company, working with clients and someday employees. We'll go with our strengths. Anything that falls outside of those areas, we discuss. Sound fair?"

Stormy bounced on the balls of her feet. "This is the best thing that's happened all year, Sunny. We can do this, I know it."

"Yeah, well, we'd better get Gramma praying. Just to make sure."

Gramma winked at them from her rocker where she'd stayed out of the conversation. "Already working on it."

That made them all chuckle.

"So, let me get the book I started, and I'll show you what we need. Hope you have enough." Sunny grabbed her purse and raced to their room—the one she'd had to share with Stormy ever since she raged back home. So much for spreading out. She traded the bag for the notebook where she kept her figures.

Downstairs, Gramma set up tea and cookies at the dining room table so they could talk and crunch the numbers.

Two hours later, they had a priority list of purchases, the rezoning and license at the top. Sunny made a call to her lawyer to ask about writing something up between her and Stormy. Then they drove to the Office of City Planners, where they filled out applications to scratch those first two items off their agenda. The license required the approval from the Indiana Secretary of State's office—plus they learned they'd need a federal tax ID number and got that application out of the way, too.

Once they possessed the license and tax ID—both of which would be mailed—they could open a joint business account. Sunny would keep the checkbook. However, in case of an emergency, Stormy would have access.

Now they were into a whole other level of entrepreneur.

Areas where Sunny had put little focus when she sought her degree. The numbers part, she understood that. The administrative aspect, especially when it came to zoning issues, she hadn't delved as deep. There must've been something in her classes at Ball State. And she still had a few of her textbooks.

That'd be where she could start. See if there're things she'd missed. City Planning would hold a council meeting to decide her petition.

After leaving Stormy with detailed notes on her vision of how to arrange the rooms—notes she'd only mentioned in passing but her sister somehow internalized enough to show Pat—Sunny used their bedroom to reread her schoolbooks and list what she might need for the meeting.

There wasn't much help in her texts. So Sunny located Stormy to see where she was with her task. Her sister had made stick figures to represent mannequins to pose in certain rooms, counted up the numbers, and called around to find out where to buy them.

Sunny shuddered at the outlay. "We can't afford that many. If we buy all those, we can't cloth them."

"I was thinking about that. Can we make some kind of consignment deal? Possibly with a shop in Indianapolis? That might help them get their product into new hands. And it wouldn't cost us as much."

That was a great idea. Perhaps bringing Stormy in on this wasn't so bad. "Okay, do you know of a place?"

"Just the one we used for my wedding. Remember going there for fittings?" Stormy glanced up from her pages, a smile tugging the corner of her mouth.

Sunny recalled the trip too. "Think they'll remember us?"

"They'll remember Windy for sure."

The giggles started, each girl making the other laugh harder. "I don't think anyone else has ever tried on every bridesmaid gown with a broken ankle. She stood on that dais while they did measurements, a book under her other foot to guess at the heel size, get the hem correct, all the while begging for knee length so it wouldn't matter. I didn't want my bridesmaids in knee length—I wanted ballet length. But I almost relented, considering what she went through. At least her cast was off before the wedding."

Sunny wiped her eyes and pulled herself together. Windy could be so funny without trying. She could also be so klutzy—the memory of her baby sister's first big break sobered those thoughts. "Why don't you call them, see about an appointment."

Stormy nodded. "Meanwhile, if we only show the flower girl and ring bearer mannequins in a couple rooms, make those choices less, that'll cut down on cost. We'll need a photographer on the payroll and a bakery. What if we have photo books with each display? Then we wouldn't need as many mannequins either."

"Good idea. It would get us started. We better set a date for a grand opening, place ads in the Tribune. Maybe on the radio, too. We should figure out a script."

The front door slammed. "Anybody home?"

Dad.

Sunny captured Stormy's stare. It was one thing to come to Gramma's and let her help them heal. It was another to face their father. They stood from the table and headed for the living room. Cue the firing squad music.

"What are you girls doing here? Come to visit your grandmother?" He dropped his suitcase and hugged them both before giving them the stare. The one where he peered into their souls and yanked out the truth before they manufactured a lie. "What's up?"

Sunny gave Stormy a quick glance before stepping up as the eldest. "Hey, Daddy. We're starting a business. Can you believe it? Going into business with my sister. It'll be so fun." Her voice squeaked.

"Stormy?"

"What she said, Daddy." Her sister blinked a couple times. "Business partners. Together. That's us."

"You girls don't call me daddy unless something's wrong. In the dining room. Now." He herded them back to the table where their paperwork lay strewn. "Sit and spill." He held up a hand. "Wait a second. Mom get in here too. Your fingerprints are on this sudden venture."

Gramma peeked in from the kitchen. "Aaron, good to see you, too, sweetie. I'll be there in a bit. I'm busy at the moment." And she popped back out.

"Guess it must be pretty bad if your grandmother won't protect you. So, you were saying..."

Sunny cleared her throat. She'd take whatever Dad dished out. "I'm not working in Indianapolis. Long story I'm not ready to discuss right now. But long story short, I helped Chloe by buying her house—got an incredible deal—and we're turning it into a wedding venue slash bridal shoppe. We've done our research, made our plans, applied for the rezoning and license, and we're going to give it everything thing we have." She took a breath and let it whoosh out.

Dad glanced from daughter to daughter. "I've always wanted my girls to be close. Do things together. Be there for each other. But somehow, I get the feeling I'm missing something important. Why would you leave your job, Sunny? And why aren't you in the classroom, Stormy? It's not spring break yet. There's more going on. I think you need to tell me." He sat there. Staring.

Sunny wondered if she'd taken Alice's Wonderland potion and was growing smaller. She had to check to see if she'd turned into Lily Tomlin's Alice Ann, sitting in a giant chair where her shoes hung off the edge, nowhere near the ground.

But no, she hadn't shrunk. Dad intimidated her when she knew she didn't live up to his expectations. Still, she wasn't ready to tell him everything. Not yet. She couldn't speak for Stormy, though she'd tried to deflect him onto the new business and away from recent disasters.

"Fine, if you don't want to talk."

"We don't." Sunny glanced at Stormy, who had echoed her words.

Dad shoved up from the table and headed for the kitchen. At the swinging door, he looked back. That gaze of disappointment stared them down. "You both realize I love you, right? You can tell me anything."

Sunny nodded. "Yeah, Daddy, we know. It's just not the best time. We love you too."

He pushed into his mother's lair, and she knew he'd try to worm it out of Gramma. Hopefully, her grandmother would stand firm against her baby boy.

Friday, March 6, 1970

PAT PICKED UP THE HANDSET and put it back. What was he thinking?

Well, that was obvious. He was thinking of the spunky blonde with the swinging ponytail who made his pulse beat in rhythm to Ricky Ricardo's conga drum. When she smiled, the entire room blazed her name. Sunny. No female had ever caught his attention like this.

And then his sister's face floated by. A cloud trying to obscure the light, reminding him he owed Venita. He'd promised her, and if he wanted to be a man of integrity, he needed to keep his promise. But what was integral in destroying that historic old house?

Just as he reached for the receiver once more, the phone rang. His private line. It had to be Venita.

"This is Pat."

"So?" Definitely Venita.

"So, hello to you too, sis. How are you?"

"I'm anxious. What did you learn in Kokomo?"

He sighed. "The mansion already sol—"

"I knew it! I can't catch a break with this."

"Calm down."

"Don't tell me to calm down. I told you something would happen if you waited." Great, now she blamed him.

"And I told you Dad had me involved with a negotiation I couldn't leave. I drove there as soon as my schedule allowed and I'm planning to go again." He was? Yeah, he was.

That brought a pause. He heard her dialing back her outrage.

"Again? You mean there's a chance?"

How did he form this without trapping himself? "I think there's something worth investigating. Besides, I'm not sure it's your best option. There are a couple other possibilities."

"Why would you think that? The location on that one is perfect."

This was harder than he'd imagined, and he fought to keep another sigh from escaping. "The house you want to raze is a classic old mansion. The historical society will fight you tooth and nail. You might be in litigation forever and still lose." Whew. He crossed his fingers, hoping he'd found the ticket.

"That's why I needed to buy from the other owner. It would have come from the original family without those preservationists getting involved." She knew it was historic? Where was her soul?

"Venita, I think if you saw the place, you'd have second thoughts. Let me get my list put together and I'll give you some great choices—and the locations will be prime." His digits grasping the receiver crossed and hope sent a prayer skyward. Just in case Someone up there cared.

Her sigh transmitted a bucket of disappointment through the telephone line, dumping it squarely on him. "Fine. But don't give up on the original site. I want that one if there's any chance. Call me soon with a progress report."

"I will. Hang in there, Venita. It's all going to work out."

"Right. You'd think that way. Later." She hung up before he said bye.

Pat stared a moment at the handset before an idea presented. Where had he put it? He searched until he found the scrap paper with the phone number, the one jotted with a large, precise script, and dialed. "Pat Whitcomb calling. May I speak with Chloe Ferguson?"

Soon the stereotypical sweet little old lady's voice came through his receiver. "Mr. Whitcomb, is it? This is Miss Ferguson. How may I help you?"

"I'm hoping you might help me reach Sunny Day, please? I don't have a phone contact for her." He smiled and hoped that friendliness poured through the line.

There was a pause. "I don't know you. Not sure I should give that information. What if I just say she's staying with her grandmother, Hazel Day? You take it from there. If you've a mind to go through her family." Sweet little voices could deceive—had she dared him?

She chuckled. Yep, she'd tossed out a challenge.

"That's fine. I'm happy to look that up. I appreciate your help, Miss Ferguson."

"Not a problem, Mr. Whitcomb. Goodbye." He could've sworn he heard her giggle as she signed off.

With a press of his intercom button, he got his secretary busy finding the phone number for one Hazel Day in Kokomo, Indiana. Two minutes later, he dialed that number.

"Hello?"

"Hello. Is this the Day residence?" Always another hoop.

"Yes, with whom do you wish to speak?" The voice switched to business-like.

"May I speak with Sunny? You can tell her it is Pat Whitcomb."

The tone relaxed. "Sure. Just as long as you're not...I'll get her." Though he was positive they covered the mouthpiece, he still heard the yell. "Sunny! You've got a phone call!"

He snorted. That reminded him of life at Trey's house. Big voices. No servants answering and quietly delivering messages.

"This is Sunny." The warmth of her smile came through, basking him as if he sunbathed on a beach.

"Hey, it's Pat. Just wanted to check in. How are plans progressing?"

The line grew quiet. For a moment he worried that his name wiped out the rays. Then she was back. "Um, Pat. I'm glad you called. Do you mind if I ask you some questions? We can make them in theory, or I'll pay you. Otherwise, I think I need another meeting with my lawyer."

"Ask away. I'll let you know if it's something where you should seek your personal legal adviser." She needed him. A foreign giddiness forced him to remember, he'd only seen her once.

"It looks like there has to be a city council meeting to discuss and approve the rezoning application. Technically, we're a residential area, but the commercial zone is so close, less than a block away. Plus a few houses have dual zoning allowing hairdressers and childcare to work out of their homes. I guess I can move, live at the mansion. Not excited about doing that yet. Still, if that's what's needed. So, my big question is: Would it be better to try for the dual zoning approval or commercial? And what roadblocks might I face?"

Pat sucked in against his teeth and winced. This bordered on giving legal advice. Best if he kept it hypothetical. "Let's return to your 'in theory' line of thought." He paced his office as if before a jury, wrapping and unwrapping the phone cord around him. "It'd be easier to get a dual rezoning ordinance than a commercial one."

Nervous energy made his deodorant less effective. His undershirt stuck to his body. And it was snowing outside. He needed to focus. "A commercial ordinance is not impossible to acquire because of the other businesses' proximity." In his mind's eye, she furiously scribbled notes.

Pat resumed pacing. "They could require a person to produce...adjustments. No telling what those might be, but figure anything from smoke alarms, fire sprinkler system, landscaping, parking considerations—who knows?"

Sunny echoed his "who knows?" and he imagined her mimicking his shrug.

He returned to his chair, sitting on the edge while starting a to-do list. "One would also need to notify neighbors of this hearing. I believe it must cover everyone within a quarter square mile, but that's something to explore as it changes from city to city. The smart move would be to have a presentation of the plans ready, allow for questions, and offer flexibility so neighbors feel validated. Then the counsel understands the presenter will work with them. Does that make sense?"

The silence made his stomach churn. Had he scared her? He'd been careful of his wording, but had he pushed his toe over the line?

She let out a rush of air. "Whew, that's tons more than in any of my textbooks. Thanks, Pat. Guess I've got some stuff to accomplish."

"When is your hearing?"

"Next Tuesday. If Stormy and I jump on this, we can get the invitations to our neighbors. Might take all Saturday, but we'll hand deliver so no one's missed."

"Want help with that?" Why did he say that? Fine, he knew why, but it was a stupid blunder. As much as he wanted her to accept his offer, he needed her to decline. If they were to get to know one another, he needed to take this slow.

"I hate to put you to work, but you are welcome to stop by. You don't have to get involved in this growing mess." She chuckled, but it tremored as if nervous. He hated how her needing him made him feel invincible.

"My day tomorrow is clear. I'll be there. Put me to work." He laughed despite knowing it was dangerous ground. This could bite him in a heartbeat.

"Great. Well, it looks like Stormy and I have gobs of postcards to make."

"Might I suggest something? If you have access to a mimeograph machine, you only need one master copy for multiple postcards on mimeograph paper. Then you crank out as many as you care to and cut them apart. It'll save you time and effort." Ha. That wasn't even legal advice. In theory. Just plain management. He grinned.

"Gramma mentioned her church has a machine. I'll ask if they'll let us use it. Thanks, Pat. Never would've thought of that idea. You give me hope, you know that?" Her voice enveloped him in a hug.

Was that so bad? "Happy to be of service, ma'am. Oh, where shall I meet you tomorrow, and what time?"

She gave her grandmother's address, and they settled on ten in the morning to give the day time to warm before having to walk the neighborhood. Unlike his sister, her goodbye was pleasant, inviting future calls.

His sister. How would she view this turn of events? As betrayal. Without a doubt. One more piece of evidence that the whole family was against her and she couldn't trust her own brother.

Perhaps she had a point. He was pulling for Sunny over Venita. But it wasn't as if he planned for Venita to lose. Or even plotted against her. He wanted to do what's right, his conscience shouted that in fact. And he needed a good relationship with his only sibling. Those two things weren't mutually exclusive, were they? They shouldn't be.

Scant concerning the Whitcombs was as it should be. They should show love for each other. Instead, they used one another.

And if he were honest, he was just as guilty. He went home when it met his needs, and to avoid his mother's nagging. He bowed to pressure so he wouldn't have to deal with his father's wrath. Where was his backbone?

Buried with his sense of injustice. Still, his conscience was digging them out. Bit by bit. Maybe one day soon he could face his family and let them know that he indeed loved them but longed to pursue the type of law that made a difference in society.

In the meantime, though, he'd continue to straddle the fence, helping Sunny where he could and try to appease Venita. He never considered himself a tightrope walker, but that was an appropriate description. Perhaps he'd better practice his balance. Besides, what could it hurt to offer non-legal assistance to Sunny?

His brain took up the chant, "Famous last words."

Chapter Five
Friday, March 6, 1970

S unny searched for her grandmother, room by room, without luck. She finally peeked outside and located her on the front porch swing, wrapped in her favorite cable-knit cardigan, staring into the space of the chilly weather.

"Gramma, are you okay?"

She glanced up. Sunny detected the split second of returning to the moment in her eyes. "Sure, lovey. Just deep in my thoughts." She shifted, adjusting her sweater. "What do you need?"

"Do you think your church would let me use their mimeograph machine? I've got to prepare those council meeting notices. Stormy and I must deliver them tomorrow."

Gramma stopped the swing with her toe and stood. "I'm sure they will. I'll make a phone call. You'll require your own supplies, though. How many copies?"

Sunny juggled some fast calculations in her head, enough to know she'd better check. "Not certain. Let me figure that while you dial." She raced into the house to find a city map of Kokomo.

With the map unfolded and laid out on the dining room table, she stared. They needed to cover north from Mulberry Street, south to the creek. Then from Western Ave heading east to Washington.

When she multiplied the number of residences and businesses in the area, guesstimating about twenty places per block, it was far more than she expected. Close to one thousand. Give or take. Sunny collapsed on her arms over her figures, banging her nose on the inlaid maple. "Ouch!"

"What's the matter?" Stormy stood over her, her hand patting Sunny's shoulder.

She raised her head and rubbed her beak. "I just realized how much walking we'll do tomorrow. We've gotta divide this up, no going together, and I've got a feeling we'll finishing on Sunday."

Stormy tugged at the page sticking out from under Sunny's elbow. "What do you mean? How many notices must we give?"

"About a thousand."

Stormy's sudden breath intake matched the way Sunny felt. "We'll be walking forever! And we've still gotta print the pages."

"Gramma is talking to someone with the church to see if we may use their machine. We need to buy paper and find a blank mimeograph sheet to type it up. I should be able to fit four notices on the master so there's only two hundred fifty sheets to cut apart. That's some good news."

"If that's your idea of good news, keep your bad." Stormy veered toward the kitchen.

"Hey, you're the one who begged to be included. You're a partner now. No backing out."

Her sister turned back. "I know. Need a sec to wrap my brain around it. And dig up massive determination for all that footwork. If you can develop an organized plan of attack, that could help."

Sunny sat straighter. Yes, an organized plan of attack. Definitely. "You go gear up or whatever you gotta do but bring me back a couple cookies. I might have something. Give me a few minutes." She didn't even wait for Stormy to leave. A solution was forming. Sunny needed to jot notes to make it materialize.

When Stormy returned with the plate of snickerdoodles, Sunny's something had gelled into a workable idea. "We'll start at the NE corner of our territory and come in one block west and south to park. There's three of us. Each can take a NE block. Cover all around it and meet back at the car. Move west and repeat until we've reached the NW corner. Repeat with SE to SW. That will leave the center area and one line of three blocks running horizontal east to west—we'll call them the spokes. We'll cover the eastern spoke before starting the SE to SW group, each of us taking one block, and the western spoke afterward. That leaves the middle block. By then we'll be tired, I'm sure, so how 'bout we do that one together? Let's stop for a break at the halfway point, before starting the SE/SW group. Yes. We can do this. Boy, I'm glad Pat called and volunteered to help. It'll take some pressure some off." In truth, that speech had been to encourage herself. If it brought Stormy onboard, all the better.

Stormy stared as if she'd just heard the explanation in a foreign language. "Tired, nothing. We'll be exhausted."

"How long does it take you to walk the block? Ten minutes? Add a little for attaching the notices on the doors. So, fifteen minutes, twenty max. You're doing one out of every three blocks except for the last. So, forty-eight divided by three is sixteen with a break after eight blocks. That's two, three hours walking with short car rests while we move to the next area. Times two with lunch in the middle. Not so bad, is it? We'll finish a lot sooner than I first thought."

Stormy plopped in the chair beside her. "When you put it that way, yeah, I think that's doable. What's first?"

"If Gramma has a mimeograph master, I can type it up while you run to the store for a ream of paper. Then we go to the church." She paused. "I should see if she got us permission." She scooted out and learned yes, it was fine. The office would be open until five. And yes, Gramma had a few masters in her desk from when she led vacation Bible school last summer.

Stormy headed out on her errand and Sunny typed the notice master, including all pertinent details. She enjoyed a moment with her cookies and was capturing the crumbs with her finger when Stormy returned. Next stop, the church.

The office stood empty of people but filled with the warm chemical scent of ink. Someone had just used the mimeograph machine.

With Sunny's plan, she cut the sheets for the first part, trading off with Stormy to run the machine the second half so neither would sport a sore shoulder from rotating the handle as it spit out indigo texted copies of the notice page. The sister not turning cut the sheets into fourths and stacked them in groups of one hundred, binding them with a rubber band. The entire process consumed less than an hour. They were out the door with blue fingers and pride in their accomplishment.

The next morning, Sunny woke with a smile, though she was hard pressed to say why. Then she remembered. Help was coming to get the notices out—help that embodied a dark-haired, handsome man with chocolate eyes... Wait a minute.

Now she knew why he seemed familiar. But it couldn't be. He'd have recognized her, too. No, Pat couldn't be the guy from the stairwell.

But if he was, did he remember? She'd been too wounded to maintain eye contact. Maybe he never got a close look. Maybe he hadn't been impressed and never gave the incident a second thought.

Or maybe he'd learned who she was and hunted her down?

That would be creepy. Better keep her barriers in place. Besides, Brock was a hunk, charming to boot. Look where that landed her.

Sunny threw on jeans and added an orange V-neck sweater over her button-down white shirt. Bobby socks, her Keds and a ponytail. She was ready to meet the world. Plus, if Pat didn't recollect, Saturday casual was as far from business attire as she could go to keep the memory at bay.

Stormy's bed was empty and made. Sunny found her in the dining room staring into a mug of coffee. "How d'you sleep, kiddo?"

Her sister startled. "Oh, fine, fine. Just couldn't get back once my eyes popped open."

"Are you sure you're okay?" Sunny sat next to her.

Stormy shook her head. "I need to sort some things. Not ready to talk about it."

"Okay, but you know I'm here when you're ready." Sunny patted her shoulder before heading for the kitchen to scrounge breakfast.

Gramma was already there, making bacon and eggs. Her dad's favorite. Guess she wanted to appease him for not caving with the details he tried to wrangle.

"Did Dad come down?"

"Not yet, sweetie. By the way, did you ask him to help with those fliers?"

No, she hadn't thought about that. "Think he'd like to? He usually just wants to unwind from work when he comes home."

"I know, but he loves you girls so. Now that you're grown, he doesn't have as much time with you."

"He got little time with us anyway, especially once he packed us off to your house. Not that I fault him. That was the best solution, considering." She shrugged. "We had it good with you, Gramma."

Her grandmother stopped checking the bacon to give her a quick hug before resuming her cooking duties. "Why not call him to breakfast and ask if he wants to go too? I'm sure he'd enjoy being with two of his girls."

"As long as he doesn't try info-fishing while he tags along." Sunny winked before trekking up the kitchen stairs to the second-floor bedrooms. Dad's room was next to hers, and she hadn't heard him stirring when she got dressed. But now his moving around sounds filtered under the door.

She knocked. "Dad, breakfast."

The door pulled open. "Hey Sunny, good. I'm hungry. I've caught up on my sleep so it's time to fuel up." He chuckled.

"Stormy and I need to pass out fliers. Let the neighbors know about the rezoning hearing next Tuesday. Like to come with us? I've got another friend coming too." She figured she'd better add that rather than blind-side him.

"You sure you want your old man along?"

"Yes, Daddy. We want you. Pat should be here close to ten. I'll go over my plan with you all when he arrives and then we'll take off."

"Okeydoke. Let's get some breakfast." He drew her into a side hug and guided her to the steps, letting her traverse in front of him to the kitchen where he planted a quick kiss on his mother's cheek before heading for the dining room.

"Go ahead, Dad. I'll bring in some coffee." Sunny grabbed two mugs as her stomach knotted. Would Pat get the wrong idea meeting her father? Would Dad arrive at the wrong conclusion meeting Pat?

At ten to ten, Pat pulled up. Stormy had let him in while Sunny gathered their supplies.

"Hope it's safe, Sunny. I left Pat in the living room with Dad. You might want to go check."

That could spell disaster. In more languages than she knew. She left Stormy to finish and hustled to the living room.

The men sat in the fireside chairs talking, Dad starting his third degree. "So where did you and Sunny meet?"

Pat glanced up at her and grinned. "I came to inquire if Ferguson House was for sale, only to find Sunny beat me to it."

She smiled back, stopping herself from running her hand across her brow sighing "whew." He didn't remember. Her breath returned.

Or was he not ready to bring it up?

Sunny gave each person a paper bag with two hundred fifty fliers. She'd had to re-divvy them after breakfast with Dad coming. And it was Dad's idea that they stay in groups of two, so no one was alone—Pat and Sunny together, and Dad with Stormy. Her sister shot her a wary glance. It might take longer, but Dad was right about safety. They agreed, but other than those two changes, they stuck to Sunny's plan.

The time sped so fast. Pat had stories that caused her to giggle. And he charmed the blue-haired old ladies like no one else. It was fun to watch, but a little niggle made her worry. Might he try his charming tactics on her? She would not traipse that road again. No way. Still, Pat's presence kept the task enjoyable.

It was a single day. Not a relationship. And Mary Poppins did sing about "A Spoonful of Sugar." Right? He made the unpleasant pleasant.

By noon, they were ready for a bite and met at Sunny's car. Dad offered to treat at Scotty's for burgers and fries. The girls claimed a booth while Dad and Pat stood in line.

Sunny was glad not to be anywhere near while Pat tried to pick up the tab and Dad remained firm. Besides, Stormy was anything but cheerful. By the time she started to ask her sister if something happened, Stormy shook her head and then nodded toward Dad, who carried a filled tray their way.

Pat brought up the rear with the drinks.

They passed out the food and cups.

Sunny was reaching for a ketchup packet when she heard the words she'd dreaded all morning.

"So, Mr. Day, what is it you do?"

Stormy cringed.

Sunny's stomach knots pulled tight.

"I'm a session musician. Work out of LA. I come home on occasion to unwind. It's a pretty busy schedule, playing for a couple of the top variety shows, I've recorded a few TV and movie themes. Do lots of productions with Burt Bacharach. Play backup at the Troubadour when I get a chance. Those jam sessions are great." Dad grinned, oblivious to his daughters' discomfort, and bit into his burger. "That sounds fascinating. I'm a music fan, almost always have albums playing when I'm alone. In fact, on the drive up I actually heard both Bobby Hebb's 'Sunny' and the *Classic IV*'s 'Stormy.' Couldn't get over..." Pat glanced from Sunny to Stormy. "Did I say something?"

Dad set his burger on the paper, his lips pursed. "The girls are under the impression that I ruined their lives with their names. And for good measure, I sort of inspired those songs."

"Dad, you weren't the one to deal with the teasing. Then, when classmates mercifully ran out of jokes about my name, those records popped up on the radio. I couldn't go anywhere without someone breaking into song and singing their own version of the lyrics. It's one thing to be tough-skinned. It's another being tormented every day. Do you realize that when I did my student teaching, I got teased by the faculty, the parents, and the kids?"

"Poor Stormy."

"Don't sound all poor Stormy or I'll give you what for. The one good part about Rob was I could change my surname."

Stormy scooped up the rest of her food, dumped it into the receptacle, and charged out the door.

Sunny stood. "Let me go talk with her. Excuse me." A glance at her father told her Stormy's parting shot had bullseyed a nerve.

As she pushed the breaker bar, it hit her. They'd better change partners if the fliers were to get posted. That realization made her want to clobber Dad and her sister.

Great. Just great. The rest of their day would be as stormy as her sister's name.

Saturday, March 7, 1970

"YOU BLAME ME, DON'T YOU?"

Pat pulled himself away from his internal pity party to catch Stormy's gaze. They'd started up the walk to their first house, and he realized his silence spoke louder to her than any conversation.

Yeah, he sort of blamed her for not getting to continue with Sunny. But for having an opinion about how she'd been treated? That wasn't his call. "I'm thinking. Sorry, don't mean to be so..."

"Unfriendly?" She cocked her head to the side, daring him to disagree.

"Is that what I've been? Then I apologize. That was never my intent."

"Calling it as I see it. You've got a thing for my sister. Figured you blame me for not getting more time with her."

Stormy spoke her mind, for sure. And Sunny mentioned she had a talent for reading people. Perhaps she figured the direct approach was best with him. "We've just met, but I do like what I've learned."

"Well, be gentle. She won't talk about it, but something has hurt her pretty bad recently. That's why she's home." Stormy tucked the flier in the storm door's décor and walked back to him. They headed for the next house.

"What happened?" If he couldn't be with Sunny, could he learn about her?

"Not sure. It had to do with her job in the governor's office. That's all I know. Can't imagine what it would have been, but she's not as happy as she used to be unless she's seeing progress on this house project."

He grabbed her elbow and stopped her. "She worked in Indianapolis?"

"Yep. One of the young up and comers. She was on the fast track and then she showed up at Gramma's."

A flash of memory popped in his brain, like a bulb illuminating a photo pose. The girl he knocked to the floor in the stairwell at the capitol. Her belongings strewn about. *Jonathan Livingston Seagull*, dark blonde hair, eyes puffy from tears. That was why Sunny felt familiar. They'd met before.

Did she remember him? She never said a word. But if it happened during a painful time, she might not bring it up.

Should he?

"Hey, there you go. Do you often let your thoughts drift off with you?"

"Sorry. Again. You reminded me of something. I'll do this house." He charged ahead, rolled the flier and slipped it under the door handle. It gave him a moment to recover. When he returned to her, he made sure he was smiling and paying attention.

"How 'bout you share what you think I need to know about your sister?" They continued.

"Let's see. She's the glue that's kept us together. A real mother hen. Since our mother wasn't much of one. When she left, Dad packed us up and shipped us to Gramma's. We had our first taste of a proper home. But Sunny'd always kept tabs on us. Tucked us in at night, listened to our woes, stood up to our bullies, and told us we'd make it." Funny how she said it all as if reading a phone book, except when she spoke of Sunny. She slipped the flier between the door and jamb and hustled back.

"Who is we?"

"Windy and me. Our younger sister. Yeah, Sunny Day, Stormy Day, and Windy Day. But Windy's name fits. There's something breezy and light about her. She's the artistic one. Got all of Dad's talent and our mother's imagination. She can play the piano, paint, sculpt, walk into a room and rearrange one piece and make it a million times better. But she's flighty and a risk taker. Not so much out of bravery. Just from not considering the consequences. She lives in the moment. You'd have to meet her to understand, I guess. Sunny's had her hands full with her."

This dovetailed with Aaron's story at lunch after the girls left. He didn't elaborate on why he was a single parent, only that his mother had stepped in to help when he needed it. And he explained that one day in the lunchroom at Capitol Towers, he talked with Bobby Hebb after he'd gotten mail from Sunny, who was trying to cheer up her father. It touched him, so he shared parts of the letter. Bobby was inspired and wrote "Sunny."

Something similar happened a few years later after a conversation with Ruthann Friedman. She'd been hanging with David Crosby and showed up for a recording session with him. Aaron told her she reminded him of his daughter Windy and pulled out her school photo. Ruthann ran home, composed the song in twenty minutes, and offered it to Terry Kirkman of *The Association*.

Then there was an argument over the phone with Stormy overheard by Buddy Buie that inspired her namesake song. Aaron was flustered, but Buddy said nothing until he presented the words to Aaron and J. R. Cobb the following day. The next thing he knew, *Dennis Yost and the Classics IV* recorded it. He never set out to embarrass his girls and thought of the songs as lovely tributes.

Pat could see both sides of it. Yeah. Sunny's name may fit her. Still, he wouldn't want to forge through life with that label. His own surname brought enough baggage.

"Hey, Whitcomb. Are you in there?" Stormy'd stopped in the middle of the sidewalk, hands on her hips.

He sighed and motioned her forward. "On information overload, I guess. Just tell me more about Sunny. But wait while I take this house."

As he rolled the flier to tuck behind the storm door handle, the inner door pulled open.

"What're you doing?"

"Good afternoon, sir. We wanted to leave you a notice that there will be a rezoning council meeting this next Tuesday. All the information is on the paper. We look forward to seeing you there." He gave his best lobbying smile.

"Why've I gotta go to some blamed meeting? Just because someone wants to change things?"

"Sir, we're trying to include you, make sure all voices are heard. My friend has purchased the Ferguson House and plans to open her business there."

"Don't need more businesses around here. They're pushing people out of their homes, bringing riff raff into the neighborhoods."

"Sir, by purchasing the home, she's working to preserve it for the future by turning it into a money-making project."

"Bah! I'll be there. You bet I'll be there. And my voice'll be heard. You wait and see." He slammed the door. But before Pat could recover, the grump pulled it open, opened the storm door as well, and yanked the flier from Pat's hands before slamming everything again.

When he turned back to the broken cement path, Stormy had her hand over her mouth. Her eyes danced and her body trembled, though no sound came out. He joined her on the sidewalk. "Go ahead."

"So, that went well." She snorted.

"I know. No winning with him. The old geezer plain didn't want to agree."

Stormy shook her head. "You didn't read him. The guy is lonely. Did you notice his lawn? The cracked paint on the house? He lives alone and either can't afford help or has health problems that keep him from fixing things. Maybe both. Don't worry. It'll take a lot of effort for him to show up. He might, but the probability is low. Depends on how angry you made him. If he does come, I'll talk to him."

It didn't remove his concern, but her words lessened it. He could just envision the curmudgeon holding the vote hostage with his dissenting opinion. Sunny would have him to blame. *Great way to help, Whitcomb.*

"So, you want to hear about Sunny, huh? First, don't ever lie to her. She can't tolerate that. Also, if you see her rubbing her earlobe, best start apologizing. She's trying to keep from exploding. Oh, and one more thing. Only try this under extreme circumstances. Wear her down. She will finally give in and then you can present your side, but slather it with honey, if you know what I mean."

He chuckled. "I understand. So, Tuesday night, if she starts rubbing her earlobe when Mr. Friendly gets going, I apologize fast and then beg for my life until she relents."

"Bingo." Stormy grinned. "You might be her thing, Bucko. You've got my approval. Just don't screw it up." She headed for the next door.

By four-thirty they piled into Sunny's Camaro to return to her grandmother's.

Pat better understood their family dynamics and had a greater appreciation for Sunny, who invited him to stay for dinner before heading to Indianapolis. Common sense said to hit the road, but the magnetism of her smile drew out a "Sure, thank you."

Pat had to admit, he enjoyed the Day family. It was open and real like his buddy Trey's. Even with the lunchtime drama, he knew they loved each other.

He spotted Stormy brushing a kiss on her father's cheek before they headed for the dining room to supper.

Mrs. Day, Sunny's grandmother, spoke a prayer over the meal before they all dug in. He remembered Trey's parents doing that, too. Not a habit he'd developed since, outside of Christmas and Easter, religion wasn't part of Whitcomb life.

Apparently, the house's quiet had been put to good use. Their grandmother served a pork roast that needed no knife to cut. That first bite melted on his tongue. He must have closed his eyes and sighed because everything grew silent and he discovered he'd become the focal point. "Great roast, Mrs. Day."

"Thank you, Pat. And please call me Hazel." She set her fork on her plate and surveyed those around the table. "By the way, family, we will have a guest for dinner tomorrow. So, you are warned. Best behavior."

"Gramma, we're always on our best behavior." Stormy's eyes were wide, but Sunny snickered behind her hand. Even Aaron tried to cover his grin.

"Since we have company, I'll not march down the list of proof illustrating the inaccuracy of that statement. But you all know what I'm talking about, and I expect manners and courtesy." She picked up her fork and threw Pat a wink. So, she was daring her clan. Too bad he'd be stuck in Indianapolis. It could be fun.

Thunder cracked the quiet, making his heart thud. A glance about assured him he wasn't alone. A moment later, rain splatters hit the dining-room windows high on the wall, growing fiercer and louder by the second.

Sunny caught his gaze. "Guess I shouldn't have asked you to stay. Now it's not safe to drive home."

He shook his head. "I've driven in worse." And he had. Just not by choice.

Aaron pointed to his mother with his butter knife. "Mom, the girls are together in their room, right? Put Pat in the guest room. No sense in driving in this. Who knows how long it will last?"

"Oh, no need. I appreciate the gesture—"

Hazel stared him down. "Appreciate, schmeciate. You're staying. No more arguing."

"Yes, ma'am." Little intimidated him, but on the short list was Mrs. Hazel Day. Along with his sister, his mother, his father—Okay, so it wasn't a short list.

Sunny glanced his way while her eyes twinkled with giggles. "Guess that's settled."

They broke into laughter, drowning out the pings and slaps at the window-panes. Aaron was the first to gain control and wipe his eyes. "Hope we don't lose electricity tonight." The tone sombered.

"That's why we have a fireplace and candles and flashlights and blankets. No more asking for worries. We're safe and dry. Let's be grateful and enjoy each other's company." From the way she spoke, Pat figured nothing rattled Hazel.

Then the front door flew open.

Everyone turned and stared.

A bedraggled young woman dripped inside, closed the door, and sloshed toward the dining room.

Hazel jumped from her chair and began wiping the girl down with her napkin. "Windy June Day. What in the world!"

"Hi, Gramma. I'm home."

Chapter Six
Saturday, March 7, 1970

"Aaron, you can loan Pat a pair of pajamas. Plus, he'll need a sports coat with a shirt and tie for church in the morning."

Sunny nearly lost control when she glanced at Pat's expression. Her grandmother's words must have taken him by surprise. Didn't he go to church? Perhaps he figured to head home instead.

"There's no—"

Poor guy apparently hadn't learned. Just give in, man.

"Patrick, you are our guest. We will see to your needs. We leave at 9:15. Breakfast is at eight." As far as Gramma was concerned, it was settled.

Sunny followed Gramma upstairs to help get Windy out of her wet clothes. Her baby sister had taken the bus from DePauw and walked from the downtown terminal in the storm. Gramma made her some hot tea while Sunny tucked her in and sat on the edge of the bed, giving them time to talk. "So, what brings you home?"

"It's spring break." But Windy didn't make eye contact.

"Yeah, but what else?"

"Don't tell Dad yet. Please. I'll tell him when I'm ready. But I'm done with school. Not going back." She had that little girl look in her eyes, the one that offered her trust to Sunny but begged to have her secrets kept.

Sunny wiped damp white-blonde bangs from Windy's forehead, checking for a fever while she was at it. "I won't tell. But you'll have to—and soon." She chuckled. "It'll be like old times. The three of us together in here."

Windy propped up on her elbows. "You mean you and Stormy moved back too? What happened?"

Sunny folded her hands in her lap. Her sister would keep her secret, but she wasn't ready to verbalize it yet. "Let's just say I needed a change, so I bought Chloe's house. I'm turning it into a bridal shop and venue, if the meeting Tuesday night goes well. As for Stormy, she's not talking, but she left Rob and her classroom. Can't imagine what happened. Teaching's all she ever wanted. But now we're partners in the business, so that's our focus."

Windy squeezed her hand. "When it all comes out, Dad and Gramma are gonna get nailed. With a lot. Good thing they can handle catastrophe."

Sunny glanced at her baby sister. The flighty one, a will-o'-the-wisp. Little Windy summed up what teased the recesses of her mind. Could Gramma and Dad handle everything? When had her baby sister gotten so grown up and wise?

Gramma appeared with the tea, and they left Windy to relax and catch some sleep.

Hours later, after Dad brought down a pair of pjs and everyone else slipped off to bed, Pat and Sunny remained in the living room enjoying the glow from the fireplace. She'd brought in a plate of Gramma's Swedish spritz cookies and hot cocoa, then sat on the floor to watch the flames. Perfect for a rainy night.

Pat joined her. After his "thank you" for the treat, he entered her silence. It was comfortable. No need to speak. Finally, though, she figured she should mention that they'd met before. "I knew you seemed familiar that day you showed up at the mansion."

"Yeah, I had the same thought. It wasn't until Stormy and I got talking that I remembered." He held her gaze.

"You did? I was a mess. Probably the worst day of my life. Thank you for your kindness. I should have thanked you then."

He smiled. "You did. Do you want to talk about it?"

She shook her head. "No. Too much..."

"Pain?"

"That, and shame. I should have known better. Let's pick a different topic. Tell me more about you. You're a lawyer. What type of law do you practice?"

"Corporate. Not what I want to do, though. I hope one day to open my own defense office. So I can help people. When I see suspects, who probably wouldn't even be suspects if they had a lawyer who would fight for them, it makes me..."

"Incensed?"

"Yes, incensed. I've a buddy from law school. We used to talk about starting a practice together. But he got married and moved to Arizona. Now he has his own law office. Got to admit, I'm a little jealous." He stretched out on his side, propping his head on his fist, and capturing her gaze.

"So, why don't you?"

He glanced away. "It's a family thing. They need me. They also paid for my schooling, so I guess there's the notion I owe them. Not sure who buys that excuse more, me or my folks." He laid flat back and stared at the ceiling.

"Must be difficult having a passion and not acting on it."

He turned to her, staring as if weighing her words. "Yeah, it is. Thanks. My family thinks I work in a great field, make enough money, I should be happy. But it drags me down."

"Sometimes pleasing family can be tough, especially when they have a certain image of you." This was the first she'd seen past his gentle smile and kind-heartedness. And she liked what she saw.

He closed his eyes. "One of these days I'll get the gumption to stand up for myself."

"You'll know when."

"You think so?"

"Yeah, I think so."

They returned to the quiet, but his hand reached out and found hers. She watched the fire while he laid sprawled, their fingers intertwined. A part of her wanted him to kiss her, or at least try. It was too soon, but she imagined it would be sweet.

But then, so were Brock's kisses. She had trusted him and missed all the danger signals. Was she so naïve that she'd fall for a guy like that again? Was Pat that type of man? She didn't think so, but her picker was definitely broken. Could she trust her own judgment? She slipped her fingers free. "I'd better get upstairs, grab some sleep. Gramma's a tyrant about church. I'll show you to your room." She stood and pointed to the couch. "Don't forget your pjs."

He obeyed, but his eyes searched hers a moment.

It wasn't time to trust him. It might never be. For now, she'd keep up her guard.

The next morning was a flurry of breakfast and getting ready. Gramma checked on Windy after Sunny noticed she was all stuffy and warm, deciding the girl could remain home today.

"Aaron, you must stay with Windy. I know it'll break your heart to miss, but God can do without your sarcasm for one more Sunday." Though he attended out of respect for his mother, Sunny knew Dad wouldn't darken a church door without that incentive. He sank back onto the couch, a smile teasing his lips.

Nine-fifteen on the dot, Gramma stood at the door, waving her charges to her station wagon. Pat was allowed to sit up front while Stormy and Sunny settled in the middle seat. Just like when they were in high school, except Windy usually sat in the front passenger seat where Gramma could keep a better eye on her.

Wabash Congregational was located a block and a half from the mansion. Which got Sunny thinking. Where would all the cars park in case of a large wedding event? Would the church allow them to use valet parking with their lot? Something to think about.

They slid into the pew the Day family had occupied for the last few decades, and somehow Pat ended up seated between Sunny and Stormy. Causing more than mild discomfort. Her heart worked its way to the base of her esophagus, making her eardrums thunder with its rapidly increasing beat. When she reached for the hymnal, her hand shook. Why was she so nervous?

Why was she asking herself stupid questions?

It was one hour. She could handle one hour. And then his fingers found hers and gave a little squeeze, sending electrical charges up her arm. Did he realize the effect he had on her? He must not. It'd be devious to cause that on purpose in church. Right?

She prayed no one asked her about the sermon because she couldn't remember a single point. A fraud. That's what she was. She glanced down the row to see if everyone realized. That's when she spotted that older gentleman who'd been by the house now sitting with Gramma at the end of the pew.

He held her grandmother's hand.

Sunny reached across Pat to Stormy and tapped her arm, before motioning with her head.

Stormy glanced Gramma's way, and then her eyes grew wide.

Pat leaned close. "What?" The question furrows between his brows deepened.

"Gramma's holding hands with some guy." She whispered directly to his ear with the least amount of voice. "Never seen that before."

He grinned and shook his head. "You Day women all have your secrets." He winked.

Was he right? Did Gramma have a secret? Then she remembered about the guest her grandmother announced last night. Sunny could guess who was coming for dinner.

After church, Sunny, Stormy, and Pat stood near the corner while Gramma chatted with other members. All the while that guy stayed by her side and eventually walked her to her car while Sunny and crew trailed behind. He opened Gramma's door and held it while she climbed in and rolled down her window. "We'll see you at the house, Gene. Dinner should be on the table in forty-five minutes."

He patted her hand. And then leaned in and...

He kissed her grandmother!

Stormy gasped, and all gazes turned her way.

Gramma pinked but told the man goodbye and re-rolled her window before starting her ignition. She uttered nary a word the entire drive home.

Once they parked in the driveway, Sunny climbed out and raced upstairs to her room. "I'll be down in a minute, Gramma, to help you. Just putting my things away."

Stormy followed on her heels, saying nothing until she closed the door behind her and leaned against it. "Gramma let some guy kiss her in the church parking lot and he's coming to dinner. Get up, get up, get up, Windy. You don't want to miss this."

Windy glanced from Stormy to Sunny. "What? I stay home and this happens?"

Sunny sat on her bed and felt the Windy's forehead. "You'll be staying in bed. You still have a fever." She adjusted her sister's blankets.

"Great. Of all the luck! Now I get a head cold."

Stormy placed her palm on Windy's forehead. "You always did have poor timing. We'll slip up here and give you play-by-play."

Sunny chuckled, but Windy wasn't amused.

"Why do I have to miss? It's only a stupid cold."

"You don't want your germs all over everyone. I know, timing is everything, but we'll keep you informed. Do you need anything?" This time, Sunny wasn't checking for fever when she brushed Windy's bangs from her forehead.

"No. I'm just bored. And your cat keeps jumping up on me whenever I doze off."

"Frazier? He's a sweetie. Probably checking to see if you're still alive." Sunny did a quick glance around for her pet. She'd neglected his attention lately, trying to get things done for the mansion.

"Well, tell him I died and to leave me alone."

"Aye, aye, Miss Grumpypants." Sunny stood and kissed Windy's cheek before heading for the door. "We'll be up as often as possible. Hang in there."

Stormy followed her out and down the stairs where Gramma put them to work. Her guest had already shown up and was in the living room watching TV with Pat and Dad.

"Girls, I need you to be on your best behavior. I know I said this last evening. Please understand how important this is to me. Gene is special. Be nice." Gramma had asked nothing like this before.

"We will, Gramma. It, he, well, I guess we're just a little surprised is all." Sunny paused from slicing a tomato for the salad.

"Why? You think I'm too old to have romantic feelings?"

"No!" Sunny and Stormy both shook their heads, but inside Sunny realized she'd sort of assumed that. No idea why, though.

"Okay, let's get this meal served. Stormy, call the men."

Gramma led the way with her pot roast on the serving platter.

Minutes later they were all around the table. Gene, Gramma's boyfriend—boy, was that hard to consider—said grace before they started passing the dishes.

"So Sunny, I understand you've bought Chloe's place and hope to make it a business." The guy appeared to be friendly.

"Yes. We, Stormy and I, have a rezoning meeting on Tuesday. If that is successful, then it's full steam ahead. Rather, I guess that depends on what they decide we must do on our end. If it's too expensive, I don't know what I'll, we'll do." The complete weight of that decision started to lean heavily on her shoulders.

"I've got a grandson who is pretty handy. His name is Kris, and I can vouch for him. He's a hard worker and will give you a good price."

"What all does he do?" Sunny peeked at Stormy, who paid attention too.

"He's great with construction, plumbing, even landscaping. Kind of a jack of all trades. Never seen the likes of it. I taught him a few techniques, and he just perfected them to a whole 'nuther level. Want me to send him around?" Gene took another bite of roast.

A quick glance at Stormy who gave a tiny nod helped her decide. "We won't know what's what until after the meeting. If things go well, you can ask him to stop by Wednesday. If they don't, we've no idea what the next step is."

And that's when it hit her. Tuesday either gave her the go ahead, or she'd sunk everything into something she'd have to sell.

Tuesday, March 10, 1970

PAT TURNED OFF ON MARKLAND Avenue, heading west to Washington Street. Traffic hadn't been too bad. Perhaps because it was a Tuesday. Whatever the reason, he made it to the meeting with time to spare.

His secretary had called around for him and learned the rezoning commission liked to use the conference rooms at the courthouse, and this one had its entrance on the south side of the building. He checked his watch. No time to grab a bite. However, if this meeting went as hoped, perhaps he'd invite Sunny for an impromptu dinner afterward.

Funny how he could find ways to escape his meetings for her. Dump his plans and drive all this way, but he made Venita wait two weeks. Well, not exactly funny. And he'd have tried sooner if he'd known that Sunny was up here. Of course, the house wouldn't have been sold. And they would have never met. Again.

Her eyes had haunted him ever since he remembered where they first bumped into each other. She carried the world on her shoulders. Still, she kept plugging along like that's what she was born to do.

Another car parked a few spaces away. Sunny's Camaro. It was time to go in. Would she be glad he came? He'd never hoped so hard. Would've actually prayed if he thought it would work.

She glanced up as he climbed from his Mustang and the slow smile spreading across her face added glow to the dusk fading into twilight. "Hey Pat. Didn't expect to see you here."

"Where else would I be?" He locked his car door and headed her direction.

"Oh, I don't know, Indianapolis?" Her grin grew, and she chuckled, sort of throaty-like.

"It's a pleasant drive."

"Listen, Buster, I've driven that road. It's got places, but unless you're a big fan of corn fields or soybeans, you're kind of stuck."

That cracked him up. "I enjoy the radio more than the scenery. Plus no one complains when I sing. It's pretty sweet."

They were giggling together when Stormy piped in. "We'd better grab some seats. Yeah, hi Pat. I'm so shocked to see you here." She tossed him a wink. Yep, Stormy had his number all right. But as long as he had her approval, he didn't care.

Inside, they found seats near the front. Windy tagged along, and it was the first time he'd seen her not doing her drowned silver mink impression. She possessed the same family resemblance, but where Stormy was taller and more angular, Windy gave the appearance of being able to float away. She stood the same height as Sunny but was the blondest. Her features were delicate, making her eyes appear like those waif children that were all the rage in the paintings—dark rimmed lids and brows against that almost white hair. He finally understood what Stormy meant about Windy fitting her name.

He turned to ask Sunny about dinner afterward, but Stormy punched his arm. Then indicated with her head toward the rear.

Several people entered the hall, but one stood out. That unfriendly neighbor he and Stormy tangled with last Saturday.

Oh, great. Just great. Now Sunny would know how he screwed up royal. His only job was to put fliers on the doors. What a fabulous time for the floor to open up and swallow him whole. If only.

"I'm so nervous. It finally hit me Sunday. This will either give us a chance or kill the deal. You might want to be prepared to buy the house." Her glance told him how her stress had built.

"You won't need me to. It's going to work." He sounded way more confident than he felt. *Please let it work.* Okay, that might have been a prayer. Maybe he needed to talk with Trey about this God stuff.

The council chair called the meeting to order and read Sunny's petition for rezoning before opening the floor for comments.

The first one to the mic was Neighbor Guy. He shuffled to the stand and blew on the microphone. "Can you hear me? Is this thing on?" He tapped the wire mesh.

The rest of the audience groaned, but the council speaker assured him it was fine.

"Good. I just want to say I am tired of change. I don't need another business in the neighborhood. They increase traffic and who knows what else. Keep things the way they are."

The council secretary held up his hand. "Excuse me. Please give us your name and address for the record."

"Gordan Jessup. I live at 1302 W. Mulberry."

"Thank you, Mr. Jessup. Please continue."

And he did. For five minutes. Finally, once he finished, the chairman gazed Sunny's way. "Would you like to respond to this?"

Sunny stared, shell-shocked.

Would she be okay?

But Stormy patted her arm as she slipped past to the mic. "Hello, Mr. Jessup. You bring up some valid points. It is difficult when things change, I agree. I'm not sure if you are aware, but Miss Ferguson was living alone in that big house.

She's taken great pride in her home. Remember going by and seeing the lovely flowers she'd plant in the spring? Always one of my favorite memories.

"But Miss Ferguson is getting up there. Her niece offered her a place to live. But that would mean leaving her home. One that had been in her family for three generations. She'd faithfully cared for it but had no one to take over. And then she received offers to sell. But they wanted to tear down that gorgeous piece of history. That broke her heart. So, she sold to my sister, knowing the home would be maintained and well-tended."

Stormy moved closer to the man, directing her words to him more personally. "Only, that takes money. Without cash, how does one manage the landscaping? Or stay on top of those minor leaks and cracks that become an eyesore, or worse? So, by keeping the integrity of the mansion, but growing a small business under its roof, Ferguson House can continue. Do you understand, Mr. Jessup?"

Pat watched as the grumpy old man became putty in Stormy's hands. By the time she broached her question, he would've said yes to anything. She was born to sell, that was a fact.

The chairman turned to Mr. Jessup. "Have your concerns been adequately addressed?"

The old man nodded. Stormy squeezed his shoulder and his face lit up. His posture straightened, and he returned to his seat, happier to have lost than if he'd won.

"Anyone else?"

"I'd like to say something."

Pat swiveled, scanning the audience.

A hand waved above the seated crowd, followed by a man standing—a clergyman, by his attire. He excused himself as he slipped past the others in his row until he got to the aisle where he strode to the microphone. "I am the Reverend Carl Mussing from Wabash Community Church."

Hazel's church? That's not who he heard speak. Pat glanced at Sunny.

She leaned toward him. "It was a guest speaker last Sunday. This is the regular pastor."

Pat nodded and watched to see what happened.

"First, I want to say that it is commendable for Miss Day to step up to help Miss Ferguson, who was part of our congregation until she moved to Greentown. I applaud her motives and agree, we need to preserve that mansion. However, I have a problem with weddings being performed in pretty venues for the venue's sake. A marriage is a solemn undertaking. God must be the cornerstone, and that requires the church. Perhaps there is some other method to save the house?"

"Response?"

Again, Stormy took charge. "Reverend. Thank you for standing up for my sister. I'm glad you understand what is at stake and what she's trying to do. And I agree. A marriage is a solemn undertaking. Without God, it hasn't much of a chance. But is God only discovered in a church building? Another thought, Reverend: On occasion could the ceremony be performed in the sanctuary? Then followed by the reception held at the mansion? Let's go further. Can the rooms of Ferguson House be blessed with God's presence too? What about people who don't recognize God or don't believe? It happens." She shrugged. "If we offer something for them and they learn we have cooperation from the nearby church—maybe you'd allow us to use your parking lot for overflow or valet parking when it's a large event? That would be proof of our working to-gether and could give a favorable view. A little of the Good Samaritan, wedding style. Can you see that happening?"

The pastor studied Stormy a moment before responding. "Mrs. Crawford, I always knew you had a way with words. You should have gone into the ministry."

He cracked a smile. "Yes, I can see your side. I will withdraw my objection for the time being." He patted Stormy's shoulder and returned to his seat.

Stormy glanced around the room and smiled before slipping past her sisters and Pat to her seat.

"Anyone else?" The chairman waited before continuing.

"We're calling a short recess so the counsel can come to an agreement. We'll return in five minutes." He scooted back his chair from the table stretched across the front of the stage. The rest of the seven-member council followed suit.

Sunny turned in her seat to lean over Pat. "You were amazing, Stormy. You knew just what to say. I was so tongue tied I couldn't have squeaked out my name."

"Anyone watching could have figured it all out. Besides, I had a head start with Mr. Jessup. I saw where he lived."

Pat gave Stormy a warning glance and crossed his fingers.

"Mr. Suave here is worried you'll find out he's the one who got Mr. Jessup all riled. Let it go, Pat. Whoever placed that flier would've had the same reception. I just figured out how to talk to the guy."

Pat tugged at his collar as the room's temperature took a turn for tropical. *Thanks, Stormy.*

"You had a problem with him? Why didn't you tell me?" Sunny turned her gaze on him.

"I didn't want you to worry. And you would have, right?" Which was true. Just not the whole truth.

"Yeah, I would've. Well, it's taken care of now. Just hope there's no one on the council who needs convincing." She leaned back in her seat and began to massage her earlobe.

Pat's heart thudded to a stop. He turned to Stormy, who sat there grinning before she leaned over to whisper at his ear. "She's self-soothing. It's not always anger that sets her off."

His heart thunked into gear as he nodded.

The council returned to their seats, and the chairman spoke into the microphone. "Miss Day? We've decided to issue you a dual zoning license. Have you moved into the house?"

Sunny stood and proceeded to the floor mic. "No sir, not yet. But I can first thing tomorrow."

"That will work. The other thing is you must ensure there's adequate parking. I realize you have no feasible way to construct parking for a large wedding on your property. But parking for thirty cars is what we ask. You have ninety days to get the lot ready. If you do that, this temporary license will be replaced with a regular one. We wish you the best with this endeavor and want to publicly thank you for trying to protect one of our city's great historic homes. Meeting dismissed."

The council stood and moved from their table. Those in attendance headed for the door.

Sunny didn't move.

Pat made his way to her.

She looked like she faced an oncoming car, ready for impact.

He pulled her to him, and she allowed him to hold her until the room had cleared. Finally, he drew back and lifted her chin. "Sunny, we need to go. Would you like a cup of coffee?" What concerned him more was helping her snap out of this fog than trying to finagle a date.

Stormy and Windy sidled up on either side. "We'd love to get some coffee."

At that point Sunny met his gaze. "I have no money for a cup of coffee. I don't know how I'm going to pay for the parking lot. I think I won only to have lost anyway."

And that's when he knew. He must find a way. Make this happen. For her.

Chapter Seven
Wednesday, March 11, 1970

Sunny unloaded her Camaro for the second time in under a month. At this rate, she should leave it all in boxes. No, she shook her head. It would be nice to have her privacy again.

Though living above a business where employees come and go...

Okay, so at this point it's only her sister. Since they all lived in the same town now, that was bound to happen. With a sigh, she heaved the last box from her car. She'd run back to Gramma's later for Frazier.

And after hauling everything but her kitchen items upstairs, she decided she'd better take a walk around the property to figure out where to put the parking area, just in case she won the lottery, or it started to rain money.

An alleyway off Phillips Street led past the back of her house. Could that be an entrance? She walked the grounds with a pencil and sketch pad, getting a rough layout, and then hopped in her car to go to Wabash Congregational, bringing a tape measure and her Polaroid camera. If she counted out thirty spots, she'd have a better idea of the area involved.

However, when she transposed the information from the church's parking lot to her sketch, all she saw was danger to the ancient sycamore and a loss of her garden. She needed that for the big weddings.

Instead of going back to the mansion, she headed for her grandmother's. If nothing else, Gramma could start praying again. That was Sunny's last hope.

As she pulled in the driveway, Gramma came out to greet her. "I've been trying to reach you, sweetie. Kris is inside."

"Kris?"

Her grandmother linked arms with her, practically dragging her to the porch. "You remember, Gene's grandson. He's here to talk with you about a job."

"Oh, Gramma. I haven't money to hire anyone. I'd be glad to if I did. Right now, though, I can't. I don't know what I'm going to do. I just researched what it will take to add a thirty-car parking lot. It's not good." Sunny almost mentioned the sycamore but couldn't speak the words.

"Don't worry about that now, hon. Come inside and meet Kris."

Sunny allowed her grandmother to lead her to the dining room where Kris sat with a glass of milk and a plate of cookies.

At least she figured it was Kris. He was the only one there. And he was hard to miss as he filled the chair. Not fat by any means, but those muscles rippled under his waffled long-sleeve polo as he reached for his snack. With sandy brown hair and gray eyes, his face lit a little more with each oatmeal raisin bite.

He gave off a mellow impression. Not that she was interested.

However, that type of company working while she fought her stressors might be a peaceful change of pace.

She offered a handshake. "Hey Kris, nice to meet you. I'm Sunny."

He wiped his hand on his pant leg before shaking hers, talking around his food. "Yeah, same here. Do you get these cookies every day?" He swallowed hard.

Sunny laughed and sat in the next chair, dropping her sketch pad and camera on the table beside her. "Gramma keeps her jar filled. Wait until you try her snickerdoodles." She cleared her throat and pulled on her professional face. "So, your grandfather says you're one of the best handymen around. Can you tell me a little about your experience?"

"I had some trade school after graduation. Shop was my favorite class, only place I did well. Except for some math classes. Geometry made sense to me and I use it a lot with my work." He chewed his lip and tipped his head to the side. "Actually, I thought I already had the job. Even had a messenger drop off a paycheck to me before lunch."

What was he talking about? "I don't understand. I'm the owner and we've just met. Who else interviewed you?"

"Some guy on the phone. Said he was part of a corporation with an interest. I've got the check here." He pulled it from his pocket and handed it over.

The amount staggered her. If she hadn't already been sitting, her knees would have buckled, and she'd be on the floor. "How...did he...what was this for?"

"Explained it was for my first month's pay and any supplies I needed. He said to rent some machinery, a leveler and a grader, for outside work." He swiped another cookie.

"I see." That's when she focused on the company name and signature. Whitcomb International. Patrick G. Whitcomb. Should she kiss him or kill him?

Whitcomb International? Oh, not those Whitcombs! Kill him was winning.

The room closed in tighter. The air got sucked out. Sunny grabbed at the table while little sparks flickered before her face. From somewhere far away, she heard voices.

"Hey, are you okay? Uh, Mrs. Day, I think you need to get in here."

Things spun, and her eyes grew too heavy. She started sliding, so heavy...

"Sunny? Hey, Sunny girl, come on, wake up." Gramma's voice.

She cracked open her eyes.

"There you are. Stormy, get some cold wet rags. Windy, go find your dad." Gramma held her hand and was rubbing her wrist.

She realized she lay on the floor so pulled in a breath and tried to sit.

Gramma pushed her back. "You stay there. What happened?"

Sunny swiped her hair from her face as pieces came back. The check. Pat had written a giant check to Kris, hired him for her. But then, oh yeah, more details filed through her memory.

Pat wasn't just Pat Whitcomb, the corporate lawyer. He was Patrick G. Whitcomb of the first family of Indiana and heir apparent to the dynasty. That's who she'd almost bared her soul to.

Thank heavens she hadn't.

"Gramma, did you know?" How far did this conspiracy go?

"About what, sweetie?" She took the cool rag from Stormy and wiped it over Sunny's forehead and back of her neck.

"About Pat? Paying Kris? Who Pat really is?" She pushed herself up to sit despite her grandmother attempting to restrain her.

"He called this morning and asked for Gene's number. I knew nothing of what he planned. Just figured he was your friend."

"How can he be my friend? I didn't even know who Pat Whitcomb was. Guess I still don't. All he said was he was a lawyer, but he's *a Whitcomb*, Gramma. One of those Whitcombs. I had no idea. I thought he was a normal person."

Gramma helped her into the chair. "Who says he isn't. Family, fame, and money aren't one's personality. Did he ever tell you he wasn't of that family?"

Sunny shook her head. No, he hadn't out and out lied to her. "It was a lie of omission. He left out crucial information."

"Did he need to tell you his whole life story? Could be he was concerned about the way you'd react if you learned he came from money. Would you have treated him different?"

"No, I don't think so. Well, maybe. I don't know. I never had the chance to find out." She stared at the check that had landed on her placemat when she fainted. Fainted. What a stupid thing to do. Windy brought Dad, who demanded the whole story. This time Sunny revealed what Pat had done and who he was. Then she slid the check in front of him.

Dad plopped into his chair at the end of the table. "Wow."

"Yeah, wow. What do I do, Dad? I can't accept this from Pat?"

Kris cleared his throat. "It's not written to you. It's written to me. Kris. Are you making me go home and not earn it?"

Sunny startled at his voice. She'd forgotten he was there. And he was right. Did she cut him out of a payday because of her pride?

"Fine, I'll put you to work. But I've gotta find a way to pay Pat back. Which means I need to get this business going fast."

Windy moved past her and opened the sketch book Sunny had left on the table. She held up the Polaroids tucked inside before studying the drawing. Then, she grabbed the pencil, added a few marks and passed it to Sunny. "What about this?"

Sunny stared at the changes. Ones she'd never have envisioned. But they were perfect. It utilized the area without harming the tree or destroying the garden. "That's brilliant, Windy. I wish I had your talent."

Dad came around the table to peek. "That is a great idea, sweetie."

"I thought you were mad at me for dropping out of school." Windy stared him down, her arms crossed.

"I am. A little." Dad grimaced and sat in his chair.

"I'm not going back, Daddy. I'm done with the university. Sorry."

Dad grew extra quiet. Then he blew out a breath that made the curl on his forehead flutter. "I think I've got a way to help you, Sunny."

She met his gaze, hope rising again. "How?"

"Well, this is really up to your sister. But you could take Windy on as your third partner. She'd buy into the business like Stormy did, only she'll use the money that was to be hers when she graduated." He turned to Windy. "There won't be the new car, like for Sunny and Stormy. Still, you'd have a job." Dad looped his arms around Sunny and Windy. "Let her be your designer and photographer. What do you girls think?"

Sunny remembered the money gift that purchased her brand-new Camaro when she finished at Ball State. And Stormy got a GTO when she received her teaching certificate. That kind of money would sure help, though it wouldn't completely pay Pat back. "What do you think, Windy?"

Her sister glanced from Dad to her, grinned and nodded. "I like it. Yes, let's do this."

Sunny slipped from Dad and embraced Windy. "Yes, let's."

"I was feeling a little left out, I confess. But, oh, thank you, Daddy." Windy pulled him tight, hugging him and standing on tiptoes to kiss his cheek.

"What do I do now?" Poor Kris. She kept forgetting he was there.

"Get ready to work. I'll take you over to the house and Windy and I can show you what we need. But first, I'd better copy down this phone number from your check. There's a certain lawyer I owe a talking to." Sunny flipped the sketchbook to a clean page and wrote Pat's office contact. "There, here's your check. Cash it. I'll be paying you from now on. Doubt I can pay quite this much, though."

"That's okay. I live pretty simply. Glad to have some work."

Sunny stood. "I'll be back in a couple of minutes. Then we can go to the house. Just need to make a quick call." She headed upstairs, taking the extension with the long cord into her bedroom where she wouldn't be overheard, and dialed Pat's number.

"Whitcomb Enterprises, Patrick Whitcomb's office. How may I assist you?"

Her hand started to sweat, and she nearly dropped the receiver. She cleared her throat. "I'd like to speak with Mr. Whitcomb, please? Tell him Miss Day is calling." And he'd better have some answers or else.

"PAT HERE. SUNNY, IS THAT YOU?" Why was she calling him at work? How did she get this number?

Then he knew. The check.

"Yes, Patrick. I have some questions."

He cut her off. "Before you ask, yes, I paid Kris. Just trying to give you a hand."

"Well, stop it. I can't do it yet, but I will pay you back every red cent. I promise, so help me. Don't ever do that without asking."

That made him grin. "And if I asked?"

"I'd have said no. Pat, this puts a money wedge between us. I thought we were becoming friends."

Uh-oh. "I thought we *were* friends. And friends help each other."

Her voice sounded tight. "How can you say we're friends when I didn't...I don't have a clue who you are? I thought you were a lawyer, but you're a *Whitcomb*." When she spoke his name, it didn't sound friendly.

And there it was. He'd wanted her to know him for himself, not for his society page presence. Too many young ladies his mother tried to set him up with only wished their names next to his in the newspaper. He liked Sunny and needed a chance at real. "You already know me better than most people, including my relatives. I never lied to you, Sunny. I simply didn't give you my family tree. Does it matter?"

The line grew quiet. "Not sure. I'm still kind of stunned. You wore my father's pajamas for crying out loud."

And he could breathe again, even laugh. "See, I'm just a regular guy who happens to have money. Plus, a name found in the *Indianapolis Star*. Will you give me a chance? I'll remember to keep a spare pair of PJs in my trunk."

"Are you trying to buy me?"

"No. Never again. At least not without checking with you. That wasn't my purpose anyway. Only attempting to help." He crossed his heart and then realized she couldn't see it. "Friends?"

"I guess. Friends. But I'm paying you back. In installments. Next time you're in town, I'll have a check for you."

That surprised him. "You will? What happened?"

"Windy told Dad she wasn't going back to school. So, he's letting her use her graduation money to buy into the business. It's now the three of us, and Windy's already started earning her keep." She explained about the parking lot change.

"Sounds like the Weather Girls will do spectacular." He chuckled. That label popped in his brain on the last drive home from Kokomo.

"Not you too. Wait, though, that's not bad. We could advertise as The Weather Girls Wedding Shoppe and Venue. Hey, I like that." She returned the laugh. "Better let you go. I'm sure you're busy."

"You caught me at a good time. And I'm glad you called. Be seeing you." Sooner than you think.

"Bye Pat." And she was gone.

He pulled out his calendar. It was thin for the week, possibly more. He weighed the consequences. Taking time off before November was stupid. Risky. Just like he explained to Eric in the letter.

Pat buzzed his secretary. "Cancel or postpone all my appointments for the next two weeks. I need a vacation. Once I'm settled, I'll give you a number where you can reach me in case of an emergency, but it better be just that—an emergency."

As he stood to leave his office, his private line rang. He knew who it was without answering.

"Hello, Venita." If only he'd moved faster.

"Where are you with the project?" Not even a greeting.

"Actually, I'm headed there to see what I can do. I'm working on it and plan to make it my focus for the foreseeable future, or until it is all settled." All true. Though not the way she might figure.

"Good. Thank you, Pat, for coming through for me. I appreciate it."

He had to sit again. She never spoke like that to him. And he wasn't really doing what she wanted. The guilt stirred acid in his belly. "Venita, I..."

"No, it's okay. I've given you a hard time in the past. But you are making this work. It feels great to have a brother for a change."

He should tell her. Come clean. But it would only make things worse. No, he'd find another spot for her. It would be fantastic, and she'd love it. That's what would happen. Then she'd never learn the rest of the story. "No problem. Gotta go. Was on my way out the door."

"I won't keep you. But keep me posted, okay?"

"I will. Bye, Venita."

"Bye," She disconnected, so he replaced the receiver. More than ever, he needed to discover a substitute location. It was getting out of hand. But first, he had to help Sunny.

An hour later, after a stop by his apartment to pack, he was on the road to Kokomo. He'd not wear Aaron's clothes again. The Howard Johnson's on US 31 would be where he'd stay. He got a room and dropped off his bags before starting a plan. One he should've made at the office. Was it a better idea to wait for morning? Or might he talk Sunny into going to dinner with him?

Dinner. That's the strategy he'd choose. It meant seeing Sunny sooner. He dialed her grandmother's house.

"Hello?"

"Hazel? This is Pat. Is Sunny available?"

The line grew quiet a moment. "I stood up for you today, mister. Figured you ought to have a chance to explain. But I'm warning you, you mess with my Sunny girl, and I'll give you more trouble than you can handle."

He had no doubt. "Yes, ma'am. She spoke with me earlier and I think it's all worked out." That woman filled his spine with ice when she took on that tone.

"Good, now we understand each other. Sunny isn't here. She's at Ferguson House with Kris and her sisters. Do you want to leave a message?"

"No, thanks. I'll get back with you." They said their goodbyes and hung up. So, what's next? It wasn't yet four o'clock. He changed out of his suit and tie into more casual attire and headed for his car. In fifteen minutes he was at the mansion.

Sunny's Camaro sat in the drive. He locked up and went in search of her.

Pat discovered the girls huddled at the side of the house, peeking at something. "Did you see those muscles?" Stormy's voice.

"Well, he is sort of cute. Like a cross between a surfer and a football player." That was Sunny!

"I think he's kinda boss." Windy. "He could've gotten ticked at how we were all talking around him, but he didn't. And he wants to work."

"Yeah, you just enjoy the view." Stormy.

"I'm not blind." Windy. "But there's more to a person than their muscles. Or their manners." She turned away and spotted Pat. "Girls, we have company."

Sunny and Stormy spun his way, and somehow Sunny stood out from her sisters, capturing his attention. Blonde hair swinging from a ponytail and hazel eyes that locked gazes with him. She seemed to glow with personality, and he craved to bask in that light.

"Hey. I was in the neighborhood and thought I'd stop by."

Sunny strode toward him, covering the space between faster than he anticipated. "What are you doing here?"

He cleared his throat. "I checked my calendar and have some vacation days coming so wanted to ask if you might use my help." He dropped his voice so only she would hear. "I'm asking Sunny. Please?"

She blinked a few times, her lips rolled in over her teeth. Then she heaved a sigh. "Thank you. I appreciate your volunteer labor. Not your money, though."

"Does that include taking you to dinner?"

Stormy and Windy zeroed in on that with "Oohs" and "Ahhs."

A sweet tinge of pink rose in her cheeks. "I'd need to go home...No, my things are here now. Guess I'll have to go upstairs and change. Wait on the porch." She strode for the door. "I'll be back." Once inside, she stuck her head around the edge of the door, calling her sisters. "Hey, you two come with me. I don't need you keeping Pat company. Heaven knows what you'll say."

Stormy walked past him and winked. "Sorry, Pat. Guess there's no more stories today." Windy followed, giggled, and wiggled her fingers at him.

He got comfortable in a porch chair. Ten minutes later Sunny emerged wearing a plaid skirt and pale pink angora sweater. The coloring was perfect for her. Plus, she had her hair down and wore a touch of makeup. Not that she needed it, but it gave her a sophistication. Took her from cute to lovely.

He stood as she approached, slipping her arms into her jacket and slinging her purse strap over her shoulder while she walked. "Where shall we go?"

He reached to assist. "There's a restaurant I pass each time I drive up. The Casa Grande? How is the food?"

"Great. That will work. Do you want to take my car?"

He shook his head. "Sunny, this is a date. I asked you, so I'm driving. And you look wonderful. Just wanted to get that in."

He flashed his grin but mentally crossed his fingers that she was good with it.

She blushed again. "Then lead on, Macduff." And she motioned for him to go down the porch steps.

"Nope, not how I was raised. Ladies first."

She took a couple steps but peered back at him. "We might have to discuss that tonight. How you were raised, I mean."

He winced, knowing full well the topic had to come up sometime.

Two steps more and she halted, her message this time for her sisters. "Why don't you two bring your things over tonight? At least enough for a sleepover. Oh, and tell Kris he's done at five. He'll start tomorrow at eight. Don't need the machines roaring too early in the morning. Later!" She waved to them and headed for the car as if she couldn't hear their twitters and giggles.

Was this normal sister treatment?

He opened the passenger door for her and then climbed in on his side, his hands starting to sweat in the cool evening air.

His Boss 302 fired up at once. That Mustang took corners like nobody's business. Tonight, though, he brought his best behavior. No need to scare her before she knew him better.

Fifteen minutes later they were seated in the restaurant, perusing menus. He'd craved this time with her. Now that he had it, his tongue forgot how to communicate. Each second that ticked all went to waste.

"Try the T-Bone. That's what my dad always orders, and he says it's great."

An opening. Well, he'd charge through it before his fear could hold him back. "Thanks. I was looking at that. What will you order?"

"Actually, I enjoy the frog legs. Stormy made me try them on a dare, but the joke was on her. I like them." She smiled, and it stole his breath.

"My sister and I never had a close relationship, not like you and your sisters. Don't know if it's because you're all girls or if it's something lacking on our part."

She put her napkin in her lap. When she glanced up, her smile was gone. "I think it's because we need each other. Our mom walked out ten years ago. But she really left years before that. I don't know what I..." She paused and blinked. "...what we could've done, but there's no way to change the past."

Pat covered her hand. "I'm sorry."

She didn't pull away.

"What happened?"

"I was supposed to be watching the girls. Windy's always attempting something. Kinda like she has to figure out for herself why she's told no. That day she climbed up on the block fence—it was six feet off the ground—and decided to walk it. I think she'd read about the Flying Wallendas. Anyway, she fell, broke her leg. Daddy rode to the hospital with her but put me in charge of Stormy. Mom was there. But I'm the one he told." She shook her head. "Next thing I see is a taxi pulling up out front and my mother walking out with her suitcases."

"She didn't say anything?"

"What was there to say?" Sunny shrugged. "No, she said she was sorry. That was it. She climbed in the cab and rode away. We've never heard from her since. When Dad got home, I don't think he was surprised. But I wish I would've kept her there, at least until he came back. Maybe they could have talked things out."

"Sunny, it wasn't your fault."

"Yeah, that's what Dad says too." The server arrived to take their order and Pat knew she was done. She'd cracked open her private self as much as she was going to tonight. But he now understood her better.

Chapter Eight
Wednesday Evening, March 11, 1970

S unny climbed the porch steps of Ferguson House as Pat escorted her to the door. "Want to sit outside a few minutes?"

"It's a little chilly." He paused, and she sensed he'd accept an invitation inside. But that would not happen. Not with her sisters here. Not with them gone, for that matter. "Okay, then I'll see you tomorrow if you still care to help."

She searched his eyes, unsure how much to trust him. She'd told him more than she'd planned tonight at dinner and needed to see how he treated that confidence before she allowed more.

"I do. See you in the morning." Was he leaning in?

She wasn't ready for that. "Um, don't make it too early." With a wink to correct the mood, she grabbed hold of the knob.

He reached above her and held the door open. "I'd enjoy doing this again, Sunny. I want to know you better. Kinda hope you'd like to know me."

She let the storm door stand guard between them. "I would, Pat. But I'm juggling a lot of unfamiliar issues. I won't rush into a relationship. If you're willing to move slow..."

"I am. You're worth it, Sunny. Good night." He waved and headed down the steps.

She watched, and at the base, he turned back and grinned.

Like she hoped.

"So, did he kiss you? What happened?"

Sunny spun to find Stormy and Windy hanging over the banister.

"You were spying on me." She didn't need to ask. It was a fact. One she should have anticipated. "No, but I think he wanted to. Let me get in my jammies and we'll talk."

"Let's do it down here. I'll make some cocoa. Better yet, I'll start the fire while Windy makes the cocoa. Gramma sent some Swiss Miss packets. It's safer that way." Stormy headed for the hearth before she finished speaking.

"That's not fair. I can start a fire." Windy's fists were propped at her waist.

Stormy raised a long thin stick of kindling, using it as a pointer. "No one doubts you can start a fire. It's the doing it safely in the fireplace that has us worried."

Sunny chuckled.

"Not funny. Fine, I'll make the cocoa, but you get changed fast. We need details." Windy turned for the kitchen.

Upstairs in her new bedroom, Sunny shucked out of her skirt and sweater, hanging them in the armoire, and slipped into her pajamas, robe and slippers and then scooped Frazier into her arms to bring with her. The poor fur-baby kept getting moved around. He needed a little TLC and would enjoy the warmth of the fire.

By the time she arrived back at the living room, Stormy had the fire blazing and Windy brought in mugs of hot chocolate drink. Not the same as home-made, but Swiss Miss had gotten Sunny through more than one late night study session at Ball State. She curled up on the sofa.

"We need pillows and blankets." Windy took off for upstairs.

"Good, this gives us a minute. I love Windy to pieces, but do you think she's going to be able to do this?" Stormy plopped next to Sunny and stroked Frazier's head.

"Yeah, she will. She'll be in her element, what with the design, and we won't have to hire an outside photographer. She can even get started getting shots to put into advertising. There must be outlets to run color ads."

"Fine, but you've always been the rescuer for her. This time we may need to let her fall and have a backup plan."

"She won't fall. I gotta believe this will work. Like it's our calling or something. Every time I come up against an obstacle, somehow it gets moved or another path opens." Sunny peered into her sister's eyes. "I don't understand, but I think we might make it."

Windy arrived with an armful of pillows and blankets. They spread them out on the antique Turkish rug, like when they used to play camping at Gramma's when they were kids.

Sunny released Frazier to roam, following him with her gaze, still in awe of how Chloe basically packed up only her clothing and a few personal effects, leaving ninety percent of her furnishings to her with the house.

They each chose a mug before finding a place on the floor.

Stormy hopped up to turn off the living room lights and then rejoined them. "Okay, girls. It's Truth or Dare time."

Sunny and Windy both groaned.

"Sunny, truth or dare?" Stormy invented really scary dares. But she could ask questions that were as intimidating to answer.

The bottom line? Sunny sat comfortably before the fire. She didn't want to get up. Time to brave the consequences. "Truth."

"Why did you leave Indianapolis? Tell us everything."

Just as she expected. Guess it was the night for stories. "I started dating this guy I met on New Year's Eve at the office party. Tall, so handsome he was almost pretty. And he sought me out. I fell for him. Big time, though I tried to slow his horses a bit. He was all 'Sunny, baby' this and 'Baby doll' that and would get pretty mushy. I hate to admit I liked it, but I needed to see some substance. Instead, he'd only take me to lunch. We rarely went out in the evenings. We made dates a few times. He only showed maybe once. Always had an excuse.

"So, Valentine's Day was my line in the sand. And he didn't step up. No call, no message. Not even all weekend. I vacillated from worry to anger. Finally, I decided enough. Unless he had a valid reason—hospitalized with amnesia or trapped in a mine—I was finished."

Sunny sighed and wrapped her arms about her knees, remembering. "Monday morning, I'm at work when I get this gorgeous bouquet of roses. Signed 'Love Brock.' That's it. I tossed it all in the trash just as he showed up. Told him it was over. He'd lost his last chance." She glanced at her sisters. Their gazes were glued to her face, eyes round. Sunny took a breath. "As he started to argue, a woman approached my desk, announced she was his wife, and that I was out a job."

Windy gasped. Stormy looked like she wanted to explode.

"I had no clue. They left. I returned to work. Then I got a call from Human Resources. His wife made good on her threat. I was fired. That's why I came home." She wiped away the lone tear that broke past her resolve.

"That witch!" Stormy had always been her champion. Sunny loved her more for it now.

"To be fair, he was married."

"But you didn't know." That was tenderhearted Windy.

Sunny shook her head. "No, I didn't, but I probably should've seen the signs. And I would not have dated him after knowing."

Her sisters enveloped her in a group hug.

When she pulled back, Stormy motioned. "Your turn."

Sunny took in a deep breath. "Okay, Stormy. Truth or dare, and I've got a great dare for you."

Was that fear flashing in her sister's eyes? "Truth."

"Why did you leave Rob and your job?" Sunny stared back. "Don't leave out a thing."

Stormy slumped. "I knew you'd ask, just hoped you wouldn't. But your dare terrified me more." She heaved a breath, making her bangs flutter. "Rob's been pushing to have a baby. I'm not ready. I love kids, but...Mom messed us all up, you know? Anyway, they passed out the new contracts for next year and I didn't get one. I cornered my principal and learned Rob told them not to worry about giving me one since I wouldn't be back next year. We were starting a family."

She pulled her legs up and wrapped her arms around them, clasping her hands in front and leaning her chin on top of her knees like Sunny had when she'd gotten to the heart of her truth. "I was stunned. He didn't talk to me at all. So, okay. He talked about having a baby. But to say that behind my back? By the time I discovered the snafu, no vacant teaching spots were left. Worse, no one at the district thought to check with me. They just accepted it from Rob because he's a principal. So, I took half of our joint checking account and half of our savings—only what I've put in—and came home. He couldn't talk to me before he did something stupid, I don't want to talk to him."

"Do you still love him?" Windy whispered the words while she reached for Stormy's hand.

"Yeah, but I'm too angry to think about it. I'm afraid of what I'll say if I see him. He's got to give me space. I love teaching. It was the best. Could be I'll figure how to incorporate teaching into what we do. Eventually. And if things get tough, I can check for a job in Kokomo, though breaking my contract by leaving as I did will probably black-ball me. Stupid temper. But I couldn't face them after what Rob did."

That called for another group hug.

Since Stormy had answered, that left Windy's turn. "Truth or dare, kiddo? And I think you need to choose truth because I don't feel like a hospital run tonight."

"You don't have to ask. Since we're all being honest, I came home because of Tim." Windy brushed a stand of hair from her face. "I thought we were getting married. Everything pointed to that. Then I tried to call him last Friday, but no answer. So, Saturday I trudged to his dorm and requested the desk to call him. They didn't even bother. Said he'd dropped out of school the day before. Then they asked if I was Windy. When I told them I was, they gave me a note. Turns out, he was failing too many classes. Made him eligible for the draft. His number is two. Guess he tried talking to his professors and advisor, but they said they'd given him enough chances and he'd messed up more than they could help. He left for Canada. Never even said goodbye."

With Sunny on her right and Stormy on her left, they sandwiched her into a hug. "Aw, honey, it's going to be okay. Your first bad heartbreak is always traumatic."

Windy's tears became sobs.

Sunny rubbed her back and drew her close. "Windy, it'll work out. We're together now. You'll see."

Stormy tapped her shoulder and caught Sunny's glance with a studious stare. "It's more than that, isn't it?"

Windy pulled away and wiped her palms over her eyes. "Yeah. How did you know?"

Sunny snorted. "You're asking Stormy? Which of us can keep a secret from her?"

Windy smiled at that.

"So, okay, kiddo, out with it. Give us the Paul Harvey version." Stormy softened her words by brushing hair from Windy's face.

"You won't hate me?"

"We love you, sweetie. Don't we, Stormy?"

Stormy nodded. "Yeah, we really do. We've put up with you forever, kid. You'll have a hard time ditching us now."

Windy clasped her hands and held them tight in her lap, never taking her gaze off them. Her words tumbled out soft, low, and Sunny strained to hear. "Like I said. I thought Tim and I would get married. I'd even begun sketching wedding dresses. So that long weekend before classes started in January, we took a little vacation. One thing led to another..."

Sunny met Stormy's glance over the top of Windy's head.

They knew the rest of the story. "Sweetie, are you...?"

Windy nodded, chewing on her bottom lip. "Yeah, I'm going to have a baby." She grabbed Sunny and Stormy's hands and squeezed. "Please, please, please! Don't tell Daddy!"

Stormy said the words racing through Sunny's brain. "If you don't tell him, he'll figure it out."

And that was a fact.

Thursday, March 12, 1970

PAT PARKED ACROSS THE STREET from the mansion, hoping his Mustang would be safe from danger. With big machinery, he didn't enjoy taking chances.

He doubted he'd be required to handle that type of task, but he came dressed in jeans and an IU sweatshirt in case it was time to get dirty.

He glanced at his watch as he locked his car. 7:50. And he had coffee and donuts for everyone. Okay, so maybe he was buying their goodwill. A little. But if it made points with Sunny... He grinned.

After mounting the porch steps, he knocked. There was a scrambling sound followed by the front door being cracked open. A bleary-eyed Sunny peeked around the side. "Pat, what are you doing here at this time of morning?"

"It's almost eight o'clock, sleepyhead. Didn't you leave word for Kris to get started at eight?" As if on cue, an old Ford pickup parked in the drive. Kris climbed out.

"Eight? It's almost eight? Girls move it! We overslept!" Scurrying shuffled in the background. "Sorry. Give us a minute. Sit on the porch and tell Kris we'll be out soon." She slammed the door.

Pat cracked up as Kris joined him.

"What's so funny?"

"They overslept. Bet they were up all night talking." About him? *Don't get a swelled head, Whitcomb. You aren't always the main attraction.*

"Whatcha got there?" Kris eyed the drinks and goodies.

"Here." He handed off a coffee and set the rest nestled in the carrier on the little round table between the porch chairs. Then he opened the bag and offered it to Kris, who pulled out a glazed and sat to enjoy.

Pat took the other chair and sipped his coffee. He hoped for the long john but figured the girls should choose first.

They were outside in a few minutes and after a short lecture on spending his money on her, Sunny and her sisters each chose from the bag. The lonely long john remained. Now he almost felt slighted that his favorite wasn't good enough.

"You like those?" Windy nodded toward his pastry.

"Yeah, I do."

"Hm. I always called it old people's chocolate."

Pat choked on his first bite.

Sunny pounded on his back.

After taking a sip of coffee, he got his bearing. "Old people's chocolate? I'm not that much older than you." *Am I?*

"She named it that because that's what Daddy and Gramma always choose. We remember they like the maple flavor, so we got used to leaving it for them." Sunny moved to her place along the balustrade.

"Then you have no idea what you're missing, missy." He winked at Windy and took another bite.

Kris stood. "Want me to get started?"

"Sure. What did you do with the keys?" Sunny was halfway to the door.

"Kept them. It was easier." He didn't wait for a reply but headed down the steps.

"Should I have hung on to them?" Sunny glanced at her sisters.

"I don't know why. He was coming back today. If he stole it during the night, we would've heard him. Plus, it's his name on the rental slip." The ever-practical Stormy.

"Guess you're right."

Windy peeked up. "So, where do we start?"

"How about Stormy shows you what we've planned for inside and you determine if you can make it better. If it looks photo-worthy, get a shot. Try sketching some ad ideas. Stormy, follow up with that shop in Indianapolis. Can we do the consignment thing? Then let's prioritize the list of what we need to start. I'll take Pat to the carriage house, see what needs done there. I'd like to make it one of the venues, for mid-sized weddings."

Stormy put out her hand. "Come on, this is our beginning. You know what to do."

Sunny and Windy stacked their hands on top of hers.

"On three. Weather Girls Weddings. Ready? One...two...three"

In unison. "Weather Girls Weddings!" They fluttered their fingers to above their heads and laughed.

Warmth spread in his chest. She appreciated what he'd done.

"Let's go, Pat. I'll show you around." Sunny linked arms with him and guided him down the steps, following Kris's earlier path. Already the sounds of a giant motor filled the air. It grew so noisy they had to put their heads together to talk.

She led him to a large backyard bordered in flowerbeds just starting to awaken with daffodils and tulips.

Then she stood on tiptoe and spoke to his ear. "This is where I envision garden weddings."

He bent to her, pretending Stormy hadn't already showed him. "It's wonderful. I can see the possibilities. And that tree over there. It's not in the way of the parking lot?"

She shook her head. "Nope, that's the one Windy saved. Did I tell you the story of the sycamore?"

His turn to shake his head.

She tugged on his arm until they were at the carriage house. The door was padlocked, but she pulled a small ring of keys from her jeans pocket and unlatched it.

He yanked the stubborn barn-door style enclosure open. "Wait until I get the lights."

But she didn't. Instead, she followed him to the pull-string hanging from a single bulb on the ceiling. They both reached for the cord.

"Be my guest." He stepped back.

"I thought you were mine." She winked and tugged.

Now that they had light, he closed the door, hushing the machinery noise.

"Thanks. I'm worried Kris is going to go deaf before all this is done. By the way, will a gravel parking lot suffice until my budget allows me to pave it?" Sunny swatted a spiderweb away.

"They never specified paving, so I think you are safe." He wished she'd just let him pay for it.

"Good. You're right. So, let's see what's here. We may find things to use for display. Or sell."

The building had become a storage facility over the decades. Trunks of all sizes lined the side walls while the end one housed floor-to-ceiling shelving protuberant with boxes and crates.

"Be careful. If there're spiderwebs, there're spiders." Pat scanned about while he warned.

"I'm not afraid of spiders."

"Maybe I am."

She glanced at him, cocking her head, as if trying to decide if he was serious.

"I said maybe." And got a laugh for his effort. If he didn't spot a spider, she'd never know. "What are we specifically searching for? Or just getting an idea?"

"An idea. Chloe couldn't remember what had been stored out here. Her family lived here since 1892 when the house was completed. Possessions they brought with them, plus what they accumulated over time, could've ended up boxed. Though it's possible the earlier stuff is in the attic. That's next on my list to explore."

He pulled some of the crates down that had been shoved onto the shelves and gingerly pried one open. The newspaper stuffed as packing dated to the 1950s. "Don't think these items are genuine antiques. But the dates only apply to when it was packed. They could be older. Want to check?"

She started through the box as he brought down another. "Oh, it's someone's doll. And there're older toys in here. This one might be useful. Perhaps the historical society can help with it."

She closed it up and set it aside to start the next. "Knick-knacks from World War I era. They had a gold star." She peered up. "I wonder who they lost. Perhaps it was for Chloe's intended."

Box by box, she checked through before he hauled it to the stack she deemed. The newspaper dates varied from post-war up to 1955. Chloe must have packed these boxes.

She paused a moment. "What time is it getting to be?"

He checked his watch. "Nearly eleven." When he glanced up, she'd rocked back on her heels and swiped the side of her wrist over her forehead. "You've got a streak of dirt."

"Where?"

He leaned closer and ran a finger over her cheek where the line of dust clung. "Here." Her skin was velvet to his touch. "Want me to wipe it away?" How had he dared to ask?

Her eyes grew big, and she nodded.

He turned his hand so that the back of his fingers brushed against her skin, sending sparks up his arm that shocked his heart.

She swallowed, her gaze locked with his.

He'd never wanted to kiss someone so much. And he'd never been so afraid of doing it wrong. Her name formed on his lips.

"Sunny."

She didn't retreat, and her coffee-flavored breath feathered his face.

His hands reached to draw her close when the door opened.

"Sunny, want us to make a run to Scotty's for lu—Oh! Sorry!" Windy spun away, taking the moment with her.

Sunny pulled back.

Pat stood and brushed his palms over his jeans. "Sorry. Should we go to the house?"

She smiled. "Yeah. We need to wash off this grime."

He followed her out and snapped the lock in place before heading for the house's rear entrance.

She turned to him before they entered. "You do know there's going to be giggles and silly remarks. Just be prepared."

Though the outside temperature registered mid-sixties, he could've been stuck in the desert. That was one arid, warm thought.

But Sunny took it in stride. They washed at the kitchen sink as her sisters came in, behaving exactly as predicted.

Pat offered to grab lunch, but Sunny said no, since he brought breakfast. Stormy and Windy said they had enough cash and left in a blue GTO.

Once they were gone, Pat hoped to have another opportunity, but Sunny kept her distance. At least she still spoke to him.

He glanced out the front window as a familiar station wagon pulled up. "Hey, Sunny, your grandmother is here."

She ran to the door and yanked it open.

Hazel mounted the porch with a large basket. "Figured, you might be hungry about now. Pat, when did you get here?"

"He showed up yesterday, so I've put him to work, as long as he keeps his wallet out of it." Sunny took the basket from her.

Hazel eyed him. "Where are you staying?"

He raised his hands in surrender. "At the Hojo's out on 31."

"You just check out of there today and come to my house. It's the least we can do to repay you. Right, Sunny?"

"Right. Actually, that's a great idea. How long can you stay? I should have asked before this."

Pat glanced from one set of piercing eyes to the next. What had he gotten into? "Thank you, that's nice but—"

"No buts. Besides, if you are at my house, I know there's no hanky panky going on."

"Gramma!"

"I'll stay. No hanky panky. Understood." He was in surrender mode again. Mercy, that woman scared him.

"Good, we have that settled. Where is everyone else?" Hazel followed Sunny to the kitchen and their voices carried down the hall back to him.

"Stormy and Windy went to Scotty's for lunch. We didn't know you were coming. Guess I need to get the phone hooked up. Transferred the utilities first thing because I knew we needed to see. Plus, I was afraid of a pipe burst in case there was a sudden freeze." Her voice trailed off.

Pat returned to the window to stare. And think. Had Hazel pegged him? No, he wasn't that kind of guy. He genuinely cared for Sunny. Actually, he could imagine a future together.

But that would mean introducing her to his family. That scared him more than Hazel.

Then he realized who else would need to meet Sunny. Which would spark questions.

Venita.

He sighed. Better find another property for his sister, and fast.

Of course, that meant he'd have to look.

Chapter Nine
Friday, March 20, 1970

S unny stretched, knocking the kink out of her back from putting in the new flowerbeds. It wasn't like she started from scratch, but she needed this yard to be heady with fragrance and a lovely diversion from the gravel parking lot emerging a few yards away. Kris should have it completed in a few days.

That guy was a hard worker. Quiet, liked his food, but ran off every calorie with his efforts at getting her up to code. She just hoped she could keep paying his salary or at least put him on a retainer.

So far, she'd found several things the historical society agreed to buy, though she had seen no cash from it yet. But interest was high. One step at a time.

The weather had cooperated, too. Other than the downpour that blew Windy home, March came in like a lamb. And she knew what that meant. Hopefully, all her gardening work wouldn't be destroyed as the month exited lion style.

Then there was Pat.

He left her a mass of bubbling confusion. At the moment, he was scrubbing the carriage house since they'd cleared and made room. Plus, he volunteered for that messy job. Those panes hadn't been scoured in decades. Had he ever washed windows or mopped floors in his life?

What was he doing spending his time here? He obviously wasn't married, or someone would search for him.

Still, Stormy was married, and Rob's strategy centered on calling to get rebuffed so Sunny couldn't rely on that assumption.

Her sister had yet to speak to her husband. Sunny almost felt sorry for the guy until she remembered what he did. That was one a stupid move. Stormy would talk to him sometime. Right?

She shrugged, the movement helping with her kinks, and packed up her gardening tools. With a little luck, and a whole lot of Gramma's prayers, this would turn into the garden venue she imagined.

As she entered the rear door, voices carried from the front. Sounded like Gramma's, but she heard another. Gene, maybe?

She took off her garden gloves and set them with her things on the drainboard before heading down the hall to investigate.

"Hey Gramma, Gene, what brings you two over?" She hugged her grandmother and shook the man's hand.

"We wanted to see how things progressed. Gene hadn't seen the inside yet. Do you mind if I show him around?"

Sunny shrugged. "No, feel free. I just planted some lilies and gladiolas out back. Hey, check out that grandson of yours, Gene. He works like a fiend. I'm telling you, I think if I could keep him fed, he'd work round the clock."

The gentleman chuckled at that. "He's a chip off the old block. Pretty proud of that boy."

"With good reason. Well, off to see how Pat's faring with the carriage house. Once he has it all spic and span, I can turn Windy loose on it to get some design set ups and photos for our portfolio. Have fun." She brushed a kiss on Gramma's cheek and returned to the back door.

On the way to the carriage house, her brain conjured all sorts of scenarios from Pat in a Cinderella position scrubbing the floors, to him standing there like Mr. Clean without a speck of grime on him. The reality was far from what she'd imagined. He appeared to have rolled in the muck before hosing it out. Streaks of black and gray ran down his cheeks where back spray from the hose dripped through the dirt splattering his face. His hair was a mish-mash of spots matted flat to his head from moisture and little spikes that poked out in different directions.

She tried. Oh, she tried to hold the laughter in, covering her mouth and even biting the tip of her tongue. Despite her barriers, it exploded with a snort, bringing tears to her eyes and a wobble to her knees.

"It's not that funny."

She nodded with emphasis. "Oh, yes, it is Mr. Perfect. You need a mirror."

He ran his hand over his hair, doing nothing to improve things. "You think I'm perfect?"

Her sides hurt, and she wrapped her arms about herself, still giggling. "Not...at this...moment. Oh!"

A gleam glistened in his eyes and he pulled her close, rubbing his dirty face next to her cheek.

"Ew! You're all sweaty." She pushed back, but he held on. "Yuck, you're drenched."

"You liked it so much, just thought I'd share." He chuckled at her ear as the rough stubble of new whiskers grazed her jaw.

She pushed again and stumbled backward.

He caught her, his eyes morphing from twinkles to concern. "You okay?"

She nodded. Even with his grimy face, Pat remained the most handsome man she'd ever met. When he got this close, her lungs forgot to breathe.

He drew closer. His finger traced from her temple to her chin, slowly tipping it until he could lower his mouth to hers.

His breath still tinged by the apple he'd munched on her porch at noon.

Without a nudge from her brain, her heart sent her arms around his neck, drawing him nearer still. Bottle rockets fired from her toes and electric impulses pinged throughout her body, leaving her a mass of tingles. If this was a kiss, she'd never experienced kissing before.

When he released her, she'd lost all sense of time and place.

He glided his palms up and down her arms. "Wow."

"Yeah, wow." The present returned. She was in the carriage house with Pat who appeared nothing like himself but, oh, he was everything she'd ever dreamed of wanting. That thought brought flame to her cheeks. She hid her face in her hands.

"Are you okay?"

When she peeked through her fingers, he again appeared concerned, but there was vulnerability in his eyes. He hadn't planned that, she could tell. She also knew it had moved him, like it did her.

She nodded, "Wasn't that the question that started this?"

He chuckled. "I guess it did." Then he sombered. "Sunny, I didn't mean...I just, you're so dog-gone beautiful."

She glanced away as his finger stroked her cheek. "You couldn't have done that if I hadn't let you. Let's get you inside to clean up." She veered for the exit without checking to see if he followed.

He did and held the door.

She stepped through, then stopped in her tracks, motioning him back so she could peek around the door at what caught her attention.

"What is it?"

"Look over there by the tree." She pointed at her grandmother and Gene standing in an embrace beneath the sycamore's branches.

"You're spying on Hazel and Gene? Would you want them spying on you?"

"That's not it. Look, on that branch that swoops low. Do you see it?"

He peered through the door's newly cleaned window. "The bird?"

"Not just any bird, a cardinal. It means true love, that they're destined to be together." Her heart happy-danced for Gramma. She'd been alone for a long time.

Pat turned her to him, grabbing her full attention. "How do you know that?"

"Because of the legend. The one Chloe told me about."

"What legend?"

She stared at him. "I never told you?"

He shook his head. "You started to say something about the tree, but we were sidetracked. Never got back to it."

She motioned toward the spreading sycamore. "Chloe explained it to me. If a couple kisses beneath its shade, and a cardinal lights on the branch, it means true love. They're destined to be together a long time."

"How did Chloe know? I thought she never married." At least he wasn't totally putting her down. Yet.

"Chloe had a sweetheart, but he was in the army, heading overseas in World War I. She asked him to kiss her there, they were engaged and would marry when he returned. But he said he wanted to wait until he came back, a special welcome home kiss. Only he died in France, he never made it. So, she never married. But she knows plenty of people that the legend worked for. That's why it was crucial to save the sycamore from the parking lot."

"Sunny Day, you're a romantic."

"You think that's all it is? Now I wish I'd never told you." Great. He was going to make fun of her. She peeked again. "The coast is clear. Let's get you inside."

"You worried your grandmother wouldn't like you spying on her."

Her fists adhered to her hipbones. "You don't get it. I'd never interrupt that opportunity. Gramma's been alone but for Dad and us girls. My grandfather died of the Spanish Flu aboard a transport ship before even arriving in Europe to fight. He never saw his son. Gramma raised him by herself and then had to raise the three of us. It's time she had a love life. And if that legend holds, she's found true love. I'm happy for her."

He raised his hands in surrender, just like he did when Gramma gave him what for. "Sorry. Won't say another word."

"Oh, c'mon." She led him to the kitchen sink to wash off the worst. Enough so he could return to Gramma's without ruining everything he touched.

She left him at the faucet and wandered to the living room.

Stormy and Windy were moving furniture in the small parlor.

"Hey what happened to you?"

"What do you mean?" Sunny surveyed her clothes and arms.

"Your face. You got some streaks on your cheeks." Windy pointed and turned her toward the antique mirror on the wall as the memory of Pat's kiss bloomed.

"Now you're blushing." Stormy sounded gleeful. "What gives?"

"I've no clue what you're talking about." It was stupid to lie to Stormy, she'd figure it out in a heartbeat. But why give her the satisfaction? Better to change the subject. "Oh, Gramma and Gene are getting serious."

"How do you know?"

"We, I caught them kissing. Under the sycamore. And a cardinal landed on the branch. It's for real."

Her sisters squealed, and Windy did a twirl. "That's so romantic!"

"I'm so happy for her." Sunny plopped on the love seat.

"Think they might consider letting us throw them a wedding here? It'd be great advertising."

Stormy landed next to her. "Great idea. I'll see if I can talk to her. How big should it be? Might we use this room for an intimate event? Or maybe a sunset service upstairs on the terrace beneath the turret. However, if she wants bigger, friends from church perhaps, the carriage house could be better."

"It's so, so romantic. Let's do the carriage house and I'll decorate it with strings of lights from the rafters." Windy's face got all dreamy.

"No!" Sunny and Stormy's voices blended in unison.

Sunny jumped and spun Windy to face her. "You are not climbing a ladder to string lights. Not going to happen. If we must put a guard on you, we will. Do you understand?"

"May I please give directions to someone else to do it then? It'll make that place special."

Sunny sighed. "Who do plan to coerce into doing it?"

"Not you two. Kris. He'd do it."

"For a ham and swiss." Stormy snorted.

"Okay, so the guy likes his food. He works it off. And he's been amazing help. Plus, did you know he's an artist?" Windy waggled her head, figuring she knew something her sisters didn't.

"How d'you learn that?" Stormy had a habit of saying what Sunny thought.

"I asked." She shrugged and headed for the door. Before going out, she glanced back. "And I still say it's romantic."

Sunny shared the laugh with Stormy, but her mind floated out to the carriage house. How could a body who kissed like Pat be void of romance? Or didn't it surface when she was there.

"He kissed you!"

Sunny stared at Stormy, knowing her thoughts were popping free to read on her face like a lemon juice ink message when given heat. Boy, did she have heat.

"Maybe."

Stormy plopped on the loveseat. "I knew it. Yep. I think it's time you two found yourselves a cardinal and checked out that tree."

Sunny grabbed a pillow and smacked her sister in the face.

But the truth was, she'd already imagined his kiss beneath those branches. And she had no doubt if it ever happened, a cardinal would appear.

Saturday, March 21, 1970

PAT DROPPED THE LAST of his freshly cleaned clothes into his suitcase. He'd had no intention of Hazel doing his laundry, but she insisted. Why couldn't he stand up to Hazel Day?

Forget Hazel, why couldn't he stand up to any woman?

His sister bossed him, his mother manipulated him. He even let Sunny intimidate him. Well, he really didn't want to argue with her. Plus, he saw her side, but he never told her. He just held up his hands like she was robbing him.

Come to think of it, she *had* stolen his heart.

He couldn't close his eyes without her face forming in his mind. And that kiss? He'd wanted to kiss her from the moment he saw her. But she kept distance between them while he helped. They never had a moment alone. Plus, she'd been too exhausted when they finished working at the end of each day to plan a date. Getting things ready to be opened on time zapped them all.

Then yesterday, the stars aligned. He'd even tried getting playful with her, and it was fun. That kiss, though. It was the best of all. He'd never wanted to kiss someone so much. Turned out better than he'd imagined.

She might assume he'd planned it. Dreamed it? Yeah, but planned, no way. A kiss like that was impossible to plan.

Despite it all, he had to admit, her dream was becoming a reality. The downstairs was nearly set. They divvied the second floor with private quarters on one side and dressing rooms on the other. The third level ballroom and terrace still needed work. Most of that waited, though, until Kris finished grading the parking lot and rented a buffer for the hardwood floors.

Now his vacation was over. He must get back to his job.

Leave this beautiful chaos for his well-ordered existence. Just when he'd found his heart's desire.

It was true. Sunny Day brought him light and sincerity and truth. When he was with her, and she flicked him that glance that said she was content to be right where she was, he stood ten feet tall. Her hand in his gave him grounding. How did she do that?

She filled his senses pushing everything else out of mind.

One more reason he needed to leave.

Last weekend he'd manufactured an excuse to search for alternate properties for Venita. Discovered a couple to present. No one was moving on them, so he'd take the listings to her in person—an empty lot off 31 near Indian Heights and another on the other side of Country Club Hills near the new high school. Neither had the charm of Chloe's old property, but it was the best he'd ferreted out. One of them needed to work.

Because there was no taking Ferguson House from Sunny.

He'd fight to keep that for her.

Would he? He stared at himself in the mirror. As much as he imagined himself her protector, would he really stand up for Sunny if push came to shove? He never stood up for himself. What made him think he'd stand up for anyone? Even her.

He hefted his bag downstairs.

Hazel was in the kitchen, as usual. She must live in there.

After setting his case by the front door, he followed the sound of her singing to where she pulled fresh chocolate chip cookies from the oven. The aroma bathed him in all sorts of happy. Maybe she'd let him take one with him. "All ready, Hazel. Just wanted to thank you again for letting me stay."

She spun to the sound of his voice. "I was hoping you'd at least hang around and have lunch. I talked the girls into coming for a bite."

He smiled at her barely veiled attempt at matchmaking, though he wished she might make this happen. "Thanks, but I need to get home and ready for the week. I've been ducking calls I should have taken. Gonna pay for that."

She patted his cheek. "Well, I'm glad you stayed as long as you did. I've got a bag of cookies for you to take—no arguments." She shoved the sack into his hands.

"Am I that predictable? I was hoping for one."

"You've got a dozen. You've also got a place to stay whenever you're in town, Pat. Don't even have to call ahead. You are welcome anytime." She pulled him into a hug. "I've adopted you, you got that? You're part of the family now. No pretending to be a stranger. Drive safe."

He pulled away and blinked. Man, he loved this family.

"Thanks." He held up the cookies. "And thank you for these. Wish I could say when I'll be back. But I will. Keep the light on."

She winked at him and followed to the front door where she watched him plod down the porch steps to his car.

Why did he need to leave again?

He drove to Phillips Street, then to Sycamore to head out to 31. Every block shouted to turn around. Go back. But as much as he loved this town, it wasn't his home. He was still a visitor and home summoned. Plus, he had responsibilities. Promises to keep. Miles to go. He should have dropped by Ferguson House to say goodbye to Sunny, but since she'd been avoiding him, he figured he'd call later. This all made him nervous, out of character for a competent corporate lawyer.

He flipped on the radio. Bobby Hebb crooned his big hit and Pat had a sudden pang of jealousy, like the guy was singing about *his* girl.

Was Sunny his girl? Wanting her to be and making it so were two different things. He had no idea how to merge those thoughts, so he pressed harder on the gas.

Twenty minutes later he tucked the speeding ticket in his glove compartment, signaled, and moved back into traffic at a speed that wouldn't attract more state troopers. Just what he needed.

After another half hour of driving, he pulled into his private parking slot and lugged his suitcase toward the elevator. A return to his normal existence. Not life. Life was what he experienced with the Day family. They loved each other and argued and hugged. That was family, that was living. He wanted that so much he could taste it.

His phone summoned before he could unlock his door. He abandoned his load with his keys still dangling as he made a mad dash, grabbing on the sixth ring.

"You're home." Venita. She couldn't let him even get inside.

"Yes, just walking in the door. Hello to you, too." He dropped to the couch.

"Where have you been? I've been trying to reach you for days."

She'd never understand. "I was still in Kokomo. Got some prospects for you. Are you in the city? We could meet for dinner." It would be neutral territory.

After a pause, he thought he heard her smile. "I'd like that. What are you in the mood for?"

"Honestly? A pizza. I tried one while there from Pizza King that was amazing. Don't they have a location in town?"

"I wouldn't know. Pizza? Seriously? Fine, I guess."

He pulled the phone book to him and turned to the yellow pages, finally finding a Pizza King not too far from him. After giving her the address and setting a time, he closed promising to bring the new information.

That bought him a chance to pop some *Jiffy Pop* for lunch—the only food left in his kitchenette—and add more cookies for dessert. Afterward, he put his clothes away and grocery shopped before getting ready to meet his sister.

He grabbed a shower and remembered the leather slacks Venita had gotten him for Christmas. The gift was so not him, but it might add brownie points if he wore them. And since he was only meeting with her, fine. He hated how they made him feel pretentious, not like he was going "natural." He added a paisley button-down and headed to Pizza King.

The place was cozy, with a couple tables for in-house service. But that was no problem. The fewer patrons who viewed her tantrum when she went ballistic with him, the better. Could be she'd accept these. But he knew, this would not appease. She'd hit the roof.

Venita arrived a few minutes after and agreed to split a sausage mushroom pie. That was a laugh. His sister would have maybe one slice. He'd have three. The rest would get boxed for home. Still, cold pizza made great breakfast when he was in college.

Once the order was placed, they sat at the table in the far corner.

"So, what did you find?" She leaned forward, her forearms bracing her, and she appeared to be open to what he had. If he were a praying man, he'd send one up. Now.

He pulled out the Kokomo map and the addresses for the locations. "This first place is a vacant lot. The owner lost what was there in the Palm Sunday Tornado and never rebuilt. But I put out feelers. He seems amenable to selling for the right price. It's close to the highway for easy access, but not so much that traffic noise would create a problem. There's shopping and businesses nearby."

"The town's small enough there's always business nearby. I wanted something with character, that matured over decades. This is too new an area. What else have you got?"

If that's her reasoning, she wouldn't like the other choice any better. Country Club Hills was a newer development, too. But he charged ahead and pointed it out on the map. "This one's got a structure on the tract. But you can buy it for a song. It's gone into default and the bank wants to unload it. You'd have young marrieds and those with new careers starting out. They'd be drawn to your high-rise apartment idea."

She shook her head. Like he knew she would. "No, these won't do. I need that original property, Pat. Are you sure that new owner won't sell?"

He tried for pitiful. "Yeah, no. She's not selling. I'm sorry, Venita. I tried." *Maybe not the way you wanted...*

She sighed loudly. The pizza guy glanced their way. "I had my heart set on that place. I should try to talk with her. Woman to woman."

"No!" Just the thought scared him spitless. "No, she's pretty adamant. You'd only make her angry and then where would you be? Nah, it's time to let this one go. I'll see what more I can uncover. I haven't tried Greentown, or there's also Russiaville, and Alto. Perhaps Burlington. Maybe moving out from the center of town will help."

"You're sweet, Pat. I hate for you to keep fighting my battle, but what else is there?" She reached out and covered his hand.

He was stunned. They'd never behaved this close. Oh, he was a rotten brother. "It's the least I can do, Venita." The very least.

Their pizza arrived, but he suddenly had no appetite. He juggled life like an undercover spy. It left him feeling dirtier than when he cleaned the carriage house.

He better tell her. He needed to tell her. But as he opened his mouth, the coward in him took over. He shoved a slice covered with sausage and mushrooms in his big fat yapper.

Without a doubt, as sure as his teeth sunk into that cheesy delight, this moment would come back to bite a chunk out of his backside. Oh, yeah.

Chapter Ten
Thursday, April 2, 1970

S unny shoved the chair in at her desk in her new office. Together with her sisters, and at Windy's brilliant suggestion, they'd turned the butler's pantry into her private place where she could concentrate on figures and whatever she needed to do. By using furniture already there, it kept the charm of the house, appearing like it belonged.

They'd also planned a grand opening date of April thirteenth.

A Monday. At least it wasn't a Friday. The chances of getting in on the June wedding blitz was infinitesimal. But something might bring customers their way. Who knew? She just hoped it wasn't too soon. Still this business needed income. That'd only happen if it opened.

As she strolled through the first floor, she noticed her sisters' touches and was assured again that going in together was the best idea.

However, living together above the business they ran meant they spent an awful lot of time together. Too much togetherness wasn't healthy. Hence hiding in her office was a nice touch.

This evening, Gramma wanted them all at her house for dinner. Said it was important and brooked no excuses.

"Ready?" Unsure where Windy and Stormy were, Sunny hollered from the base of the staircase.

Seconds later, Windy floated down the staircase while Stormy charged in from the front porch with a "Just waiting for you." They took Sunny's car and parked at the curb since the drive was filled. She didn't recognize two of the cars, but Kris's truck sat on the street, too.

Stormy gasped. "No, he wouldn't." She recognized a vehicle.

Sunny opened her driver side door.

Windy, in the front, got out, too. "Aren't you coming, Stormy?"

"Not if he's in there. What's that meddling old woman thinking?" She crossed her arms over her chest.

Sunny leaned in. "I'm not taking you home. Gramma said it was important we be here."

"Couldn't care less. Go on in. Bring me food when you come back."

Sunny straightened.

Windy glanced at her over the top of the car before leaning inside. "Are you sure?"

"I'm very sure. And don't either of you tell him I'm out here or I'll never speak to you again."

"If that's what you want." Sunny closed her door and Windy followed suit. Somehow, she knew an explosion was due before the evening ended.

Gramma met them at the porch. "Where's Stormy?"

"In the car. She won't come in if Rob's here." Sunny hugged her grandmother.

"And she made us promise not to tell him." Windy added her hug.

"Well, you didn't tell him, you told me. I'll have a chat with that girl."

As Gramma headed off the porch, Sunny felt the explosion's rumble. This would not be fun.

Part of her wanted to watch. Someone might need First Aid. Instead, Sunny guided Windy toward the dining room and away from the front windows.

Dad sat at the head of the table, in his usual spot. Gene was in the place next to Gramma's where Windy usually sat. Kris sat next to him with a vacant chair on his left. Windy grabbed that one leaving Sunny the choice of sitting on Rob's right or left. It didn't matter. The remaining would be for Stormy. Both would cause a ruckus. With Gramma's best china and crystal on the table, she hoped it wouldn't get too awful. She'd waved a generic hello to everyone but noted the woebegone expression taking over her brother-in-law's face.

The front door opened and closed a few minutes later, and Gramma appeared alone. "We'll give Stormy a chance to wash up and then I'll serve." Her smile was tight, but apparently, she'd won the skirmish.

Stormy arrived soon after, glancing at each filled chair and noting the only one left. She glared daggers at Sunny before yanking out the seat and plopping with a whole lot of huffy.

Sunny shrugged back, refusing blame.

Gramma grasped hands with Gene and Sunny, motioning for everyone to join up. Stormy's sigh couldn't be missed, but she obeyed under her grandmother's laser stare.

Gene spoke grace. After which, not much else was said. This dinner table never was so quiet. It made Sunny's stomach flip enough that she was nervous eating her favorite meal from Gramma's kitchen. Still, she dipped up some Chicken Marseille, a dish only prepared for the most important dinners, and passed it on to Rob before taking the green beans, almandine style, from her grandmother.

When everyone had a full plate, Gramma tapped the side of her crystal goblet with her spoon. "It's so quiet, I probably didn't need to do that. But I want this to be official. Gene needs to speak with you." Her hand slipped over by his and he squeezed it a moment.

Then he stood. "Hazel and I have grown closer over the last year. I love her deeply and have asked her to be my wife. We wanted to announce this to you all, you are our family. Kris, I'd have had your parents here if they were able. We'd like your blessing and want to set a wedding date. Oh, guess I should add, Hazel said yes." He winked at her as the once quiet table filled with voices expressing congratulations.

"Gramma, where are you thinking of having the wedding? What size do you want?" Romantic Windy drove straight to the heart of things.

"Well, I learned there's this new place in town. Hoped to book something there. I don't need a white gown, but perhaps a bridesmaid's dress would do?" She glanced over at Gene a moment before continuing. "We'd like to keep it small, but with all our family and friends from church, it might be too big for your intimate settings."

"The carriage house would be perfect then. Kris, you'll help me with the rest of the décor, right?" Windy had him trapped before he could say a word.

The poor guy swallowed—he'd kept eating—and nodded. "Sure."

"All we need is a date, Gramma. I'll put you on the books." The tingles in Sunny's stomach changed from dread to excited. This might be their first event. Depending on when. Could they pull this off? Great, the dread tingles were back.

"We were thinking May sixteenth, that's six weeks from now. Is that too soon?"

Sunny glanced at Windy, who beamed with joy, to Stormy who'd remained withdrawn, but managed a shrug.

"It will work. Oh, I'm so excited for you. Welcome to our family, Gene." Sunny hopped from her seat and hugged the guy before Windy shoved her out of the way.

Gramma's grin told her this was good. She'd never seen her grandmother so happy. The loving gazes she had for this man filled Sunny with hope. Honest-to-goodness, worth-waiting-for love existed in this world. Maybe, just maybe she'd find it.

It could be Pat, but who knew. He'd gone back and hadn't called. Did he regret that spur-of-the-moment kiss? She didn't want to believe it, but with no calls, the idea was taking root.

The meal continued with plenty of conversation from all but her sister and Rob. Once dessert—a sugar cream pie to die for—was served, Stormy excused herself to the living room.

Sunny caught Gramma's glance and nodded before she followed.

Stormy sat as though she were pulling herself inside, her legs drawn up under, her arms crossed tight across her chest, and her posture slumped.

Sunny sat next to her and pulled her close knowing tears were on the verge of falling.

That's all it took. Stormy sobbed in her arms while Sunny stroked her head. What was there to say?

Just as Stormy calmed, a shadow darkened the light spilling from the dining room. Sunny looked up to see Rob.

"May I speak with my wife, please?"

Sunny pushed off to stand.

But Stormy pulled her back. "Stay."

"I should let you two talk in private."

"No, I want a witness." Stormy sat straight and wiped her eyes with her palms.

"Fine, if that's how you want it." Rob shoved his hands in his pockets. "Stormy, why? I don't get it. Why did you leave? Take half of our savings? What's going on?"

Stormy hopped up from the couch and stood toe-to-toe with her husband. "It's the money. That's all that bothers you. You cheat me out of my job, and you're worried about the stupid money."

"Your job? That's what this is? I thought we agreed we were starting a family."

"No, you agreed. You didn't listen. I'm not ready and if this is how you plan to act, I may never be ready." She poked her finger on his chest to emphasize her final words.

"What do you mean?"

"I mean, I...mean...I want a divorce." She ran up the stairs and a second later a door slammed.

"She can't mean that." He rubbed his hand over his face.

"Rob, I think she does. Teaching meant the world to her, and you yanked that away."

"But I thought she agreed. I was at that principal's meeting. When talk of contracts came up, I casually mentioned the possibility. Just an off-hand remark. I didn't know anyone took it as gospel. The contracts were issued before I could tell her." He sunk onto the sofa. "What do I do? I don't want to lose her. I really want a family together. Sunny, I love your sister more than I can say." His elbows propped on his knees and his gaze stared at the floor while his fingers ran deep parts through his hair.

She resisted the urge to drape her arm over his back. He'd screwed up and needed to own it. But she did pat his shoulder. "Then, Rob, don't give up. Start with an apology. Be patient. Maybe try wooing her."

He glanced up. "Wooing her? Where'd you get such an antiquated word?"

"It might be old-fashioned, but it works. She's gonna resist. We know that. But if you want her back, don't stop. And remember, listen to her heart. That'll prove to her you really love her."

He sighed. "When did you get so smart?"

"Always have been. You just prefer someone more exciting."

She patted his arm again and headed for the stairs. It was time to check on Stormy.

Sunny found her sister stretched across her bed, clutching Mr. Murphy and sobbing into him. Sunny couldn't fault her. That bear had soaked up enough of her own tears, it was used to the process. She sat on the edge of the mattress and tucked some strands behind Stormy's ear before pulling a couple tissues from the box and handing them over.

Stormy dabbed her eyes. "Is he still here?"

"Left him coming unglued on the couch. He's in a major bad way, Stormy. I don't believe he did this to be mean or force the issue. He's really clueless."

"Did you explain in simple words? You'd think the youngest guy to get a principalship in the district's history would comprehend basic English."

"I know. I'm not saying to give him another chance. Or even go talk with him. But you might want to ease on the gas, divorce-plan wise, until everything's in the open." Sunny peered into Stormy's eyes, insisting on a returned gaze.

"We'll see. With Gramma's wedding and getting the carriage house ready for it, I won't have time to consult a lawyer in the immediate future."

It was a concession. That was enough for now.

When they finally came downstairs, Rob had gone. Sunny kissed Gramma and Dad goodbye and gave Gene another hug before motioning to Windy that they were out of there. That girl had been in deep conversation with Kris. How'd she get him to talk?

The ride home was silent. Both of her sisters seemed lost in their own thoughts and Sunny had sufficient thoughts of her own crowding her mind. She actually relished the quiet.

But when she pulled in the drive, a familiar Mustang sat parked on the street. Her heart pounded in her ears and she couldn't step out of the car fast enough.

Pat relaxed on the porch. Looking like he belonged there. Like she could see him there greeting her every time she arrived home.

She stood watching him over the top of her Camaro while her sisters said hi to him and went inside. Good. They needed an opportunity alone. If tonight had taught her nothing else, it was that she must take a risk. She already knew how her heart felt.

But she'd been burned before when she trusted. It was time to lower her protective shields.

It was time to give him a chance.

PAT MADE HIMSELF COMFORTABLE on the porch. No one was home. They'd either grabbed dinner or went to Hazel's. He knew they'd return shortly. Waiting gave him time to think.

He'd raced to Kokomo on a whim. To be honest, he craved more than to hear her voice on the phone. He wanted to touch her face, stroke her velvet cheek, stare into those hazel eyes that swallowed him whole. He needed to be with her, and a telephone call wouldn't do enough.

His secretary uncovered a couple more spots to check for Venita. With that excuse, he drove to town and visited the properties. At least he could say he did. Then he made a beeline to the Ferguson House. It drew him like...so many cliched similes popped through his brain, each one pretty much on the nose.

Until he knew for certain she cared, he couldn't make a plan, hold a thought, or live his life. Everything screeched to a standstill.

Venita scared him when she suggested coming up herself. That would spell disaster. If his sister learned how much he'd helped Sunny, especially when with a little push he could've gotten her to sell to him? Hiroshima's fallout wasn't as bad.

Yet the deeper his feelings for Sunny ran, the more important it became that he come clean with Venita. That would be easier if he discovered her the perfect place before he dropped his bomb. Whether or not he found the ideal location, Sunny must meet his family. If they were to have a relationship, that is.

Mom and Venita would pester to learn how they met. Once the name Ferguson House was mentioned, his sister would commence a countdown to blast off.

There had to be a way. The only open method seemed honesty. Normally his favorite, but his fear ran deeper. If he couldn't get past this piece of drama, how did he plan to stand up to his father. How did he announce he wanted to be a trial lawyer, a defense attorney?

He was such a fraud. He didn't deserve Sunny. What did she see in him?

Then a Camaro's headlights turned their beams into the driveway and his heart picked up extra beats. The doors opened and Sunny stood gazing his way while her sisters tumbled out and headed for the house. They waved greetings as they passed, not stopping for conversation. Sunny continued to watch him.

He stood. "Coming to the porch?"

She closed her door and ambled around the front of her car toward him.

He wanted to tell her to run. That he couldn't wait to take her in his arms.

Her weighted steps and rounded shoulders told him she carried the world again, so he met her part way and enveloped her in an embrace. "How are you?"

She tipped her chin up at him. "It's been an emotional evening. Good stuff and hard stuff."

"Want to talk about it?"

She nodded. "Yeah, I do. Let's go for a walk."

It was after dark, but the streetlight overlapped glowing circles. He laced fingers with her, and they headed for the sidewalk.

She didn't speak at first, so he waited. He'd give her all the time she needed. About three houses down, she cleared her throat. "Gramma requested we come for a special dinner tonight. Gene asked her to marry him and they wanted our blessing. Kris was there, too, though I learned his parents live out of state. That's why he's with his grandfather." She glanced up a second before continuing.

"Anyway, when we pulled up, there were cars parked in the drive and Stormy recognized Rob's right off. Gramma made them sit together through dinner. Afterward she and Rob got into it. The worst part of this huge catastrophe is they still love each other. Their whole problem is simply lack of communication. It's hard. They're both hurting so much. I don't know how to fix it."

He stopped and pulled her to him beneath the streetlamp's glow. "That's not your job. You don't have to fix their problems. Bet you've tried to do that your entire life, huh?"

She nodded against his chest. "It's my role in this family. I set the example and fix things for others. But I'm failing worse than ever."

He raised her chin, so she met his gaze. "No. You. Aren't. You're an extremely competent, loving, intelligent woman giving her all to help those around her. I wish you could see you through my eyes. You amaze me."

"I do? I think you need glasses." She pulled back.

The moment was lost. He should've kissed her. Did she want him to kiss her?

"Sunny, you really don't get it, do you?"

"Get what?"

"That you are wonderful, beautiful. That I'm falling in love with you." Oops. It didn't matter how they slipped out. He'd said the words. Now what?

She turned to face him again. "Pat, maybe you need to study your mirror. I see an amazing man who cares, who is selfless in giving, one who I..." She glanced down, and her words grew soft. "One who I'm falling in love with." When she raised her head, her eyes gleamed with moisture.

There was no stopping. He pulled her close and met her lips, hungry to absorb what she saw in him.

When she drew back this time, it was slow, and she buried her face in his shirt.

He rested his chin on her crown. "Sunny, I can't imagine how you view that in me. I'm such a mess. If you only knew. But you give me reason to find courage. Maybe you're the courage I need. Oh, man, I need more time with you. I hate this distance between us."

She nodded, not raising her face.

"I have to drive back tonight, got work to finish. But I had to see you."

Now she gazed up at him. "You drove all this way to see me knowing you must return tonight?"

"Wasn't a difficult decision. The hard part will be driving home without you." She'd said she was falling in love with him. Her words echoed in his brain. There was no intelligent reason for her to fall for him. Yet she said she was. He could fly to Indy without his car when he let that thought soar in his heart.

They walked around the block, fingers tangled, her head leaning against his shoulder. Contented together, he'd go on like this forever. Which bloomed the realization that he'd never conceived the idea that he could hate the sight of the mansion. He came pretty close, though, knowing this walk would end at that porch.

He escorted her to her door and kissed her cheek. Not exactly what he wanted to do. Still, it was better to not rush. Changes were required in his world if he ever brought her into it. "Say that you'll go out with me tomorrow evening."

Her voice came out so soft, like velvet. "You'd have to drive all the way up here again."

"No problem doing that for time with you. So will you?"

She nodded and his heart soared.

He ran a finger along her jawline and stepped back, following her with his gaze as she headed into the house, before bounding down the stairs.

The ride home became reflective of his plans, his goals, and what it would take to make them happen. To be worthy of Sunny, he must get honest with his family. Where did he begin?

With his mom. Let her know he was interested in someone. He'd introduce them soon, and she was not to set him up anymore. It was the least complicated starting spot.

If he survived that conversation with little faltering, maybe there was hope.

It was too late to call her tonight once he pulled into his parking garage. Lunch tomorrow? This was a plan. He got inside his apartment and readied for bed, setting his alarm for early.

There were details to accomplish at work. And if they were off his plate, he'd have an easier time speaking with his father. When the time came.

Only the night was unkind. Pat tossed as if he'd downed a gallon of coffee before retiring. There was no getting comfortable, no counting enough sheep. His thoughts bombarded his brain with what-ifs. Finally, he'd just started to drift when his alarm sounded. He stumbled to the shower in hopes of it clearing his head. A stop at a coffee shop on the way to his office helped.

Venita called an hour after he got in. If he'd arrived on time, she would've caught him walking in his door. How'd she do that? "Pat, your secretary told me she gave you a couple more sites to check. What did you learn?"

That he needed a word with his private secretary on sharing information with his sister.

"I drove by the places and spoke with the owners. There's one over by Alto that has the age and grace you want. He can be talked down more, fairly sure. Also, I checked another in Greentown. It's my favorite between the two. They were the only ones viable."

"Okay, should we drive up this weekend?"

Not what he expected to hear. He couldn't let that happen yet. If she got in the vicinity, she'd want to run by Sunny's. "No, I think we should talk about them first. I'll show you on the map and I took some Polaroids so you can see for yourself."

"Fine. When do you want to get together?"

He glanced at his calendar while shuffling through his plans in his head. Lunch was blocked to talk with Mom. Dinner tonight was with Sunny. "How about tomorrow for brunch?"

It got quiet for a few seconds. "Sure. But I'll need to bring Brock. I'm not letting him out of my sight."

Pat released a sigh, then wished he could take it back. His brother-in-law wasn't his favorite person. In fact, some days he didn't consider Brock a person. The guy was too slimy. But he was his sister's husband. That made him family. "Whatever is fine."

"I know you don't like Brock. So, thank you for putting up with him. I'm not feeling all that fond of him at the moment. But he will not embarrass me again. Plus, he keeps looking for excuses to go places without me." Was she crying?

"Venita, you can't force him to do what's right. He needs to choose to do it."

"But what if he doesn't choose me?"

She'd be better off without... What did they use to call men like her husband? Yeah, gigolos. That's what Brock was, but he shouldn't tell his sister. Venita would be so hurt. And she might not believe him. That would ruin any chance of them building a relationship. Of course, Pat's shading of the truth didn't help matters either. "He'd be a fool not to choose you. But you want him to love you for who you are, not for our parents' name and wealth. You are worth being loved, Venita. I hope both of you see that."

She got quiet again, and for a moment Pat thought she'd hung up. Then he heard her sniffle.

"Don't cry, sis. Please."

"I can't believe you said that. That you think that. Pat, I'm glad you're my brother. I love you."

Oh, he was as bad a jerk as Brock. "I love you too, Venita. We'll talk tomorrow." He had to make this right. There was no future with Sunny unless he did. And even if Sunny wasn't in the picture, he owed his sister better.

Chapter Eleven
Friday, April 3, 1970

Sunny tried on the third outfit, tweed bellbottoms with a maroon pullover and a macramé belt and turned to her sister. "Better?"

"The first one was fine. You've never gotten this crazy about what you wear on a date before." Stormy only helped as she was stuck in the same bedroom. Just like at Gramma's, the three girls shared. Sunny knew her sister wanted the place to herself.

Stormy had isolated most of the day and preferred solitude. It made Sunny reconsider seeing Pat. Should she cancel and stay home and take care of her sister?

"Don't start with that look. I know what you're thinking, just give me some space. I'll be fine." Stormy popped up to stand next to her in the mirror's refection. "You're always there for me and deserve this night. Go enjoy your time with Pat. He's a nice guy."

"He is, isn't he? Stormy, I don't need the craziness of falling in love right now. But if that's what's happening, I'd better tell him about Indianapolis. I mean, he actually bumped into me that day in the stairwell. It's when we first met, but neither of us remembered until we put it together later. He said you helped him figure it out when you were passing out the fliers."

"Well, aren't I just the helpful one then. Hope it doesn't make trouble for you, sweetie."

Sunny spun and pulled Stormy into a hug. "I need to be honest. No matter what. Because of that, I feel pressure not to wait. So, I plan to tell him tonight. Can you play Gramma for me and start praying?"

"I doubt my prayers will do much good, but sure. For you, anything." Stormy hugged back, giving Sunny more confidence.

"Anything? How about giving Rob a call?"

"Anything but that." She shuffled to her bed and plopped.

"I've heard you humming all day. Think I can't recognize the songs? All those Marilyn McCoo tunes—'One Less Bell to Answer' and 'Couldn't Get to Sleep Last Night.'"

"Blame Dad. He brings his work home." Stormy rolled to her side.

Sunny sat next to her. "Yeah, but when you started on 'What Now, My Love' I got worried."

"We're a musical family. It's how our emotions come out. Let's talk about you and Pat."

With a sigh, Sunny let her win. For the moment. "So, you like this outfit best?"

"It's great. All of them were. You don't get how pretty you are—and he won't care what you're wearing, only that you're with him."

"Sure?"

"Sunny! Just get downstairs. He'll be here anytime. Wait, I know what. Take my long-fringed vest. That will give you more warmth and you can pace the front porch while you wait for him." She hopped up and pulled the beaded suede vest from her armoire and handed it to Sunny. "There now. Put that on and get going."

Sunny obeyed, but at the door she glanced back.

Stormy had rolled to the other side, shutting herself off.

Sunny blew her a kiss anyway and bounced down the stairs like a teenager on her first date. She'd just peeked out the window when his headlights turned into the drive, making her heart pound in her ears and her knees wobble. This could be dangerous. She grabbed her purse and met him on the porch.

"Ready?"

She nodded, too tongue-tied to speak. He was more handsome than last night in his pin-striped trousers and wide collar button-down shirt covered by a knitted vest. His dark hair and chiseled jaw set her pulse to doing erratic things.

He joined her at the steps, melding their hands while walking her to the car where he held her door before slipping in on his side. "I'm pretty stoked about tonight. It was hard concentrating on work when all I thought of was seeing you."

Her face heated, and a nervous laugh escaped. She hoped he felt the same way after she made her confession.

"Are you okay with the Casa Grande? It seemed like a great place. Next time maybe I'll take you to Indianapolis to one of my favorite restaurants."

Would there be a next time?

"Sunny, you're awful quiet. Is something wrong?"

She forced her mouth to speak. "No, I guess I've been excited, too. The anticipation for tonight and all. Just hope I haven't built it up so much in my brain." When she realized what she'd said, she wanted to roll the window down and stick her head out like a dog, letting the breeze cool her overheating face.

But he chuckled. "I understand. I feel the same. Let's relax, be just Sunny and Pat. Like any other day?" He reached for her hand and she let him find it.

"Great idea." And her anxiety level crept down a notch. Or two.

They arrived at the restaurant, placing the identical order as last time. The Casa Grande was the only place Sunny knew that served frog legs, making it a treat for her.

The waitress had perfect instinct. Each instance Sunny lifted her fork to her mouth, she magically appeared at the table checking how things were. The first inquiry or two irritated. After the fifth time, Sunny grew beyond annoyed. She determined the woman would not catch her again and began to eat faster. Which was a mistake.

One she realized as the too large chunk of frog meat made it to back of her throat before she'd chewed it enough. She opened her mouth to speak and it lodged. Stuck. Her heart thudded, and not because of Pat's closeness.

She grabbed at his hand and squeezed.

"Sunny? Are you all right?"

She shook her head as tiny sparkles appeared in the air in front of her. Hard as she tried, her lungs couldn't force a breath in or out.

"Can you breathe?"

She shook her head again and held the table for support.

He was out of his seat now, beside her. "Something's stuck?"

She'd just raised her chin in a nod when he pulled her from the chair. As he stood behind her, he wrapped his arms about her and shoved his fists into her...she was too desperate for air to imagine exactly where, but when he did it the second time, something flew from her mouth, landing on the table. A chunk of frog meat.

She drew in a ragged breath, gulping oxygen while grasping the chair-back.

Then the momentary spotlight's heat burned her consciousness. A million trillion eyes stared. She spun and raced for the ladies' room.

The woman peering from the mirror modeled florid cheeks and mascara-streaked eyes. Well, that's a picture Pat was sure to remember.

But he saved her life. He. Saved. Her. Life. The enormity sunk in and she grasped the sink to steady herself. She'd nearly died right there, right then. But Pat knew what to do. Now she was alive.

She needed to thank him.

After cooling her cheeks and ridding herself of the mess beneath her lashes, she returned to the table and sat as unobtrusively as possible noting that their plates were gone along with the deadly piece of frog.

"Thank you." She remained embarrassed, but that didn't diminish her gratitude.

He covered her hand. "So, are you ready for dessert?" His chuckle eased her discomfort.

"Only if it's pudding. I don't think I trust myself." She glanced up and flashed a smile. "I'm still in shock. Can't believe that actually happened. You read about it, but it's only on the news or in books."

"It happened to me once."

"It did?"

He nodded. "I was a kid and wanted to get back to my friend's house. Mother made me come home to eat lunch that day. I think she was worried my friend would be a bad influence, so she kept searching for reasons to keep us apart. Anyway, I was inhaling my sandwich and suddenly couldn't breathe. Not a soul at the table noticed until Clara yanked me up and pulled that move. That's how I learned."

She started to ask who Clara was, but the server returned to the table. "The manager sends his apologies and says your meal is on the house tonight."

Pat stood. "No, that's kind of him, but we will pay. Please thank him."

The server shook her head. "Um, someone else paid the bill. That's why it's on the house." She retreated as if she figured they blamed her. Being annoying didn't make it her fault exactly. Sunny could've been more careful.

"I wish I knew who to thank. Maybe I should pay someone else's check. Pass the on kindness."

Sunny stared at Pat. Who was this amazing guy? "I love that idea." They headed for the cashier, and Sunny stepped away to give him a little privacy. But then she overheard what he asked despite his efforts to be quiet. "How many patrons are there tonight?"

"We've twelve groups dining with us this evening, sir."

"Please total up their bills for me. I'd like to pay for them."

Sunny's breath caught in her throat as if the frog meat reattacked. He could afford all those dinners? Of course, he could. He was a Whitcomb.

She watched him whip out a credit card and cover the meals of everyone in the restaurant, even adding a handsome tip for the wait staff. Sunny felt around for the bench that sat against the wall for customers during high traffic times as her legs attempted to give out.

Two thoughts collided in her brain. The first increased her love for this generous guy. The second reminded her she was of humble origins and was nowhere in his class. Both made her wonder: Why on God's green earth was he interested in her?

The cashier called the manager to handle such a large transaction who at once grabbed Pat's hand, shaking it. Repeatedly. "You are very kind, sir."

"It's our way of showing thanks to whoever picked up our tab. We appreciate it. Don't say who did this. We don't want the notoriety. Please?" He kept saying "we." Not "I." She had nothing to do with it, other than embarrassing them both. The sooner they left, the better.

He must have heard her thought as he turned then and laced fingers with her, escorting her to his car. Once they were both inside, he squeezed her hand. "Are you sure you're okay? We can drive to the hospital and get you checked out."

That'd be the perfect topper to an excruciating evening. "No. Thank you. I've had enough excitement for tonight. Besides, I'm doing fine. They'd think we were both crazy." She already thought that herself.

"Then you want to go home?" He sounded so sad, she hated to tell him that was the one place she needed to be.

"What if we take another walk? I do want to be home, but there's always my backyard to stroll."

He started the ignition. "I get that. Sure. Next stop, Ferguson House."

And next for her, she'd better tell him about Indianapolis. Unless this was God's way of saying not to share. At this time.

PAT GLANCED AT SUNNY for the hundredth time. She'd grown so quiet after her scare. Which terrified him more than he admitted.

She continued to massage her earlobe. A clear indication she was holding things inside.

Maybe if he was just honest with her, then she'd relax. But what should he say? That he was a coward and prone to bending the truth when cornered? He might as well let her in on it before she discovered for herself. But he needed a spot where they could talk, some place without interruptions. Then he knew where.

After he turned into the drive, he hustled to get her door. "Instead of a walk, let's go sit. Got the perfect place." This time he pulled her near with his arm about her shoulders. His protective nature had been aroused and he just wanted her close.

They walked along the side yard to her garden, which continued to put out enticing scents. It wasn't too dark, he could still make out the giant sycamore and its low-hanging branch.

It'd be the right spot to sit and talk. Hopefully the darkness would hide his embarrassment as he told her his deepest, darkest secret.

She stumbled and he held her secure. Not on his watch. She buried her face against his chest a moment, making his heart swell. When she was this close, he could believe he was that champion on a white horse, her knight in shining armor, all those storybook heroes who won the princess.

"How about here? I'll help you up on the branch and then join you." He sensed more than saw her nod before he lifted her to the seat.

She grasped a smaller sprout sticking out to steady herself.

Now his turn. It was a tad higher than he remembered and he was grateful for the dark that blurred his awkwardness. Soon he was next to her. The smile she flashed caught the moon's glow. "So, what do you think?"

"Little room for a cardinal to land."

He chuckled; she'd relaxed. "Doubt there's a whole lot of them flying around at night."

"Well, then, if one did light, we'd be sure it was a sign." Did she just wink? "I know you don't believe in the legend. That's okay. Even if it isn't true, it'll make a fun selling point. Windy can use this for engagement photos. If a cardinal shows up, we'll do something special. I'm still trying to figure what. One idea is starting a true love wall with the photos that captured a cardinal with the couples. Perhaps in the front hall, so everyone must walk past."

"That's a smart marketing gimmick. Once the legend gets circulated, couples will beg for a chance."

Sunny really was an intelligent woman. Not surprising. The capitol employed only the savviest. A part of him wondered what happened, but when she was ready, she'd tell him. He just hoped she trusted him enough to eventually do it.

"Thanks. The more we prepare, the more ideas multiply. Some are wild fantasies, but others only require extra time to implement. The big thing now is making sure the carriage house is fit for Gramma and Gene's wedding. They're coming over Monday to tour it and set a time for photos. I didn't have the heart to tell them I caught them kissing. It was just too private. So, I'm hoping the cardinal comes back for their pictures."

He groped for her hand. "I'll hope with you."

Conversation lulled. Part of him wanted to tell her, but that coward part was fierce tonight. Finally, with the feel of her fingers beneath his, he let her trust in him pen his cowardice in a corner. "Sunny, I need to talk with you."

"I need to tell you something, too. I've just been too timid."

"I understand since I'm feeling the same. But I better go first. Please. This is really hard." He took in a breath and released it slowly.

"You mean the part where you have tons of money and I don't?"

"What? No! What are you talking about?" Where did that come from?

"It never hit me until you bought everyone's dinner. Even in my dreams I can't imagine being able to do that."

"So, I'm some rich snob trying to flaunt my wealth?" Is that how she saw him? Could he have been so wrong?

"No, oh, no. That's not it at all. In fact, I forget you have money until things happen like tonight. It's never a big deal to you. But you were so extravagant with your generosity and kept it quiet. Plus, you repeated 'we.' I realized I don't meet that standard."

His friend Trey had pointed that out to him once. But the truth was he learned about generosity from Trey's family. Plus, he'd seen that same spirit with the Days. He squeezed her hand again, though he'd rather take her in his arms. "I included you because we're in this together. Someone paid for your meal as well as mine. It was a kind thing to do. It didn't hurt me to pass along the kindness. It was from both of us."

"Okay." Her voice remained whisper soft, so he strained to hear.

"But my family's wealth isn't the topic I need to explain. Exactly. I mean it sort of involves my family. Remember when I told you I wanted to be a defense attorney, but familial obligations blocked the way?"

"Um hm."

"My biggest problem is I have a hard time standing up for myself with my parents, and sister. I'm easy to push around, I guess, because I need my family's approval for me to accept I'm loved for who I am. I've been nervous to tell them how I feel. There's my mother who's always trying to find the right girl for me, and Father who expects me to handle the corporation's litigations."

He tried to see her face and glimpsed her gaze on him. "Then there's my sister. She's a little older and highly intelligent. But because my father doesn't believe women belong in big business, he gave her a cushy job with a title in hopes it would shut her up. It didn't. She's out to prove she's as capable as any man. That drove a wedge between us. I get lumped with all the other males who've failed her." He wanted to run his hand through his hair but dared not while precariously balanced.

"She's the one who found Chloe and pushed her to sell. If she can prove to our father that she can compete in his world, she'll be a happy camper. So, she sent me here to buy the mansion. As a favor. But the moment I saw Ferguson House my gut twisted at that bad idea. Then I got to know you. I wanted to help you. My sister doesn't know about that. I've researched other properties and told her about those. The best is a possibility on a parcel in Greentown." He concentrated on the small hand beneath his. "I want to bring you home to introduce you to my family. But I can't. Not until I tell them the truth." He cleared his throat and soldiered on.

"When I told you that you are my courage, I meant it. Today at lunch I spoke with my mother. There'll be no more setups from her. I put my foot down. It surprised her a little, but I think she respected me. The next step is to talk with my sister. So far, she thinks I've been kind, trying to find her a replacement property. We're finally getting closer, but it's over a lie. I have to tell her the truth."

He knew it was a ton to drop on her. Once he began talking, though, it was hard to stop. He needed her reaction, and the dark that helped him initiate now kept him from seeing her expression. "Have I lost you?"

Her even breathing told him she wasn't too angry, but he couldn't read her eyes.

"No, I'm still here."

"That's not what I meant."

"You are still you. I feel the same as I did." She paused. "I need to think. Just because I've fallen...Just because my emotions are constant doesn't mean everything will be all daisies and roses. I'm for you, I'll cheer you on. However, we'll never make it if the half-truths aren't corrected." She sighed and he heard the weight on her grow heavier. "There's still something..." She shrugged. "Gotta let this sink in."

It was his turn to sigh. "I get that. I really dumped on you. But, Sunny, I can't hide anymore. I've gotta be the guy you see. Somehow you found integrity. All I know is cowardice. I planned to tell my sister tomorrow, but she's bringing company, so I ducked again."

"Could we walk, please? I think better when I'm moving. It will help." Her thumb curled up around his hand and she returned a squeeze.

"Yes, let me hop down, and then I'll help you." He jumped and landed wrong. "Ow!" The ground rushed up to greet him.

"What's the matter?" She sounded worried.

What a fool. "I twisted my ankle. Give me a second and I'll lift you down." If he could stand. It took bracing himself next to the tree to get to his feet. His angry joint wouldn't allow any weight. Great. He'd have to lift her down while standing on one foot. Though she'd seemed light when he set her up there, lifting her down was an entirely different story. He nearly dropped her and ended up falling against the trunk himself.

"Whew, we're not doing that in the dark again. We need to string lights out here. Let me check your ankle." She stooped at his feet.

"I'm fine. Just a little twist." He winced at her touch.

"Forget it, bub. I've been caring for Windy her whole accident-prone career. I'm an expert. Besides, you saved my life tonight. You owe me."

"I owe you?"

"Yup, I need a chance to save yours. Lean on me. I'll help you to the house where I can get a better look." Somehow, she slipped beneath his arm so that it draped across her shoulder.

With her arm about his waist, she pulled him close. "Should I get the girls?"

That was not going to happen. There'd been enough embarrassment for one evening. He grimaced. "I can make it. Let's go."

Once they were near the house, she paused. "The back is closer. The front will be easier to navigate. What do you say?"

He was nearly all in and worried about driving home now. But the image of falling off those rear steps was more than he could handle. He spoke through gritted teeth. "Front."

She steered him that way, guiding him up to the porch, then leaned him against the wall while she opened the door. Seconds later, she plopped him in the nearest living room chair and turned on more lights.

Sweat from exertion dripped through his hairline despite the temperature.

"Stay there. I'll get an Ace bandage and bowl of ice water."

Where was he going to go? Though the thought of his foot in ice water made him want to run. Fast.

Yet, he'd fessed up, and she was still willing to care for him.

Now what did he do?

Chapter Twelve

S unny found a large aluminum bowl in the kitchen, filled it with tap water, and emptied a tray of ice cubes into it. The first aid kit was in her office. She stopped there for the ace bandage and then, with a couple towels tossed over her shoulder, carried the load to the front room.

"Give me your foot." She reached out, but he flinched and drew back, connecting his heel with the chair leg.

"Ow!"

"You shouldn't have pulled away. Now let me see." She untied his shoe and gently slipped it off. After rolling his pant leg up to his knee, she removed his sock. He had nice feet. For a guy. She peeked up at him. His cheeks flamed. So cute. "The next part isn't fun."

"You mean sitting here and letting you undress my foot is?"

"Seriously? Allowing me to take care of you is that difficult?"

She stared him in the eye, daring him to say the wrong thing.

"It's not totally unpleasant. But I'm..." He shrugged.

"You're not in control. I get that. Sometimes you've got to let someone else do what they need to do. Whether or not you like it. I need to help you. The alternative is the ER. Your call, bub."

Terror flashed though his gaze followed by a slow grin spreading over his face. "Since you've started, I guess you can go ahead."

"Why thank you, sir. Now to get your foot in the ice bath."

She guided it in but didn't miss his eyes growing twice their size. To his credit, other than a deep inhale, he never made a sound.

"How long must I leave it?" His teeth chattered.

"A couple more minutes. I'll dry it off and wrap it tight. Then we'll prop it for a while. The good news is there's little bruising. It might not be sprained, just strained."

"Oh, goody." He groaned and she felt sorry for him. All his plans, and now he probably wondered if he could even drive.

"Be back." Sunny raced up the stairs to her room. Both of her sisters were there—Windy sketching while cross-legged on her bed. Stormy hadn't moved since Sunny left. "Girls, I need some help. Pat twisted his ankle. Are you okay if he sleeps on the couch? The other alternative is for one of you to assist me in getting him to Gramma's."

Windy hopped up. "I'll help. I rarely get to."

That made Stormy snort though she never rolled over. "Ain't that the truth. Whatever is fine. I don't plan to go parading downstairs in my jammies."

Sunny motioned for Windy. Once in the hall, she put her finger to her lips and led to the kitchen. "We should be able to talk here. I don't want to move Pat, but it's better if he goes to Gramma's. I can drive his car, so you follow me with mine. Right now, he's soaking in ice water, and he'll need to keep it elevated until we leave. You okay with all that?"

"Sure. You've done it for me plenty of times. Can I tell him about my adventures?"

Sunny shook her head. "I don't think he'd appreciate them tonight. Maybe another time. Let's rescue him from the ice."

When they came through the hallway, he glanced up. "Fun, you've brought reinforcements for your torture chamber."

"Aw, c'mon Pat. I'm trying to help you."

Windy stepped forward. "Listen to her Pat. She knows what she's doing. I *know*."

Sunny chuckled at that while she knelt in front of him and placed a kitchen towel on her lap. "Put your foot on this and I'll dry you off."

He started to flinch when she wrapped the towel about his toes, but she could see in his eyes, she'd surprised him by not causing more pain.

Moments later, she finished wrapping the Ace bandage and handed the bowl of water to Windy before standing. "Take it easy getting up. I need you to lie on the couch. Stick your foot over the armrest, I'll put a pillow there. It'll be above your heart level, so will bring down the throbbing. If you lie still for about thirty minutes, I'll adjust the bandage. Then we'll get you to Gramma's."

"I can't stay the night, Sunny. I'm meeting my sister tomorrow, remember?"

"Then wake up early and drive back. But give your ankle time to rest. It will hurt less in the morning. Trust me. Please?"

He stood, slowly. "I can at least lie here. We'll discuss the rest in thirty minutes."

She grinned. One battle over. She helped him to the couch and got him settled. Was this the time to tell him? He was sort of a captive audience.

The idea grew power. She instructed Windy to check the clock and return in half an hour. She needed privacy.

Then she dropped crisscross to the floor in front of the sofa with her back to him.

"What's going on?"

"Um, I still need to talk to you. I can do it better if you don't watch my face."

"Okay?" He reached out and tucked her hair behind her ear.

She found his hand and laced fingers with him. This would be harder than she'd anticipated. "I need to tell you. About Indy." She swallowed. "I'd been seeing a guy. We met New Year's Eve. He was funny and attentive and asked me out. But he didn't enjoy dating evenings much. That caused tension between us. The few times he'd agree, more often than not he stood me up. So, when he left me sitting in my apartment on Valentine's Day with no call or message all weekend, I knew I was done. Monday morning, I received a bouquet of roses from him. No 'I'm sorry,' no explanation. Just 'Love, Brock.'"

Pat's fingers squeezed a little tighter, but she continued.

"I threw the roses away. When he showed up at my work, I announced it was over. Just then some woman strolled to my desk, told me she was his wife and that she'd have me fired. I never knew he was married. But she kept her word. I was out of there by lunch, if you remember." She wiped away a tear with her free hand.

"It's hard enough to be fired, especially when you've been promised a promotion and you did nothing wrong. But to have all your coworkers learn that you've lost your job for dating a married man, and have it announced by his wife? The humiliation was intense."

He stayed so still, no sounds.

She had to spin and read his face.

His eyes were closed, his free arm rested on his forehead, and a tear dripped toward his ear.

"Pat, I promise you, I didn't realize he was married. I'm not that type of person."

He nodded. "I know."

"Are you all right?"

"No. I have a twisted ankle." He wiped his hand over his face.

"You get what I mean. Do you believe me?"

"Yeah, Sunny, I do." He cleared his throat. "Do you have any aspirin? Between my ankle and my head, I could use a few."

She hopped up and brushed her hands over her pants. "Sure. I'll get you some, and a glass of water."

The hallway lengthened a mile. Traversing it took forever. Minutes ticked while she grabbed the pills from her office and raced to the kitchen cabinets for a glass. Hours passed trying to fill it at the sink. What was wrong with her?

She knew what the matter was. He'd said he believed her, but he didn't act like it. Maybe he wanted to, but still doubted.

It was embarrassing enough to confess it all. But if she bared her soul only for him to think she lied, there was no future together. That notion stopped her cold.

No future? He told her he'd make things right with his family, so they'd have a future. Had she just ruined everything?

No. She must believe in him. She would believe in him.

With the aspirin bottle clutched in one hand and the water tumbler in the other, she returned to her patient.

The front door stood open.

Pat, and his shoe and sock, were gone.

She ran to the door.

His car was backing from the drive.

She watched him head for Phillips Street and turn until the taillights disappeared from sight.

Sunny slammed the front door making the windows rattle. She stood staring at it like the answers were among the wood trim.

"Sunny? What happened?" Windy and Stormy leaned over the staircase railings.

When she opened her mouth to explain, nothing came out. And then a noise she'd never heard filled her ears and brought her to her knees. The noise ripped from her, deep inside her, like someone yanked every pain and hurt right out into the open.

Her sisters were there. No walking over, just instantly there. Holding her, brushing hair from her face, rocking her from side to side. Taking her aloneness. Giving her acceptance.

"Sh-sh, it's okay. You're okay. We're here. We've got you, Sunny."

They were the branch sticking out of the rapids that she could cling to, the ledge that halted her free-fall. They were her sisters.

Stormy helped her to stand, and Windy grabbed a box of Puffs. They guided her back to the sofa and sat on either side.

"When you're ready, you tell us. It's okay." Windy shoved a tissue into her hand.

"He left after you told him, huh?" How did Stormy do that?

Sunny nodded and gulped a breath before trying to speak. "He...he said...he believed me." She inhaled again and let it out. "Said he needed...aspirin. I go to get it, come back..." She shivered with the memory. He couldn't leave fast enough.

"Jerk." Sunny wanted to correct Stormy, but it hurt too much.

"What am I going to do? I didn't realize I'd fallen so hard. You know, when we went to dinner, he paid for everyone's meal. Wouldn't allow the manager to tell the other diners." She hiccupped.

"Wow!" Windy passed her another tissue.

"Why would he do that?" Stormy's brows furrowed together.

"It was my fault. I choked and he had to help me. It was embarrassing. But when we tried to pay, we discovered someone had paid for our meal because of it. He didn't know who to thank, so he paid for everyone's."

"Wow." Stormy reached across Sunny for a tissue from Windy.

"And then we have this deep heart to heart, and I think we're starting to build something, but he twists his ankle, so I bring him in. I figured it was time, and I don't want to build with secrets or lies."

Windy passed her another tissue.

"Well, if he said he believed you, then sent you on a goose chase so he could escape, I'd say he's still into secrets and lies. Even if he does spectacularly nice things." Stormy patted her knee. "You weren't looking for anyone when he showed up. Who knows, the next guy you meet might be Mr. Right."

"Maybe." But Sunny highly doubted it. Pat was not the first guy she'd kissed. But no one ever made her feel like he did. The electricity in his touch charged her to life. But his walking out the door nearly killed her.

BROCK.

She said Brock.

That dirty, low-down womanizing husband of his sister...

Pat's anger churned and swirled as he thought of what that arrogant, pea-brained male model wannabe did to Sunny and Venita.

And then he realized, Venita was the one who got Sunny fired. A vice gripped his heart and cranked tighter. He stepped on the gas with his left foot. His right straddled over behind the floor shifter so he wouldn't automatically use it and kill himself from the sudden stab of pain.

Please don't let there be police out tonight. There wasn't time for another ticket. He had to get home.

He realized he ought to plan what to say. He had to explain to Venita what her clown of a spouse did. But then she already knew. She'd had Sunny fired. Why did he keep forgetting that piece of the puzzle?

If he told Venita the truth about Kokomo, she was sure to recognize Sunny's name. Not that many Sunny Days in the phone book. Apparently, his sister was aware of Brock's philandering. Yet chose to blame the other women. *Oh, Venita, you're better than this.*

The whole way he combed through various details as if putting together an opening statement before a jury. He needed to get his sister's attention and make her see Sunny as the injured party.

But Sunny possessed the one thing Venita wanted—the mansion.

He knew his sister well enough to realize she'd take it as proof that the world conspired against her and that she couldn't trust any man in her life—not her father, her husband, and now her brother. And maybe that was sort of true, but he needed her to trust him. Only sharing the truth would fix this.

It was eleven by the time he parked in his slot. Exiting the car would be trickier than getting in. But he managed without falling on his face. He was able to handle light weight on his injured ankle, so he didn't have to hop all the way. When he'd first raced for his Mustang, his foot was so numb he didn't feel as much as he'd feared. Now the cold had worn off. And despite being propped, it hadn't been above his heart, so sensation had returned. Overall, though, he kept his male reputation intact and didn't cry like a baby trying to get into his apartment.

He never bothered getting undressed but dropped into bed, asleep by the time his head hit the pillow.

But his dreams were vivid, full of his sister determined to end him with various means like sending wild animals after him to an ax wielding robot.

His phone's insistent ring had him groping his nightstand for the receiver. "Hello?"

"Pat, I can't make our brunch. Something came up." Click.

"Venita?" He sat, swinging his legs off the side of the bed, and plunged the little black switch hook buttons. "Venita?"

Now he was awake.

Why did she cancel? He was determined to do this. For Sunny. For himself. Even for Venita, if she'd accept that.

Plan B time.

He gingerly stood. No sharp pains shot through his ankle. So, he sat again and unwrapped it before heading for the shower. He thought better in there, and maybe he'd figure out his next step. Brock. There's the key. He needed to find his brother-in-law and set him straight. No more cheating on Venita. No more putting innocent women into situations where they lose their livelihood because he wanted one more conquest.

Conquest? Had their relationship gotten that far?

No, Sunny wasn't like that. But given the chance, Brock might have pressured her. He could believe that. Well, that changed today.

But where to find the guy?

Pat dressed while he mulled his first move. He glanced at the clock and an idea hit. The house Father gave them for a wedding gift, that's where the slimeball would be. Brock wouldn't be awake without guarantees of something in it for him. The man was the laziest. What did his sister see in him anyway?

No matter. He just needed to find him. Chances were favorable the leach would still be at home. Pat inhaled before trying his right foot in a loafer. A tad tight, but not super painful. He swiped his keys on the way out his door. Venita's home wasn't far from his parents' estate, over by Geist. Twenty minutes later he pulled up in front.

The house appeared quiet. It was hard to tell if anyone was there since the garage was closed. He'd have to take the chance.

After locking up, Pat walked the brick path bordered with pansies to the front and rang the bell.

He was about to leave when the door yanked open.

"Oh, Pat. Man, you caught me at a bad time. Venita's not here, and I'm just getting ready to take off." Brock ran his hand through his hair. He answered his own door? Venita probably couldn't leave him alone with a maid.

"This won't take long. I need to talk with you."

Brock raised his eyebrows as he stepped aside allowing Pat entrance. "C'mon in then. Can I get you anything? Water? Something to hurry you along?"

"Where are you off to, Brock?"

"Oh, I've got this thing. Can't be late." His fingers combed through his hair again.

"What's her name?"

"What do you mean?" He tried to appear indignant, but that crumbled as Pat stared. "Hey, this is none of your business. What I do is—"

"What you do is chase skirts. Don't deny it, Venita already told me." Pat figured he might as well lay it all out.

"Your sister's crazy. I'm not doing that. Not my bag." He turned avoiding eye contact.

"She knows, Brock. Now so do I. Treat my sister with respect or get out. She doesn't need to live in fear of what you're doing when she isn't around."

Brock snickered. "Sounds like you came from a fifties puritan movie with happily-ever-afters and having eyes for only one gal. What a lot of hogwash."

It took everything in Pat to not deck him. "Final warning. You'll not keep hurting my sister."

"Look, I'm going to lay it out so you will understand. I do not plan to change my ways. I like women. They like me. Everyone is happy, except you and Venita. Too bad." He headed for the door.

Pat stepped in front of him. "Then divorce her. Give her a shot at a happy life."

"You don't get it, pal. I have grown accustomed to a certain standard of living. I've no intention of giving that up."

Pat always thought Brock married Venita for her money and family connections, but to hear the guy say it sent a chill down his spine.

Brock pulled open the front door. "Now if you will excuse me..."

Pat started to leave, then turned back on the threshold as an idea formed. "You do know my father can have you cut out of everything. You wouldn't get one dime from the family and he'd have you black balled even if you wanted a job delivering pizza."

That was humorous to Brock. "You and your old man should talk, Pat. He knows what's happenin'. As long as I remain discreet with my indiscretions, we're good. Just like your grandfather advised him. I'm surprised he's never told you. But then, you're just the goody-two shoes of the Whitcombs. Now goodbye. There's a gorgeous redhead waiting for me who needs to hear how beautiful she is. Can't say it's been nice—probably won't even mention this to Venita." He shoved Pat and slammed the door in his face.

Pat stared at the decorative molding on the now closed entrance, seething and unable to put his thoughts in order. The jerk slammed the door on him! The vein in his neck began to pulse. Hard.

What should he do? He needed another plan.

On the way to the car, Brock's words bounced back. His father knew? He approved, or overlooked Brock's actions as long as they remained...discreet?

Venita couldn't catch a break.

Neither could he.

Pat started the ignition, gunned the gas and left rubber peeling out of the neighborhood. He'd never felt this angry in his life.

A young teen-aged girl on the sidewalk jumped into a manicured lawn making sure to be out of his path.

That scared him enough he slowed down. The last thing he wanted was to hurt a child. Or anyone.

Except Brock.

Maybe his father.

Right now, though, his thoughts jumbled through his brain. He needed to cool off, think. Slow down his heartrate as well as his driving. That sent him back to his apartment.

Once there, he slipped the phone off the hook and grabbed a legal pad and pen. He would sort this out. Figure out the best offense. It would require him putting all his cards on the table. A true gamble.

What were the stakes?

His family. His future. And Sunny.

He'd let this fester too long. Clean. That's what he needed.

He also needed to talk with someone who could recommend and not judge. He tried Trey's number, but no one answered. Why had he thought of Trey? Well, they'd been friends forever. Trey always accepted him. But something else niggled, something he couldn't put into words. Yet. Still Trey was unavailable. What was his next choice?

Trey's parents still lived in town. They'd always made him feel like part of the family. He even received Christmas cards from them, with a label touting the same old address. Would they listen?

The best he could do was try. He dialed the number he still knew by heart. When the familiar voice answered, it threw him back in time. "Mrs. Haynes, this is Pat Whitcomb."

"Pat, how great to hear from you. We were just talking about you the other day wondering how you were doing." Her smile came through her words.

"Well, I'm facing kind of a dilemma. Would it be okay..." He coughed. *Don't let the coward win. Try again.* "Think you might have a few minutes to help me sort through this mess?"

"How soon can you get here?"

"Twenty minutes?" Could it really be this easy?

"Plan to stay for dinner. We'll see you soon. Drive safe."

"I will. And thanks." He hung up and stared at his phone. Why hadn't he reached out before? What will they say when they hear the whole sordid tale? No matter. He grabbed his keys and headed for the one place that taught him the difference between a house and a home.

Chapter Thirteen
Saturday, April 4, 1970

S unny threw her blanket aside and braved an upright position. Her head pounded. They didn't manufacture enough aspirin to fix what only time could. She padded past the mirror and caught a stranger's reflection. The poor thing staring back had swollen tragic eyes. Then she remembered: she was that poor thing.

A good dousing in cold water might help. She headed for the bathroom, catching the time on Stormy's alarm clock on the way. It was still early, the sun only starting to peek over the horizon. But she couldn't take lying there in her thoughts anymore.

There'd been little sleep—and by that she meant that there was none that she was aware of, but in case she'd dozed between crying jags, she'd allow for the benefit of the doubt.

Back in her room, she quietly dressed and pulled her hair into a ponytail. She slipped out the door, gently closing it behind her. This thing between her and Pat didn't change the fact she had a business to run.

Sunny wandered out to the carriage house to check on how things were progressing. The entire inside now sported multiple coats of white paint making it appear bigger, though the rafters remained natural and rustic. A ladder stood to the side indicating where Windy and Kris left off in their light-stringing adventure. They'd really turned the promise of her imagining into reality. Or the beginning of it. Maybe they'd move furnishings on Monday and capture ad-worthy snapshots for showing.

Gramma and Gene wouldn't need to see the pictures since they had already caught her vision, but perhaps when styled for their wedding, those photos could help advertise.

She meandered to her garden for a little pre-breakfast weeding. The cool air refreshed her worn spirit and she rid herself of pent-up frustrations by yanking out the wild things that dared to sprout among her planned beauties.

She'd made it to the final bed when the back door creaked. They needed to get that oiled. More for Kris's to-do list.

"Sunny, you out here? Oh, there you are." Stormy headed her way. "How are you doing this morning?"

"Functioning, maybe? I don't know. I'm not ready to think about it. The truth is, I've no idea why he left like he did. My guesses are usually pretty good, though. I owe him the chance to explain. Just not up to reaching out yet." She wiped the back of her hand across her forehead and stood.

"You're doing better than I expected. There's no rush, sweetie." Stormy drew her into a hug. "You don't realize it now, but this'll work out. Somehow."

Sunny pulled away. "You believe that?"

"I do."

"Then why aren't you applying your words of wisdom to you and Rob?"

Stormy gave her a half smile. "Who says I haven't? That time alone yesterday did wonders. I don't have a strategy or even a direction. However, I'm more at peace. We've got this business. We're together. So many good things happening. I'm focusing on the good."

"Actually, that sounds like a plan. We can do it." She grabbed Stormy's hand and swung their clasp between them.

Stormy grinned. "So, want some breakfast? I'm feeling adventuresome and thought I'd make bacon and eggs. Maybe if we eat early, we'll grab our share before Kris shows up and we have to feed him too."

That made Sunny chuckle. "Almost done, this is the last bed. Get started while I finish here. Be there in a minute."

"Okay." Stormy gave her hand another squeeze before letting go and returning to the rear door.

As the girls cleaned up after eating, Kris walked in the back way. He glanced around and shrugged. "Gonna keep stringing the lights in the carriage house." He turned and went back out.

"I'll help." Windy tossed her dish towel on the drainer and raced after him.

"This might be a problem." Stormy stared out at their departure.

"Think so? I don't feel any romantic vibes coming from him." Sunny joined her sister at the window.

"I know. She could be hurt again. Plus, with the baby...she hasn't told Gramma or Dad yet, has she?"

Sunny shook her head. "No, I doubt it. We would've heard the explosion. Since Dad's gone back to LA until the wedding, bet she's holding off until then."

"Yeah, bet you're right. Hey, how 'bout we dress a couple mannequins with what arrived from the consignment shipment? We can get started and have Windy show us how wrong we are."

Stormy winked.

"Good idea. Let's go." Sunny tossed her sponge in the empty sink and followed her sister to the small parlor. "You know, we could also get the dining room set for cake tasting. Chloe left her Irish linen tablecloth and napkins. That would give the perfect background for that exquisite china she donated."

"I think Windy needs to do that. No, wait. We'll arrange it and let her tell us how to improve. Much safer for the china."

Stormy laughed at her own funny.

Unfortunately, she spoke the truth.

Two hours later mannequins graced three of the downstairs rooms promoting theme ideas, plus progress had been made on the dining room.

Stormy stepped back and scanned their work. "Wish we could keep fresh blossoms in the vases. Wonder how often we'd need to change them out?"

"Maybe once a week? Could we make that part of the weekly budget?" Sunny cringed at adding something more, but it was close to being a necessity. "Wish my flowers were growing well enough to supply that. What if we limit it to strategic? A modest bouquet centered on the dining table and one arrangement in each room plus the entry?" She added them up in her head. She could start with inexpensive carnations and baby's breath and add to them with blooms from her garden. That would keep her from making her own beds too thin and still have nice arrangements throughout. She'd need to think about that.

A car door slammed out front, reverberating through the open entry.

"I'll go check in case it's someone you don't want to speak with." Stormy patted her arm as she slipped out and then called from the front. "Not him. Strange car. Some woman. I'll tell her we aren't open yet."

Sunny smiled. Her sister taking charge.

A few minutes later Stormy returned. "She wants to talk with the owner. Says she has a proposition."

"You're an owner, too."

Stormy put her hands on her hips. "I got a feeling this needs your input. Sounds like a money discussion."

"Oh, okay." Sunny glanced in the mirror above the buffet. Not exactly her most professional look, but the woman gave her no warning. She was neat and clean. That would have to be enough. With a deep breath, she headed to the front.

"You?" Sunny stared into the face she'd never forget, feeling her jaw unhinge. This was her home. No way would this...person invade her private domain, not after Indy. She straightened her spine and turned on her best glare. "What are you doing here?"

"I came to offer the owner a deal. Do not tell me that's you." The visitor spoke through gritted teeth.

Sunny bit her bottom lip while she pulled in a breath and rubbed her earlobe. Manners. This wasn't a planned attack. This woman got caught off-guard too. Plus, Gramma taught her better. Stay firm but polite. Be the better person. She forced a smile. "Afraid so. I'm guessing you and I don't want to conduct business. I'm sure I don't want to do business with you." Okay, maybe that was snarky, but she'd done her best. Sunny turned to leave. "You can show yourself out." She tossed that over her shoulder without missing a step.

"Wait. I need this property." Pause. "You owe me after what you did."

That halted her mid-step. "After what *I* did? You're kidding, right?" How could she spew those words from her mouth? If anyone was the wounded party, it was Sunny. Not this...witch. She rubbed her lobe harder.

"Look, you convinced my brother you wouldn't sell, but I can make it worth your while." The woman dared to step forward.

"Your brother? Pat is your brother?" Lightbulb time. That's why he ran. Sunny's knees buckled.

"You mean you didn't know?"

Stormy slipped an arm around her. "Pat appreciates Ferguson House and has been a great help." That must have cost her sister to say something nice about Pat, but it was the right zinger. Bullseye.

The woman paled and then grew beet red. "He's...been helping you?"

"With all sorts of things. Even spent his vacation time here. Can't imagine what we'd have done without his advice and extensive knowledge dealing with all the legal aspects."

Okay, maybe Stormy crossed the line with that last part.

However, it was another direct hit sinking What's-her-name's battleship. What *was* her name?

"No, that can't be true. He's been up here searching for other properties. He's been working for me. He promised me." Realization flashed through her eyes. "I'm going to kill him." She spun for the exit, shouting over her shoulder, "Don't even think of contacting him again. You will stay away from my husband and my brother and all members of my family." The door slammed after her, giving the windows another earth-shattering shake.

"That's what you heard last night?" Sunny shuddered at the boom. No wonder her sisters came running.

Stormy nodded and closed one eye with a grimace. "That's Pat's sister?"

"And Brock's wife. How could I have been so dumb?"

"What do you mean?" Stormy cocked an eyebrow.

"When I told him, I mentioned Brock's name. At least I think I did. He must've known who I was talking about. That's why he left. He realized I was the other woman when his brother-in-law cheated on his sister." Pat never wanted to lay eyes on her. Again. Ever. She peered at Stormy, watching her reaction. "Venita. That's her name. Now I remember."

"How did you ever forget that?"

Sunny shrugged as a wave of emotion splashed over her. Then another. Her insides quaked. "I...I...can't...breathe." Her heart pounded in her ears and every fiber of her being wanted to run. Anywhere.

Stormy guided her to the chair and pushed her over so her face was down by her knees. "Breathe in. Out. In. Out. You're going to be okay."

Gentle strokes down Sunny's back soothed. But as she relaxed, the tears came. Not wracking sobs, but quiet drips dropping onto the carpet while she kept her head low.

Finally, Stormy helped her sit upright. "Better?"

She nodded. "I just flashed on her first appearance in my life, reliving the humiliation. You know, if Pat and I ever married, she'd be my sister-in-law."

"Dodged a bullet there, sweetie."

That made her snort. "You're right. I'll keep telling myself that."

Stormy hugged her. "Want to finish arranging the dining room?"

Sunny shook her head. "Gonna lie down for a bit. I didn't sleep well because I kept wondering why. Now I know. Maybe I'll grab a nap."

"Okeydoke. I'll do what I can before checking on the kids. See how the carriage house is coming."

"Good idea, but you know Windy hates it when you refer to her that way. I'll be down after a while." Sunny plastered on a shaky smile as she headed to her room to curl up with Mr. Murphy.

Frazier mewed and jumped up with her. "Hey, Fraze." She stoked his sleek long coat. "How are you doing, buddy?"

He circled until lowering into a ball next to her. Like he understood.

"You love me, doncha?"

He purred his answer.

"At least you do. And my sisters do. And my family. But they can't really know how bad I've messed up. There's no guarantee with this venture, and I've dragged the girls in with me. Everything I touch falls apart." She buried her face in her bear. "I'd sure appreciate some advice about now. Are you positive you don't have any for me?"

Mr. Murphy remained stoically silent.

"I keep forgetting our deal. I talk and you listen. Wish you'd reconsider. No one else is ready to hear about the mistakes dragging me under." She pulled the stuffed bear close as her tears absorbed into his matted fur.

Frazier glanced her way and then licked her hand. If she only dealt with Mr. Murphy and Frazier, life would be much easier.

Sure, her sisters were there for her, but that's not how it worked. She was the eldest. She was the problem solver. It was her job to care for them. She was failing miserably at the moment. Stormy and Rob separated. Windy unwed and pregnant. Now they were taking care of her. She was a mess, her world a shamble, and she'd let her sisters down. Again.

Could she do anything right?

PAT PARKED IN FRONT of the modest craftsman-style house and locked his car. A wave of coming home again washed over him. No longer was he the Big Boss's son, or a prominent corporate attorney dealing with millions and billions of dollars. Now he was a gangly teen, relaxing with folks who had zero use for pretense.

The front door pulled open before he could knock.

"Get in here, Pat. It's been way too long." Lonnie and Sherrie Haynes met him with a group hug before pulling him inside.

He glanced around. New photos covered the walls and credenza. The kitchen had a fresh coat of paint and more updated appliances. But most everything appeared the same, and it soothed his soul.

"Sit down. I was telling Lonnie that you wanted to talk with us. I'm so glad you reached out. We've missed you, Pat." Sherrie was open and kind, just as she'd always been.

"Thank you for having me over. It's like returning to the good days. I almost expect Trey to tear down the hall any minute." He paused a moment, hoping that would happen. It didn't.

"When was the last time you talked to Trey?" Lonnie leaned back and crossed his ankle over his knee.

"A few weeks, maybe a month. Not sure. We planned to have lunch, but he had a sudden work thing."

Lonnie and Sherri glanced at each other. Some message passed between them. Then Sherri spoke. "There was an accident about ten days ago. Carol was hurt the worst. She's still in the hospital. Trey's with her when not at the capitol. He wrangled some time off, but to maintain her insurance, he's had to keep working. Carol's mom is watching the kids on the weekends. We have them during the week because we're closer to their school."

Something slammed into Pat's chest. Why hadn't he known?

Because he'd been too self-absorbed in his own mess to notice or even give his friend a call. "I'm so sorry. Is there anything I can do?"

"Pray. Be there for Trey. He probably needs a buddy to talk to."

Suddenly his problems seemed so petty, so small. "I've taken up too much time. I apologize for intruding." He stood.

"You sit right down this minute Patrick Whitcomb. You are not doing that. We've always considered you one of our own. You don't walk out on family, no matter how noble your intentions are." Sherrie was another woman he feared.

At times.

Like now.

"I hate to be in the way. And compared with what you're all dealing with, my problems aren't worth mentioning." But he sat as commanded.

"Let us be the judges, Pat. It bothered you enough to call. Maybe we can help. Start at the beginning. What's going on?"

So, he did. He covered it all from his father's disapproval of his desires, the rocky relationship with his only sibling, the amazing girl he'd met, the request of his sister, how he'd not been upfront with her, Sunny's confession—without mentioning her name—and the confrontation with Brock. Everything involved, every discussion he'd had with Sunny, he told all, no matter how humiliating. Still his pulse pounded as he relived his morning's fiasco. He was at a loss of what to do.

They weren't there, couldn't know what it was like. Why did he come here?

The Haynes listened, no interruptions. Finally, he came to the end. "So how do I help my sister? How do I keep her husband from hurting her more? And how do I fix things with the young lady in Kokomo? I feel like such a fraud."

There was no fixing this. He knew it. He'd just wasted their time.

Lonnie and Sherrie shared a glance before Lonnie became the spokesperson. "I've got some questions, for clarity. Do you love this girl with the house?"

Pat nodded. "Yeah, I do. I'd like to build something with her."

"Do you think you can do that and stay working for your father?" Lonnie's gaze penetrated.

Pat pondered that a moment before shaking no. "She deserves someone who isn't a toady for his father. And I can't imagine bringing her home to meet them until things are right with Venita."

"I agree with that. Another question: have you prayed about it?"

Pat shook his head again. He should've known it would come down to their faith. "No. You all do that, but I've never been a praying person. If I was ever tempted, though..." If he just knew how. And if it would work. And, most important, if there really was a God who would hear and care.

"Well, that brings me to the most important question, then. Pat, is Jesus your Lord and Savior?"

What did Lonnie mean? Pat had read enough to be aware of Jesus. But lord and savior? "I'm sorry, I don't understand."

Lonnie uncrossed his legs and leaned forward. "Then I have my answer. Pat, it's hard to pray to Someone when you have no idea Who they are or what He's done for you. I'm not going to blindside you or make you feel trapped. Do you want to know? I'm happy to share."

Did he? Was there really Someone who cared enough to listen and help? He'd screwed things up so badly, he knew he needed something more. Something divine? These people were good and caring. Was this the root of their goodness? He needed to know.

In fact, he longed to know. He nodded. "Please. I'll listen."

Lonnie said that from the moment Adam and Eve sinned, God established a plan to redeem mankind. He grabbed his Bible and read about how everyone sinned and fell short, but Jesus made a way by being the only sacrifice worthy to save mankind. Nothing anyone did, said, or purchased could fix things, but God offered a gift. It only required acceptance. "So, I'm asking Pat, do you want Jesus to be your Lord and Savior? To cleanse you from your sins and make you whole?"

Cleanse. Hadn't he craved getting clean, knew that was the only solution? And here it was. Waiting for him to accept. Could it really be this easy? It was as if God strategically placed examples to point him in the correct direction, straight to this moment. His heart hammered with anticipation, tightening in his chest. "Yes, that's what I want."

Sherrie moved to sit next to him on the couch. Lonnie knelt on the floor in front of him. "Then we're going to pray. Just bow your head and close your eyes. Put your focus on Jesus and repeat after me. Dear Jesus."

"Dear Jesus."

"I am sorry for all the wrong choices I have made."

Pat spoke the words.

"I ask you to cleanse me of my sins and send your Holy Spirit to live in my heart."

Pat repeated, though the idea of a spirit—holy or not—living inside him felt strange.

"Be my Lord and Savior. Lead and guide me in all I do and say."

Again, Pat uttered the phrase wondering if there'd be any difference afterward.

"Thank you for your sacrifice. I put my faith in You, Lord."

And he did. That was the bottom line. He couldn't trust in himself, not with how he screwed up everything he touched. He needed someone who understood. *Boom.* Understanding flooded his jumbled thoughts. He realized there was no other he could trust. Mind blown.

They closed with Amen together.

Funny, Pat's chest didn't hurt anymore. Breathing came much easier. And the grin pushing its way out wouldn't be contained.

"Welcome to the family, Pat. The family of God." Sherrie was the first to hug him.

"I want you to know we are praying for you. I think things will start to break loose pretty fast. Just keep looking to Jesus for his guidance. Do you have a Bible?" Lonnie pushed himself back up and sat in his chair.

Pat shook his head. "No, I don't. Where can I get one?"

"Right here." Sherrie reached over to the end table to pick up a book and handed it to him. "There you go. Now you have your own."

Pat thumbed through the pages, so many. It would take a while to read cover to cover.

"Don't start at the beginning. You can come back for that. Begin with Luke. And we want you to come to dinner often. We'll help you with questions—not that we have all the answers, but mostly, we know where to look." Lonnie helped him locate the book of Luke.

"I'll slip off to the kitchen and finish supper while you two talk." Seconds later, it was just Lonnie and Pat.

Every question Pat had, Lonnie answered. He made sense. It was no longer a duty to come clean with Venita, he was determined to. Not out of fear. But out of love for his sister. Sherrie called them to the table where Lonnie prayed over the meal. He offered to help clean up, but she wouldn't hear of it. Instead, she sent him home with dessert, some leftovers, and advice about Sunny. "Just be honest and pray about it. God will show you what to do."

He stood, already noticing a pull toward his next move. Tonight he'd get in touch with Venita, make plans to talk.

Pat thanked them, not only for their hospitality, but for helping him find what he'd searched for all his life, and promised to return next week for another dinner and more guidance.

The drive home was filled with a lightness and joy that he didn't understand, but thoroughly welcomed. So different from feeling like he was juggling to stay alive. It even got him to whistling. From the parking structure, up the elevator, and through the corridors to his apartment.

But as he turned to his hall, he spotted a figure slumped outside his door.

Venita?

"Hey sis, what's the matter? How long have you been waiting?"

She slid up the wall and stepped toward him, her eyes red and swollen. She'd been crying? When she got to him, she stopped and stared.

Before she slapped him.

"Why, Pat? Why did you lie? Why her? Of all the females on the planet, why Sunny Day?" She choked out that sweet name.

He pulled her close and held her with his left arm while slipping his key in the lock.

She struggled a bit before melting and sobbing against his chest.

Then he guided her inside to a chair, flipped on the lights and closed the door. He dropped crisscross on the floor in front of her and took hold of her fingers. Not even nervous. No fear. He simply stated the truth. "I am sorry. I owe you a huge apology. Instead of attempting to mislead you with a different location, I should've told you the truth. It wasn't for sale. And it never should be part of any plan to raze it."

"But that woman—"

He rubbed circles on the backs of her hands with his thumbs noting the calm enveloping him. "Sunny. I didn't realize the connection until last night. It came out while we were sharing some...stuff. I wanted to talk with you about it this morning, but you canceled. How did you find out?"

"I figured if we chatted face to face, maybe..." She shrugged. "But then *she* walked in the room. The same witch who tried to steal my husband, and now she's on to you." She jerked her hands away.

Somehow, despite her growing anxiety, Pat felt peace as a blanket of serenity dropped over him. "Venita. You don't know the whole story."

"She's bamboozled you too, I guess. So pretty and sweet, how could she ever fib?"

"Did you ask her what happened? When she told me, she didn't know we were related. Why would she lie? In fact, Sunny was embarrassed she hadn't figured out he was married before you told her." He took a breath. This would be difficult. "The thing is, Brock had already blown it and she'd broken up with him. He was begging for another chance when you arrived."

She jumped from her chair, shoving him backward.

He cracked his head on the floor, tiny flashes of light preceding the wave of pain.

"Oh, Pat, I'm sorry, I'm sorry. Don't die!" She knelt at his side.

He gasped and then bit back a laugh at her exclamation despite the radiating pain. "I'm okay. Give me a sec." After a moment, he sat, rubbing where he'd smacked.

"Do you have frozen peas? I hear they are great for bumps." She popped up and ran to his kitchen, returning with a paper towel and a couple ice cubes. "Your freezer is empty. How do you eat?"

He took the bundle from her and held it against his wound. It helped. At least it wasn't bleeding. "Venita. I'm sorry Brock is who he is. I tried speaking with him, but he won't change. You've gotta decide if you want to live this way or move on. I'll support you either way, but you need to know, I'm in love with Sunny. I believe you two can find common ground, but allowing her in the same room with Brock won't happen. I won't do that to her. If we have a future, and I'm praying we do, I won't be bringing her to the house for holidays if Brock is in the picture."

"So, you're choosing her over me?" Her eyes grew wide as tears streamed.

"No, I'm choosing her over Brock. I'd like to help you get out of that mess too. Divorce isn't a thing in our family. I know. But he's not willing to be faithful to you, he's already destroyed your wedding vows. Could be you only need a separation. If he gets a taste of life without you, and your money and connections, then he might change his mind. I'm not in your shoes, but I am here for you whatever you choose. Even if he stays, I'm still your brother and I love you."

She threw herself at him and he feared falling backward again, but he steadied himself and wrapped her in a hug. She plopped next to him. "I love you too, Pat, though I'm not sure about giving Sunny a chance yet. Is her name really Sunny Day?"

He chuckled. "Not only yes, but she has sisters. Windy and Stormy."

Now she laughed. "I think I must have met Stormy; she was feisty."

"Sounds about right. But Sunny is aptly named. She's like a day of sunshine and light. I love her, Venita. I just pray I haven't messed it up too much."

"You? Maybe you ought to worry that I didn't."

He glanced at her eyes, and a twinge of fear rose. Had she done something that made it beyond fixable?

Chapter Fourteen

S unny stretched as her sisters wandered into their room.

Stormy carried a tray. "Have a good nap?"

Windy sat on the bed next to her.

Sunny scooted to sit. "Yeah, I did. Thanks for letting me slip away. I just needed a bit. Now I'm ready to tackle things. What time is it?"

Stormy set the tray—loaded with a teapot, cups, a plate of cookies, and a jar of honey—on her nightstand before joining Windy. "It's four. You missed Gramma."

"Why didn't you wake me?" She swung her legs over the side.

Stormy patted the bedding. "Relax. When she heard you were napping, she was happy. Said you've been working yourself to a frazzle so wouldn't let us. She dropped off the cookies and tea. I found Chloe's tea set and figured if you didn't get up soon, you won't sleep tonight. So, this is our wake-up call."

"I like your style. You may serve when ready." Sunny grinned, memories of the tea parties they had as children flooding past. "What cookies did Gramma send?"

"Spritz. Little flowers with a drop of jelly in the center." Windy swiped one from the plate Stormy offered and held it up before popping the whole thing in her mouth. "Mm."

"Gramma also said she wants us over for supper. Says that we should make Thursdays from now on a family dinner night." Stormy handed out the cups before settling at the foot of the bed. "What do you think of that idea?"

Windy cocked her head to the side while she reached for another cookie. "It's good, as long as we can miss occasionally, if there's an important reason. She's not so demanding that she'll make us forgo stuff, right?"

"She wants to be sure we keep family first. What stuff are you worried she might make us forgo?" Sunny had an idea but wasn't about to assume.

"One of us could have a date."

"What are you doing thinking of dating? You've got other plans now." Count on Stormy to cut through to the core.

"I know. I don't need a new relationship. But I'll tell you a secret. If Kris were to ask me out, I wouldn't say no."

Sunny put her cup on the nightstand. "Windy, that's playing with danger. Don't let your heart get all tangled up with him before he learns about your future. That's not fair to you or him or your baby. Wait until he knows what he's getting into. Then if he wants a relationship, and you're ready for one, you can explore it."

"I get it. A part of me blocks out that my life has changed, and a part dreams of Tim coming home so we're a family. I don't think that'll happen, and this baby isn't going anywhere, so I better get my act together. You're right. I'll tell Kris before anything happens."

Stormy shook her head. "What about letting Gramma and Dad know? Isn't that a higher priority?"

Windy shoved another cookie in her mouth, making that her answer.

"Fine, well, we've had our tea party. I'd better get ready to leave for Gramma's. Oh! First I want to see what you got done while I slept." She stood and hugged Windy and then Stormy before going downstairs.

As she wandered from room to room, her sisters' touches greeted her from each display. They were beautiful, elegant, one even had a playful appearance. These rooms inspired weddings that would speak to brides and families. It caused her tears to return. Happy tears. They gave her hope.

As long as she didn't screw it all up.

Outside, she strode for the carriage house hoping that the added spring in her step counteracted the emotions rising to the surface. Before opening the door, she inhaled and the mingled scents from her garden instilled extra sweetness to her anticipation.

The lights strung over the beams, hanging in perfect loops and coils, infused the room with a fresh atmosphere. Along the rear wall, they'd brought furniture in, leaving a place for an altar and podium. White tulle wrapped about, and tall vases ready for arrangements graced either side. It wasn't finished by any means. Though what lacked, her mind filled in. Gramma and Gene would have a lovely wedding here. And maybe, just maybe, so would others. Her tears found her. She was grateful to be doing this with her sisters.

Plus, Kris. If not for him they'd be repairing Windy in the ER again for doing something dangerous. None of this would've been completed without him.

"So, what do you think?" Stormy drew her into a side hug.

Windy slipped up on her other side.

"I think getting you two involved was the best idea ever. I love you both so much." She pulled them all close. "We are the Days, the Weather Girls who can weather anything together."

"To us!"

"To the Weather Girls."

"Let's go get ready." Sunny kissed the tops of their heads and released them. "Last one done has to dry dishes at Gramma's!"

She raced for the house.

A short while later they parked in Gramma's drive at five on the dot. Warm aromas tinged with oregano wafted as they opened the front door drawing Sunny straight for the kitchen.

"Hey, Gramma, what smells so good?" She planted a kiss on her grandmother's soft cheek before taking a peek in the oven.

"Lasagna, and it can come out now. You know where the mitts are." Gramma winked as she sliced the french bread.

Sunny pulled the pan from the rack and placed it on top of the cold burners. "Yum! Oh, Gramma, this looks delicious!"

"Stormy, please fill the glasses. Windy, you can get the salad out. Table is all set, so once I've finished with this bread, we're ready." Her grandmother turned on the broiler and set the lengthwise split loaf, slathered with garlic butter and Parmesan cheese, on the top oven rack while expecting the girls to do as she'd directed.

They did.

Soon they were all at the table, holding hands while Gramma said grace. Then they could dig in.

"This is so good, Gramma. I haven't had your lasagna in ages." The taste brought back waves of memories...like their first night after Dad sent them to live in Indiana...that dinner after Kevin Madden broke up with her before prom. What about that time she'd inadvertently destroyed Dad's favorite signed Burt Bacharach album by trying to change the needle in the player's arm and put it in backwards... "Okay, Gramma. What's going on?"

Her sisters stared at their plates, but Gramma calmly forked another bite of salad, chewed and swallowed. "Whatever you mean, Sunny?"

"This is your comfort-for-Sunny meal. I know why you're doing this. There are a couple blabbermouths at your table."

Stormy dropped her fork on the plate. "Fine, Sunny. Windy and I knew you needed this, so we told Gramma. It's not like she didn't know what happened in Indianapolis. You told her when you came home. So, we didn't spill any secrets. We just wanted to give you a good evening, that's all."

"Stormy's right, sweetie. They didn't tell me anything new except about your visitor today. It's providence I wasn't there. I'd have popped her a good one."

The idea of Gramma duking it out with Venita tickled her to no end. "That I would pay to see. Okay, thank you, Gramma. I appreciate this. Though much more and I'll need to buy bigger clothes."

"I doubt that. You've been working too hard for that to be needed. Take a good gander in the mirror, hon, and you'll notice you've lost weight with all this physical exertion." Gramma took another bite.

"You think I'm skinny?"

Her grandmother shook her head. "Didn't say that. But you have lost a little. When things settle down, it'll be fine. Just remember to not skip meals." She sipped her iced tea, then set the goblet back and dabbed her lips with her napkin. "There's something else."

"What?" All three girls, in unison.

"That's my question. I know there's more to what's happening. After Rob's visit, it's obvious there's some healing that needs to happen with you, Stormy. But my intuition tells me more's going on with Windy and Sunny. So tonight, we get to the bottom of it." She smiled as if that made her plan acceptable.

"Windy June, you are first. Why did you quit school at Spring Break instead of finishing up the year?"

Stormy jumped from her chair and swiped Windy's plate. "I'll clear the table. Sunny, you get the glasses. Gramma, we'll wash dishes and clean the kitchen."

Sunny tossed Windy a sympathetic glance and gathered the goblets before following Stormy.

Her sister grabbed her arm as she passed through the swinging door and nearly made her drop one of Gramma's crystal pieces. "What's gotten into Gramma? Think she knows?" Stormy's voice hissed at her ear.

"Why are you so worried? You're getting off Scot free." Sunny set the glasses on the kitchen table and started the dish water before donning an apron.

"I don't like it. It makes no sense. She never lets me off with anything."

Sunny started by washing the crystal. "Well, maybe if she gets blindsided by Windy's predicament, she won't play psychologist with me. Grab your towel."

Stormy did but spent several seconds holding the goblet rather than drying and putting it into the cabinet. "We never could pull one over on her. But what got her onto Windy's trail?"

"No idea. As horrible as I feel about Windy's predicament, she's gotta tell Gramma. And I can't imagine what she has in store for me." Sunny moved on to the plates and utensils.

"That's got me stumped, too. You've told us everything. Right?"

Sunny kept washing. "Yeah, right."

The heat of Stormy's gaze bored through her, but refused to meet it. There were deep thoughts she only confided with Mr. Murphy. And she wasn't ready to share them with anyone else. Not even her grandmother. Who loved her. No matter what.

The swinging door swung open and Windy came in, her eyes red, but smiling. "Your turn, Sunny." She took the dishcloth from her and fairly drove her from the sink. "Get it over with. You'll feel better."

That Sunny doubted. But she dried her hands and headed for the dining room.

Gramma sat at her place. No one had taken her plate and she still ate. *Oops.*

"I'm here, Gramma. What shall we talk about?" Sunny's hands wadded the apron she'd forgotten to take off.

"Sit down, sweetie. I'm worried about you."

Sunny obeyed, sitting on the edge of her chair.

Gramma covered her hand. "I watch you throwing yourself into this new venture and I know you thought you were doing it to help Chloe at first. And then your sisters—" She held up her hand, stopping Sunny's denial. "Yes, I realize they helped with money, but you'd never have agreed if you didn't believe you were helping them. And even though they're your partners, you still feel like it is your business, your responsibility. Right?"

Sunny's free hand crept up to her earlobe. "Right, I guess. I got them into it."

"They had some say, you know. And they must carry more responsibility."

"But I'm the one who pulled them into this crazy scheme. I need to protect them—"

"That's the word, sweetie. Protect. You've been doing that for them your whole life. Take a peek. Your sisters have grown up. One's even having a baby. You don't have to be responsible."

Sunny's eyes burned. "But I'm supposed to be. I've always been the one to take care of them. And I learn that with me gone to Indianapolis, their lives got messed up. I should've been there for them. They should've been able to count on me. Instead, I'm torpedoing my own life and now I've pulled them into this risk that could backfire and leave us all with debts we can't pay off until we're ready for social security."

"It's not your job. They're adults. You can emotionally support them, be there if they need you to listen, but they must learn to stand on their own two feet. They won't if big-sister Sunny always makes things right."

Sunny wiped her face. "When we lived in LA, Dad always told me to watch the girls and Mom. Said I was his responsible one. I blew it with Windy. I could've stopped her from walking on the block wall, but I was tired of being the party pooper. And I had gotten to an exciting part in the book I was reading, so

I didn't pay attention. She fell, Gramma, because I wasn't doing my job. Then when Daddy rode with her to the hospital, and Mom left. I couldn't get her to stay. Dad would've if I'd been able to make her wait for him. But I blew it there too. We lost our mother because I didn't do my job, Gramma. So how can I stop now? Stormy and Rob are split. Windy's gonna have a baby and not married, no father in the wings. I've failed them again. Dad gave me this job to do, but I can't measure up to his expectations. My own chaos spills over. I lost my career because I didn't pay attention to the signs. I should've seen, figured it out before everything exploded. How can I be their example if I'm so screwed up?"

Gramma stood and pulled Sunny against her, rocking side to side while all her failures tumbled out. "Do you have any idea how amazing you are? I need to talk with my son concerning the pressure he's piled on you over the years. Can't believe he meant for you to take this so to heart." She pulled back. "Remember when you all first arrived? I'd tell you girls something, but your sisters looked to you for approval. I'd never seen a fourteen-year-old with so much respect from her younger siblings. It intimidated me. A little. But you my darling, we became a family because of you. No one's perfect, Sunny May. It's how you handle the imperfections, what you learn, and how you move forward that tells the tale. You'll be fine. God put a strength in your heart to stand firm in adversity. But you don't have to do it under your own strength. Look to Him. He is your guide. Listen to His voice. He is perfect and won't let you down."

Sunny hiccupped. "You're right. I needed that. I have been trying under my own power. I've also been envisioning this with another person in the picture. But he's gone. I know I should've been asking God for approval and direction. Hope it's not too late to start." *Hic.*

"It's not. Want to pray about it?"

Sunny nodded.

They sat back in their chairs. Gramma grabbed her hands and began to pray.

And Sunny handed over the weight from her shoulders to Someone more equipped to carry it.

Sunday, April 5, 1970

PAT PARKED IN THE HOSPITAL LOT. At the front desk in the lobby, he gained his information. Morning visitation had just started, and Carol Haynes was on the second floor. Her husband was already with her.

He chose the stairs rather than the elevator, arriving at the end of the corridor where Carol's room was located. The door stood part-way open, but he still knocked on the jamb.

"Come in." He recognized Trey's voice before seeing him.

Pat entered and produced a bouquet of daisies as though it were a magic trick. "Ta-da! Thought these might brighten your day." He grinned as a slow smile spread across Carol's face.

Trey hopped up, clapping him on the back before taking the flowers from him. "Hey, man, thanks! I'll go search for a vase." He slipped from the room leaving Pat in an awkward gaze with Carol.

She broke the silence. "So, what have you been up to?"

"Probably more than you. Looks like they've got you pretty stationary for the moment."

She grimaced. "Yeah, two broken legs, cracked ribs and a removed spleen."

"Ouch! When you do something, you don't mess around."

"Don't make me laugh, it hurts." But she still smiled.

"I'm sorry, Carol. I didn't know until last night."

She shrugged. "No problem. I'm getting better. It's Trey and the kids I'm worried about, well, more Trey than the kids really. The grandparents are giving them the time of their lives. But Trey has to keep working so the paychecks keep coming. When I get home, I'll still be pretty useless. He'll fret that he's not taking care of me."

"Know when they plan to let you leave?" Pat pulled a chair up closer to the bed and sat.

"I think what's holding things back is figuring out my home care. An assistant for while Trey's at work would help, but our insurance doesn't cover it. So, he's trying to figure how to make it happen."

Pat opened his mouth but changed his mind in time as Trey came back.

"A nurse is taking care of the flowers. She'll bring them in after while. So, what have you been up to, bud?" Trey sat in his chair.

"Well, I had dinner with your parents last night."

"They told me. Also said you made an important decision." Trey grinned.

"I did. Never knew such peace. My sister was waiting for me when I got home. Turned out to be an answer to prayer. We talked like we've never talked before. Oh, and I've met someone."

Carol tried to move, and Trey sprang to her side. "Need help, hon?"

She shook her head. "Want to hear about this someone. Tell us."

They may as well have asked him to talk about his favorite subject. He grinned. "Her name is Sunny. Holding her hand is like strolling in sunshine. She's beautiful and intelligent and kind and funny. Has a bit of a temper, I mean when Sunny gets hot..." Her face floated through his mind. "She has this habit of rubbing her earlobe when stressed that is so adorable—"

"He's got it bad, babe."

Carol nodded. "So bad. When do we get to meet her?"

"I need to fix things between us first. I messed up. Massive. Not sure how to make it right." A sigh escaped. Now that things had improved with Venita, it was time he corrected his mistake with Sunny.

"You've come to the best place. Carol is an incurable romantic. If she can't help you plan something wonderful, it's a hopeless cause." Trey winked at his wife.

"Glad someone listens to me. Sometimes. Okay, tell me more and I'll give you ideas."

They spent the next hour doing just that. When Pat finally said goodbye, he left with a strategy.

Before implementing, though, he needed to run by his apartment and make some phone calls. The first was to an agency—home nurses on call. He arranged for them to contact Trey saying they'd won a contest. The agency agreed to convince the Haynes they were entered when admitted to the hospital. Their prize was free nursing care for two months, to be used however they wanted or saved for a later date in case of an emergency. He hoped that would keep Trey and Carol from figuring out he paid for it.

Then he contacted Hazel and shared his plan. She agreed to help and to get Stormy and Windy on board. That meant he now had to gather supplies.

He phoned a few places he found in the yellow pages, but no one had what he needed. Then he remembered who did. Should he? To make this a happening, he'd better. He dialed the number and asked to speak with his mother.

She agreed, after a brief explanation, to let him sort through the Christmas decorations. Somehow knowing her son was doing something for the woman who'd stolen his heart got her excited. Even willing to help.

It was fun going through the boxes with her there beside him. He doubted she'd ever been in the attic. They had people. Those charged with transporting the crates from storage. Those paid to handle the displays. Those who returned the crates to storage once the holidays passed. Together, he and his mother probably destroyed someone's well-devised plan. Too bad. This was love, and that trumped.

He found something he didn't expect in the fifth box. It might not be exactly what Sunny envisioned, but it would tell her he paid attention. Hopefully, it would prove what he wanted her to know. With his mother's permission, he tucked it into his jacket pocket.

"Here, I found some." His mother waved him over. "Is this what you're searching for?"

He kissed her cheek. "Yes. This is perfect." After checking, he located four more similarly filled crates and moved them to the doorway before helping his mother climb down.

"Never dreamed the attic was like that. Maybe I should hire a decorator to make it less warehouse looking."

He chuckled, following her with the first box. "It's fine as it is. Seriously, Mother, you're not going up there again. Are you? Who cares what it looks like?" He hoisted the rest to the floor and closed the entrance.

"I know you think I'm a fuddy-duddy who shouldn't be climbing, son, but I'm aware of what an attic is. There was one at your grandparents' house while I was growing up. I enjoyed slipping up there to read or have make-believe parties. I haven't always been a Whitcomb." She winked at him. He had an ally with his mother. "I want to meet her, this woman who has captured your heart. She must be someone pretty special."

"She is. I will bring her soon. If this works out."

"It will." She wrapped her arms about his waist and hugged. "You always were my affectionate one. Go win her affections. I'm rooting for you."

He scooted the boxes to the elevator. She held it open for him and they rode to the first floor where she called for a couple of servants to help carry the crates to his Mustang.

After getting two into the trunk, they crammed the last three into his backseat. The downfall of a sports car.

However, now he was Kokomo bound. Hopefully Hazel had Sunny busy out of the way. Plus, he didn't need another speeding ticket, so he kept it to only five miles over the limit. Boy was his foot itching to press the gas harder.

At the mansion, Sunny's car was gone, but Stormy's GTO stood in the drive. She raced out as he parked, like she'd been watching for him, and circled around to his door, holding it closed. She made a motion to crank down his window. "Before you get out, tell me your intentions. If you're going to hurt her again, you can go home to Indianapolis."

He cracked up.

She wasn't amused.

He sobered. "I have no intention of ever hurting your sister. I love her more than I can say but need to show her. Will you help me?"

"Right answer. Yes, I'll do it. Gramma gave me a quick rundown of your plan. She thinks she can hold her there until sunset. I also got Kris to come over, so we have help. Ready?" She opened his door.

"Ready. The boxes should remove easier from the passenger side. Got two more in the trunk." He climbed out and they transported the first load to the backyard where they waved down Kris before fetching the last of the crates. Now to get started.

It took longer than he'd planned, but they got the final part completed, so Stormy went inside to make sure everything worked.

That was his cue. He set the special piece on the sycamore branch. He hoped Sunny would see it the way he meant it and not as making fun of her. He second guessed himself. What if this didn't speak his heart to her? What if he'd hurt her so much she couldn't hear his message?

What if he'd ruined everything?

Stormy came back out. "You did good, Pat. Trust me, this is perfect. Your hard part will be getting her to come outside. Remember what I told you about her. Those keys to success. You can do it." She punched his arm.

Kris carried the last ladder away, then wandered over to observe the fruit of their labor. "Looks groovy, man. She's gonna lose it. Cool." He stood with his hands on his hips surveying the yard.

Stormy caught Pat's gaze. She was having as hard a time as he to keep from laughing. Neither of them had ever heard Kris express that much of an opinion.

"Should we begin off and then on? Or on from the beginning?"

Pat had a vision in his head. However, how to start still eluded.

"Off. You get her out there and I'll handle the inside part."

"Thanks, Stormy. I couldn't have done this without you. Or you, Kris. I appreciate both of you helping."

Kris shrugged. "No biggie. Gotta go. Monday." He waved over his shoulder and pulled out from the new parking lot.

Stormy turned to him. "You're okay, Pat. Wondered if I should take out a contract on you, but you're cool. Don't ever make her cry again. Got that?"

"Yes, ma'am." He swallowed. That was one promise he really wanted to keep.

Chapter Fifteen

Late Sunday Afternoon, April 5, 1970

G ramma pulled out another box, and Sunny kept her groan internal. She wanted to return to Ferguson House. There was so much to do to meet their Grand Opening deadline.

Instead of getting shorter, her to-do list seemed to grow by the hour. But Gramma insisted these things would help her with the displays. So far, they'd found a WWI uniform belonging to her grandfather and several old-fashioned framed photos along with Victorian period artifacts to display throughout the mansion.

This current box was filled with loose pictures with a few albums buried beneath. Gramma *ooh*ed and *ahh*ed like she'd discovered long-lost friends—and sometimes that's exactly what she'd found. She shared stories about each one until Sunny could recognize people she'd never met when new snapshots turned up.

They sat together on her couch—Sunny in the middle, Gramma and Windy on either side. Ordinarily this would've been a joy. The exact thing Sunny would normally love to do with Gramma. Those stories and photos filled holes in her heart, helping her see the legacy handed down from earlier generations. She'd never met Gramma's parents, they died before she was born. Her grandmother was an only child, as was her father. No first cousins or aunts and uncles on her paternal side. She had no idea about her mother's family, other than they resided in Texas. Somewhere.

But Gramma chose today to open up and share. Therefore, no matter how strong the draw to return to the mansion, Sunny would honor her grandmother who'd done so much. She'd listen to every story with her whole heart, latching onto the details that seemed to move Gramma the most. And she'd squash that nervous tick trying to drag her back where hours of work waited.

Of course, she'd be up half the night finishing what should've been completed already.

"Oh, I forgot this photo was ever taken. This was the day I was promoted to high school with my best friends—there's Chloe and Margaret and Pauline. We're holding up our grade cards. Hey, maybe mine is in here somewhere. I usually did very well with my studies. Had a brain for numbers, like you, sweetie." She dug through the other things in the box.

Windy picked up a different photo and studied it a moment. "Gramma, is that Chloe in this picture with some army guy?" She handed it over.

"Yes, it is. I took it that...oh. That was taken by the old sycamore. Her beau was shipping out the next morning. He didn't come back." Gramma shook her head before wiping her cheek. "She loved him so much. He wouldn't kiss her beneath the tree because he wanted to make it special when he came home."

Sunny glanced at the snapshot, and something caught her eye. Was that a bird on the branch? She peered closer. Since the photo was in black and white, it was difficult to decide if it was a cardinal. But it sure seemed like one. "Gramma, did you see this?" She pointed to the bird perched over Chloe's shoulder.

Gramma nodded. "I never showed this to Chloe. Didn't want her to know."

"Know what?" Windy's gaze roved between them.

"That the cardinal was on the branch. She might've felt guilty for not getting him to kiss her, believing that if he had, maybe he'd have come home. Or she might've clung to hope, only becoming crushed because the legend failed. But either way, it would've hurt her, and I couldn't do that to my dearest friend." Gramma set the photo aside. "That needs to stay with me. I realize a photograph with a couple and the cardinal would be wonderful, but if Chloe saw it, it'd break her heart."

"I'll make sure she never sees it. We can present it in an antique frame and set it in one of the theme rooms. I can't believe she'd ever go through them all. It could hide in plain sight." Windy grinned, like she'd solve the problem. It was obvious she wanted that photo.

But Sunny understood. "No, she'll attend Gramma and Gene's wedding and will want to check what we've done. Actually, I plan to encourage her to do it, give her a special tour. It'd be nice to have her approval."

"Oh." Windy sounded almost heartbroken herself.

But Gramma patted Sunny's knee. "She's going to love it. You've been respectful of her family heritage. This will bring her a lot of joy."

"With the amazing resources she left for us to use, it's hard not to honor her with what we're doing. Chloe was very generous. I can't imagine ever leaving so much of my life behind." Sunny mentally shuffled through her own belongings she'd hate to part with.

"The Apostle Paul said he released everything to strive forward to the prize of glory. It's all just stuff. The memories remain. And when we're with our Father in heaven, we'll have the best of those memories because we'll view them as He sees them." Gramma pulled Sunny and Windy to her. "Run the race, girls. Win that crown. I love you so much."

"We love you too, Gramma." They returned the hug.

Then Sunny drew back, making a point of checking her watch. "I enjoy doing this with you, Gramma, but we'd better get back to Stormy. I hate that we left her working alone over there."

"She did say there was someone she decided to speak to." Windy tipped her head and widened her eyes in a you-know-what-I-mean gesture.

"Think she's finally talking to Rob?" Sunny glanced at Gramma who shrugged, not getting excited.

Windy also raised her shoulders and produced a thin smile.

But what else could it be? What if it wasn't a successful conversation? What if she needed her big sister there to help guide her through this?

"Sunny, you agreed to allow them stand on their own two feet. Don't take that back. God is a better adviser. Let Him do his job." Gramma always could see through her.

Her grandmother was wise. But the old recording needle in her brain still found the worn grooves in her life's record. She needed a new album. "Whatever the outcome, I can be there for her. And that means we'd better get moving. It's dinner time and I'll bet she hasn't eaten." Sunny stood.

"Bet you're right. We should stop and pick up something. How about Scotty's?" Windy started loading up Sunny's arms with boxes of the things they'd decided to use.

Gramma slipped out of the room and hustled back with a paper bag she set atop. "You'll need cookies."

Sunny hefted the load and moved toward the porch. "Guide me down? Hey, why aren't your arms filled, Windy?"

"Uh, I'm getting the doors for you."

Seriously? "Right." *Grrr.*

"Be careful, girls. I'll see you tomorrow." Gramma waved from the porch.

They stowed the boxes in the trunk. Anything breakable had been wrapped and rewrapped for added precaution. After all, Windy was the one helping her. Okay, so maybe it wasn't fair. But did anyone outgrow being a klutz?

She pulled in at Scotty's and Windy volunteered to run in, nearly jumping out before she'd put the Camaro in park. Said it was so Sunny could relax in the car. Her sister even refused the money she'd tried to slip her. Said it was her way to say thank you. Okay. That was nice. Made her feel a little guilty about the klutzy thoughts.

So, how did she encourage Windy to hurry? Sunny's sole goal was to get home. Home. The mansion daily grew more home-like. With many special touches continually added. She'd grown attached to the place, more than she ever dreamed she would. Sunny glanced at her watch. Six-thirty. Her stomach growled. Great. Now she was hungry and irritated. Not a terrific combination. She tapped her fingers on the door panel.

Ten minutes later Windy returned with their meal. Though tempting, she restrained from laying rubber in the parking lot and pulled off onto Washington. They were homeward bound. At last.

When she parked in the drive, Windy popped out faster than she'd ever seen her sister move. After gathering the food from the restaurant, the girl fairly ran toward the back. Straight to the kitchen via the rear door? Well, that meant she was less likely to spill on the beautiful hardwoods. Maybe her baby sister was growing up.

Sunny shook her head and stacked all the boxes in her trunk with the cookie bag square on top. Then she carefully lifted the load and used her elbow to close the lid. Negotiating the front steps wouldn't be easy. Once there, though, she'd set things aside and open the doors—which Windy conveniently forgot about.

Grrr. Again.

Just as she turned to put her load on the porch table, the front door banged into her, knocking her to her bottom and sending her stack all over the wooden floor.

She glanced up.

Pat stood over her his palm extended. "I'm sorry, Sunny. May I help you up?"

She batted his hand away. "No, thank you. Look what you did!" Sunny crawled, refilling the boxes, checking for damage. All but the cookies appeared intact. At least that was something.

"What are you doing here anyway?"

Pat handed her a photo that had fallen loose. "I wanted to talk with you. Explain what happened."

She sat back on her haunches. "I know what happened. Figured it out all by myself once your sister dropped by."

He winced. "Yeah, I'm sorry about that too. I needed to sort it out."

"Glad you got that done. Or did you?" She snatched an album out of his hands.

"Venita called me the next morning to cancel our brunch and hung up before I could say anything. I had no idea she was headed here."

"Get to the point, Pat. My dinner is inside getting cold and I'm sure you broke our dessert." She picked up the bag of cookies and shook it in front of him.

"I did talk with her. I told her everything."

She paused and gave him more than a once-over. "Everything?"

He nodded. Good thing the porch light worked. Twilight had settled, or it would've been hard to see his face. She needed to do that. See his face. His very handsome face. That appeared so sincere. "Everything, Sunny. I even told her that I'm in love with you. That I want a future with you. And I'll never bring you to a family function if Brock's there. I made sure she understood. I won't ever do that to you, Sunny." He stooped to slip a handful of photos back into a box.

She absorbed his words. It wasn't a scenario she'd considered —seeing Brock again—especially since she'd figured it was over with Pat.

Still, he protected her. He loved her enough to tell his sister.

She blinked about a million times.

"Don't cry, Sunny." He drew her to a standing position. "Here, let me help you get this inside. I have something to show you."

"You get the door." He stacked and scooped it all, minus the paper bag that Sunny held, and took her load inside. "Where would you like this?"

No words, she just pointed to the table under the front window.

After he set it down, he reached for her hand and laced fingers with her.

She didn't pull away.

His heart pounded. Whether from her touch or the anticipation of showing her what he'd done, he couldn't tell. Probably both. But if they weren't outside soon, he'd lose his ever-lovin' mind. "C'mon. You need to see this."

He led her down the hall to the kitchen where Stormy and Windy glanced up with knowing smiles while wolfing down their burgers. Stormy even popped him a thumbs up.

He inhaled a shaky breath. "Out here. Close your eyes. I won't let you fall."

She obeyed but trailed her fingers to feel her way out the back porch.

"You're doing great. Just down the steps onto the garden path." Bit by bit, he guided, and she followed, relying more on him the further they ventured. Finally, they were there.

He stationed her where she'd get the full effect. Then he glanced at the window.

Stormy peered awaiting his signal.

He nodded and she did her job.

The backyard flooded with light from hundreds of white Christmas bulbs strung throughout. They made a crisscross pattern overhead from tent poles anchored alongside and were woven in the trees and shrubs. It turned the garden into a fairytale land. Exactly how he'd envisioned it, which was good.

But watching Sunny's face was more important. Her eyes roved the yard, growing bigger by the second. "You did this?"

Her voice was breathless—he'd stolen her breath. Yes. He controlled himself and didn't let out a whoop. "I had help. Stormy and Kris. I couldn't have gotten it done in time without them." Hopefully, that wouldn't steal brownie points, but he was determined he'd be more than honest from now on. No omitted details. Completely and vulnerably transparent.

That was his solemn promise to her.

She pulled him into a choke hold of an embrace, bouncing and tightening with each bounce. "I can't believe it. It's perfect! We can have outdoor evening weddings. It'll be so beautiful."

"Sunny." He tugged at her arms. "Sunny, need to breathe."

"Oh." Her face grew pink—and he spotted that lovely color in her cheeks in the soft glow.

He pulled her close. "I love you. You may choke me anytime. But you might let me up for air on occasion."

She raised her head and grinned. "I guess I could do..." she pulled away and stared at the sycamore. "There's a...is that a car..." In slow motion she moved toward the tree, her fingers entwined with his and pulling him along with her. "Is that a cardinal?"

He reached up and handed her the Christmas decoration—a cardinal ornament. Even up close, it appeared rather lifelike.

She cupped it in her hands, stroking the red velvety covering. "I thought it was the real thing." Was she disappointed?

"Sunny, I couldn't guarantee you a real cardinal at this time of evening. There was no way. But I can guarantee that I will love you with everything I have as long as God allows. This was my best method to show you." He sat her on the branch before following. "Look, we only met less than two months ago. My heart knows what it wants, but I'm not about to rush you. There's no hurry. Take all the time you need."

She put her finger to his lips, then set the bird next to her.

"Kiss me."

"What?"

"Kiss me. Chloe's love wouldn't kiss her beneath the tree before he left for war. But Gramma got a photo of them standing together and a cardinal lit on the branch. A kiss then couldn't change history, but it would've been a gift to Chloe." She took a breath. "Yeah. We're just getting started. But I want to start right. So, with this guy for our cardinal, kiss me. Please."

They were balanced so precarious; he needed to move slow. But as he leaned closer, she did too until their lips met and nothing else existed. He resisted pulling her close though that's what he longed to do.

What he *would* do. Once they were out of the tree.

Why had he set her up there?

She drew back. "This will be good, Pat. We'll be good. Thank you for humoring me."

He smiled at her. "I'm happy to do that anytime, my Sunny one. Let's get down."

She grinned and nodded.

He hopped down first, this time not injuring himself. Then he reached for her and placed her gently on her feet. So near his breath ruffled her hair. This is what he wanted. What he'd imagined would happen once he got her out here. His pulse hammered in his ears with anticipation. He drew her close, breathing in the coconut scent of her shampoo that painted mind images of pleasant days on a tropical beach. He wove his fingers through her curls, bringing her face to his where he could kiss her the way she deserved to be kissed, thoroughly, from his heart and soul. And he received her response as her arms grew tighter about him, drawing him into more passion than he'd ever known existed.

He needed to pull back.

As Pat drew in a ragged breath, he glanced over her shoulder and blinked. There was no way. He whispered at her ear. "Turn around, slowly. Check out the branch."

She did. Her hands went to her mouth.

There, next to the ornament, sat a real cardinal. Just the thought brought tingles. No one would believe this.

"Pat." Her voice, so soft, spoke his name with wonder. "The legend is true." She turned in his arms and caressed his face. "But with or without a cardinal, I love you."

The back door squeaked. He needed to oil that for her, but for tonight it made a terrific warning of impending company.

Stormy and Windy ran to them.

"Did you see?"

They both nodded with excitement. "We did!"

Great, her sisters were watching them? He should've known. Hadn't this family any sense of privacy?

"It's after dark and a cardinal landed on the branch. That's mind-blowing!" Stormy at least didn't bring up anything more personal.

"It was so romantic." Windy glanced at him. "The cardinal I mean. You were okay too, Pat."

The lights must be raising the temperature. He felt the heat building up his neck and skull. "Gee, thanks for your critique. I was hoping for that."

Sunny grinned and buried her face in his chest.

He pulled her close figuring he might as well get used to it. When you fall in love with one Weather Girl, the others were certain to be nearby. A sort of packaged deal. That was fine with him, as long as he had his Sunny. For her, he'd accept her sisters in the bargain. There'd never be a dull moment. That's for sure.

"You know what this spot needs?" Windy bounced her index finger on her chin. "A wrought-iron bench that circles the trunk. Maybe in a leaf motif and painted white. That's what it needs."

Sunny turned around and shared a glance with Stormy. "You are right. But those things cost a lot."

"I'll buy it. It will be our memorial bench." That'd be cool. Maybe even a plaque with the date. No need for more. He and Sunny would always remember.

"I don't know..." Sunny chewed on her bottom lip.

Great, they were going to disagree over money already?

"What about if you hired Kris. He could make it."

Everyone turned back to Windy again.

"Kris knows how to do that?" Stormy didn't sound like she believed it.

"That's the type of art he does. He uses Gene's garage. If you covered the supplies, maybe something on top of it for his labor, I'll bet he'd do it. He likes it around here. What do you say?"

Sunny turned to him, not her sisters. His heart swelled with her trust.

"I'm fine with that if you are." She smiled and he drew her close again. Who cared if her sisters watched? Well, he did. A little.

"Absolutely." He cleared his throat. "Now if you'll excuse us, Windy, Stormy, I need to discuss the details with your sister." He kept his eyes on Sunny and barely discerned their giggles as they receded toward the house. "Where were we? Oh, that's right. I was about to kiss you again."

"Good. I was about to suggest that very idea." She met him halfway. But when she kissed him, it was all the way, straight to his heart.

Epilogue
Saturday, May 16, 1970

S unny helped her grandmother straighten her veil. It was short, attached to a small fascinator that matched her teal wedding dress. She carried a bouquet of calla lilies with teal and white ribbons dangling.

"Do you think he's as nervous as I am?" Gramma peeked out the window overlooking the carriage house once more.

"I'm sure he is. However, he's not backing out and neither are you."

Gramma spun from her view, indignation splashing all over her face. "Back out? Why would I do that? I'm just excited is all. Been forever since I've shared my space with a man."

Someone knocked, Sunny opened the door.

Her father stood on the other side, handsome in his navy suit with the white dress shirt and matching wide embossed tie. He'd grown a mustache which, added to his longer sideburns, gave him a rakish appearance.

It reminded Sunny of just how much had happened in the last six weeks.

For one thing, Windy finally told Dad she was going to have a baby. He took it better than expected, though by no means calmly. He'd been the first to suggest adoption, but Windy was determined. Even though the family realized there'd be whispers. Maybe some out and out rude comments. But Windy would keep her baby. Period.

Her sisters would stand by her. Period.

Another surprise, Venita came to see her. This time she apologized for her behavior. Having had a minor taste of what Brock was like, it wasn't hard to offer forgiveness. It might've been harder for her family to let it go, but now Venita and Sunny got along when thrown together at events. Like dinner with Pat's parents. Without Brock in attendance.

A week after Pat put up the lights, Venita called to say her husband was gone. He'd cleaned out their joint bank account and disappeared. The senior Mr. Whitcomb hired an investigator who located Brock in Las Vegas where the missing spouse had applied for residency—*he* was getting a divorce.

Venita decided not to fight and let him keep the money. Said it was a small price to pay to remove him from her life. Besides, she still had her private account and the house. Plus, that property in Greentown? Turned out to be a gem. Her plan was working. Even her father was impressed.

Then there was her Pat. He stood up to his father. They agreed Pat would continue to work for the corporation, slowly phasing out of his tasks so that by this time next year, he would have opened his own agency as a defense attorney. Sunny was so proud of him.

Stormy and Rob remained at odds. That would take more time to heal. And Sunny hoped it would. Heal.

"Well, Mom, it's time. You still want to do this?" Dad winked at Sunny, pulling her into his joke.

"Of course, I want to do this. In fact, let's get this show on the road. Isn't it 2:30 yet?"

Dad pulled Gramma into a hug making Sunny tear up to see them embrace.

Stormy arrived just then. "It's filling up quick. Glad you chose the carriage house. The line's out the door."

Gramma went to the window again. "Get them seated so I can start down. Stormy, tell them to grab whatever place is available. They've got two minutes, and then I'm coming."

Stormy's eye grew wide before she raced for the stairs.

"Gramma stop it. You promised to let us handle things. If we can't pull this off for you, we aren't ready. So, trust us and cool your jets. We'll get you married. I promise."

Her grandmother stared, and Sunny knew she'd crossed a line. But then Gramma smiled. "You're right. I did promise and it is your business. I'll just be over here in the corner, trying to breathe."

Windy showed up and whispered to Sunny. "Stormy says she's not coming back up here. But to tell you if Gramma wants to come down, we're ready."

"Did you hear that, Gramma? It's time. Let's get you married." Sunny grinned while her father offered his arm to his mother and led the parade down the stairs, out the front door, down the porch steps and to the entrance of the carriage house.

Stormy stood at the door, ready to open on cue. The music sounded. The door pulled wide. Dad walked Gramma down the aisle to Gene, whose eyes glistened in the light from the small bulbs shining from overhead.

Sunny linked arms with her sisters and watched from the back of the carriage house. Windy planned the decorations. They gave a quiet, neutral atmosphere and could be used for any style wedding without taking over. That girl was a wonder.

And Stormy? Sunny shook her head. The way she finagled everyone into doing what she required, and with a smile to boot. Well, almost everyone.

Gramma was a special case. Still, Stormy was as gifted at her part as Windy was with hers.

Since word of Gramma's upcoming nuptials got out, a few customers checked into their new business. There'd been calls for appointments almost every day. The Weather Girls Wedding Shoppe and Venue was more than a dream now. This venture had a chance. It might become a success.

But her greatest win was the guy who took her breath away. The one who ensured there'd be a cardinal for her, just in case. Who believed in her dreams and invited her into his.

She scanned the room for his handsome face but didn't find him. But then she felt a tap on her shoulder. She spun into arms that held her secure.

"I now pronounce you husband and wife. You may kiss your bride, Gene."

Sunny turned back to watch that kiss.

Pat laced her fingers with his and kissed her hand.

She glanced up at him as he mouthed, "I love you."

She mouthed back, "I love you too," and leaned against him, drawing strength from his presence. Their chance, when the pastor made their announcement, would come. She knew. There was no doubt.

A little red bird told her.

Acknowledgments

Abba Father, thank you for weaving my past memories and childhood home into this fun story.

To my wonderful P.I.T. crew who prays me through each story keeps me accountable—Annie, Deb, Lori D., Julie, and Dorothy—you ladies have worked overtime this year! Thank you! I love you all!

Thank you to my cover artist, London Montgomery. I do love your covers!

My Beta Readers and Street Team, you are such a huge support. Thank you! And extra thanks to Lisa Canton who went above and beyond.

Thank you to my Pencildancer friends—Jennifer Crosswhite, Diana Brandmeyer, Liz Tolsma, and Angela Breidenbach. I've really had to lean on you all this year. Thank you and I love you!

And speaking of Jennifer Crosswhite, my editor and friend. You are the best! You make this craziness fun!

My extraordinary family has stepped up their encouragement and support in this insane season—Phil, Jaime, Jonathan, Alyssa, Juan, Natalia, Meg, Mat, Owen, Kami, Mom, Amy, Rick, Rusty, and all my extended loved ones. I couldn't do this without you all.

And, as always, E.B. I still miss you.

Author's Note

I'M NOT SURE EXACTLY when this idea first dawned, but once it took hold, I fell in love with the notion of three sisters named for the songs written and produced in the 1960s. I've always been enamored with the music of that time period—it's what I grew up with and music speaks to me. I feel like there's a story behind each song, and I began to wonder what the story might be for "Sunny," "Stormy," and "Windy."

My husband is sure that it's a dangerous thing to let me wonder too much. However, it's never stopped me.

But what if each song had a similar inspiration? What if one person had somehow said something to each of the people who actually penned the songs?

And what if the girls' last name was Day?

Now I had an idea. And this is what bloomed out of it.

One other thing I should mention is that there is a place you can visit in Kokomo called the Seiberling Mansion. I've toured it many times and it is the inspiration of Ferguson House. At one time it was the site of Indiana University's Kokomo campus until it was outgrown, and the current site erected. But many a teacher who taught in the Kokomo schools got their teaching credentials from there.

Since *The Casa Grande Restaurant* holds many memories for me, as does *Scotty's Hamburger Joint* and many other spots, I had to include them. More will show up in the rest of *The Weather Girls* trilogy, so be ready.

Please be aware, though Kokomo is a real place on the map, and actual locales are mentioned, this is still a work of fiction, and the Kokomo of my imagination is not to be confused with reality. This is only for fun and not to be construed as factual.

One more thing. If you enjoyed this story and want to know when the next book releases, follow the link to my website where you can sign up to get the latest information and a free novella. I love hearing from readers, and we can connect there as well.

You can scan here for my website.

Or use this link.

jenniferlynncary.com

Abundant blessings,

Jenny

PS Keep reading to get a sneak peek of the next book in *The Weather Girls* trilogy, *Stormy*.

About Author

Historical Christian romance author Jennifer Lynn Cary likes to say you can take the girl out of Indiana, but you can't take the Hoosier out of the girl. She is also a direct descendant of Davy Crockett, which along with her Indy upbringing, adds fodder to her sweet/clean books. She and her husband make their home in Arizona where she shares her tales of heritage and small-town life memories with her grandchildren.

You can contact Jennifer via her website jenniferlynncary.com

Sneak Preview of Stormy

Prologue

April 25, 1948

Los Angeles, California

THE BABY CHEWED HER FIST as Aaron Day paced the hospital room with her. His second daughter. She was as perfect as her big sister though she'd already displayed her own temperament. Looks-wise, she possessed the makings of being another beauty like her mother.

He wandered to the window, talking low while Cheryl, his wife, tried to rest. This darling cutie was a tad bigger than her sibling, taking longer to enter the world. But she was here.

And needed a name.

He gazed out over the vista of their growing metropolis. So many modern-day pioneers forged their way to this mecca, full of hope and talent to fuel their dreams to succeed.

He and Cheryl had tasted that success and stayed. A modest but comfortable income could be made without getting famous if one developed a dependable reputation and a quality product. Aaron had done that; his work was steady.

Cheryl, though, was forced to put her movie career on the back burner. For the time being. She'd shine on that silver screen again. He had faith in is lovely wife.

"Look out there, baby doll. They say it never rains in California but guess no one told the weatherman." Pelts

pinged off the window's glass as a muted rumble sounded before the sky cracked a split. "Got a whale of a storm brewing, sweetie. Maybe that's what we should name you."

The baby let out a lusty cry and Cheryl rolled toward them. "Is she okay?"

"She's perfect. Naming her Stormy April."

"Oh, Aaron, not again? Those girls will never forgive you."

"They'll come to love their names. Stormy will take the world by storm, you just wait. She's going to do big

things."

Cheryl closed her eyes. "Fine, Aaron. Just remember, when she complains about it, I'm sending her to you. I'll

keep my bargain about you naming the girls. But I'm making sure they know this is your idea."

"No problem. I'll tell her how she rode in on a bolt of lightning and electrified our lives." He glanced back at

his daughter and held her close. "Yes, my little Stormy April Day. You'll be a force of nature. I have no doubt."

Chapter 1

May 16, 1970

Kokomo, Indiana

"THINK THEY'RE GOING TO AGAIN?" Stormy peeked over the top of her younger sister Windy's head. Their other sister Sunny had slipped away from Gramma's wedding reception with her boyfriend, Pat. Anymore it seemed like they were always searching for a spot to start kissing. It was better than watching an old romantic movie on the late show. They could pass for teenagers instead of twenty-something professionals—almost too cute.

Only, if they got caught spying, Sunny would give them what for while Pat's face changed from pink to crimson. That was almost too funny.

"I'd bet on it. Oh, they moved around the tree. Did they see us?"

"Uh hm." Someone behind them cleared his throat.

Both girls spun.

"Robert Crawford. Why must you sneak up on me?" Stormy threw out the question in hopes of deflecting any toward her. Besides, he was the last person she wanted to see. Why did Gramma invite him anyway?

"Sorry." He shoved his hands in his pockets. "Thought we could talk a little. How've you been?"

Stormy swiped her bangs off her forehead, grasping a moment to retain her civility. This was Gramma's special day, and she'd not let her temper ruin it because a certain husband had to show up. Gramma could invite anyone she wanted. But inviting the guy her granddaughter wanted to divorce was kind of a sneaky trick. That old meddler needed to stop hoping and plotting. Gramma had her own marriage to concentrate

on now. Stormy's was beyond fixable at this point. Probably.

"Same as always." She paused, and then her manners kicked in. "You?"

"Fair. Gearing up for the end-of-the-school-year hustle." He hardly glanced up to meet her stare. Like

the child no one chose to play with. The analogy cracked her heart gaining him some sympathy.

Drat! Not good. No sympathy for the guy. She bit her lip, reminded herself why they'd split, and got tough. "You have your vacation in a few weeks. Then you can do what you want." *And leave me alone.*

"Guess you're right. Could we talk? I'll get you some punch." *Like ginger ale and sherbet could solve all their*

problems.

No, she needed to be firm. Things had been too busy with getting their new business, The Weather Girls Wedding Shoppe and Venue, started followed by Gramma's shindig. She hadn't had a moment to contact a lawyer. However, it was on her to-do list. The longer she dragged this out, the harder it would be to finalize their divorce.

Just the word brought a cold chill. However, if she couldn't trust him, she shouldn't stay married to him. "Rob, I don't think there's a lot to say." *And if she did let loose about how he tanked her teaching career, she'd couldn't predict what she's say—and in front of her sister. They didn't need an audience.*

"I'll get you some punch, you two can sit over there." Windy pointed to an area of the garden away from the majority of guests. "Or go inside. That's a better idea anyway. Head on in the mansion and I'll bring your cups." She put her hands on their shoulders, pushing them to the front of the house before motioning them up the steps.

"Thanks, Windy, we'll sit on the porch." Rob forced a smile and her little sister winked at him.

Right. Thanks, loads. Windy.

Rob stepped aside to allow her to ascend before him.

Stormy stood. "Rob, why? It's over."

"Windy's gone for punch. We should at least wait for her." He nodded toward the porch.

"Fine." She mounted the steps and plopped into a chair making sure he had to sit with the table between them. No reaching for her hand, no physical touching that might weaken her resolve. She crossed her arms for emphasis. "What do you want to say?"

"Stormy, I was wrong. I'm sorry. I spoke out of turn and never dreamed they'd take my comment as gospel and not give you a contract. If I could yank the words back, I would. I wish you'd believe me." He had that puppy-dog look in his eyes, the one that usually made him irresistible.

She sighed. He'd never lied to her before. That she knew of. He had broken trust, though. That meant every time she glanced at him, she saw what she lost. "I guess, I believe you. It's not that easy to move past the shock, the hurt. I..." Sharing her feelings hadn't wasn't part of the agreement, only listening.

"I get that. I do. I miss you more than I can say. If you'll postpone any divorce action and give me a chance to make it up to you, I will. I promise."

"I'm not coming back. At least not now." She blew out a breath. "I won't go see a lawyer for a few weeks. Okay? We've got a lot to do around here anyway. I'm not making any promises, so don't get your hopes up." She nailed him with a stare to send the message home.

"Promise. No raised hopes. Just know I'm not giving up. Keep that in mind."

"If you make a pest of yourself, you won't like the consequences."

He lifted his hands. "Not a pest, simply available. Okay?"

"Okay." She leaned her head back and closed her eyes. "It's been a tough year. First the Beatles break up and then you and me. I don't see them getting back together either." A tear slipped and she swiped it away before he could notice.

Windy returned with two cups of punch. "So, you kids doing all right? No blood spatters or severed heads."

"Gross, Windy. We're more civilized than that." Stormy ran her hand over her face and glanced at Rob. For a moment she thought he seemed grateful that she hadn't sliced him to ribbons.

That was the strangest part. He'd always been sure and logical, not the risk taker. The grounded half of their duo. He constructed his plan and then executed it. Even if the problem resulted from an excited slip of the tongue, sneaky didn't fit his style.

Neither did this. Why did he appear so lost?

Her conscience told her that. She'd pulled the rug out from beneath his one-year, five-year, and ten-year plans. They'd made those plans together and she'd bailed.

With good reason.

But still.

Windy waved and headed to the reception in the backyard garden. Gramma had been their first customer and planned her wedding in the carriage house. It turned out lovely. Stormy knew Windy took advantage to get some great publicity photos. Now they just needed to bring in more customers.

The Weather Girls Wedding Shoppe and Venue had been the brainchild of her older sister, Sunny, who rescued historic Ferguson House from falling into the hands of a developer who wanted to raze the lovely old mansion.

It took all three girls pooling together to save it and start the venture, but it was more than money. Each worked in her own niche, bringing a unique talent to the table. Sunny was amazing at numbers and business. Windy was the artist and photographer. She had the eye for improvement.

And Stormy? What did she bring besides baggage and pain? Her ability to read people, move them into doing something and imagining it was their own idea. Comes in handy when working in sales. Or with third graders. But she never saw Rob's betrayal coming. Maybe that's why it devastated.

Still, she did believe him. Unsure if out of habit or her skill, but she did. That was the sad part. She just wasn't trained to backpedal. Her mother had betrayed her too. To Stormy, the woman no longer existed.

"Guess I ought to get going." Rob patted the arms of his chair before pushing himself to his feet. "Thanks for talking, Stormy. And for believing me. I won't give up. I can't." He trudged down the steps, then turned. "Tell Hazel I'm happy for her and Gene and thank her for inviting me. G' Night."

So, it was true. He didn't gatecrash. Gramma really did invite him, and it wasn't a fluke. Stormy wanted to throttle the old woman. She was most likely in the middle of cutting her wedding cake.

Stormy reminded herself that murder's not good for business. Probably wouldn't photograph so great in the wedding pictures either.

Those that Windy was supposed to be taking.

Did she get any shots? Or had she played around, doing things as she felt? Someone needed to take that younger sister of hers in hand. She had no time to be flighty. Not with a baby on the way.

Stormy leaned her head back and closed her eyes. They had tons of baggage between the three of them. Beside what they dealt with growing up, they each brought struggles home when they all showed up in February. Sunny had worked through much of hers. That gave Stormy hope. Still, Windy flitted along as if nothing had changed. She was on an adventure with her sisters. Until she gained a clue that being an unwed mother would be the toughest thing she'd encounter, she only kidded herself.

Maybe Stormy was kidding herself, too. Could she and Rob find any other alternative besides divorce?

She was sure he still loved her. And to be honest, she still loved him. Yet pain continued to stab from when her life exploded.

This wasn't the time to become psychologically aware. She was on the clock too.

Stormy headed for the backyard. Big band era music played from the speakers and a dance floor sported several couples slow dancing to "Sentimental Journey." Her father manned the turntable keeping the songs flowing.

"Where's Rob? You didn't chase him off, did you?" Windy popped up at her elbow, her camera hanging from a strap around her neck.

"No, though I wanted to. Gramma invited him, the old manipulator." She glanced about for her grandmother just as she received a tap on her shoulder.

Stormy spun. Gramma and Gene stood behind her.

"Where's Rob? You didn't run him off, did you? He was my guest."

Stormy's face bloomed with heat. "No Gramma, I didn't run him off though I would have appreciated a heads up that he was coming."

"So, you could hide and not do your job? Kokomo isn't that big, Stormy. You're going to run into him on occasion. Best get used to it."

"You weren't trying to do more than help me become comfortable in his presence, were you?" Stormy's fists went to her hips.

"My wedding, young lady, and I'll invite whoever I want. I've always liked that young man. He's a go-getter."

Gramma wiggled her fingers at her as Gene danced her away in his arms.

Windy patted her shoulder. "Should we find Sunny and talk? I've got plenty of shots for the time being."

Stormy shook her head. "We'll do tons of that tonight when we go to bed. I'm fine. For now."

But she wasn't. Between feeling like a professional puppy kicker and being blindsided by her grandmother, Stormy was anything but fine. She imagined Rob driving home, her old home, and letting himself into the dark, quiet house.

Did he turn on the lights or move by feel to their...his bedroom? What was he thinking? Had he been praying about all this?

Had she?

Yes, some. In fact, she'd moved on from praying for bad things to happen to him to asking that she'd stop feeling all this hostility at the mention of his name.

Maybe, by accepting he hadn't done it on purpose, she might be moving in that direction. She wasn't ready to pray for reconciliation. But it would be nice to quit wavering between pity and resentment.

Rob parked his Cutlass in his driveway as the dread of going in alone took over, making him turn the ignition key. What law stated he must return home right now?

After backing away from their Greentown address, he shifted to drive and headed to the highway. Where did he want to go?

Anywhere but home. It hadn't been a home since the day he found Stormy gone. No note. Not a clue for the longest time. It took three calls to Hazel's house to learn she was safe but wouldn't talk to him.

Fine. If that's what she wanted... Then she skipped work, called for a substitute, and informed her principal she was done. Refused to return. He still saw Don Tanner's face when it finally registered Rob was as much uninformed as he.

But something he said—the mention of Stormy coming to his office to sign her contract for the next school year and there not being one—got him thinking. No, they'd never take it as fact based on his hopeful outburst.

Yet they did.

Teaching was Stormy's passion. Never in a million years could he imagine her not a teacher. Maybe taking a sabbatical to start a family. But not stop. Still, that's happened. Now she'd broken her contract. Good luck securing a new one. She'd been so angry she really had cut off her nose to spite her face—or crashed her career to spite her passion.

He pulled into the T-Way parking lot and found a space. If home wasn't his destination, he'd better figure out something to do besides wasting gas cruising. He was too old to be cruising. After loosening his tie, he considered his options. Walk the mall until closing (which happened in about an hour except for the theaters), grab a root beer float at the Dog n Suds, or an ice cream at the Frozen Custard.

Yeah, just what Stormy dreamed of—a fat, overweight, tubby...he'd go on, but he'd depressed himself enough.

A walk through the mall until they closed wasn't too pathetic, right? Plus, he'd get exercise to boot. Better than the alternatives. If he wore himself out, maybe he'd get some sleep. Now with a plan, he restarted his car and pulled out onto 31, heading for the Markland Mall.

Saturday night and the movie theaters were the biggest draw. When he noticed that *Ballad of Cable Hogue* had hometown boy Strother Martin in it, he almost bought a ticket. But with Sam Peckinpah directing, he realized he'd be in for a violent shoot'm up. Rob wasn't into that, not with sleep a priority. Another time, Mr. Martin.

Of course, there were other movies. Liza Minnelli's *Tell Me That You Love Me Junie Moon* felt too artsy. *A Man Called Horse* with Richard Harris, too painful. He had enough of tween-aged student problems to choose *PufNStuf* and *Let It Be* only reminded him the Beatles broke up. Guess he was lucky *Love Story* was no longer playing—that'd be enough to put him over that proverbial edge. So much for a movie distraction. Walking the mall won.

Montgomery Ward was having a White Sale. Plenty of sheets and towels and pillows at bargain prices. Not that he needed any, but whatever kept him from his own dreary thoughts. He wandered into the store. There was always the hardware department.

"Rob, what are you doing here?"

He glanced up to spot Glenda Whitehall, another teacher from Stormy's school. "Oh, hi, Glenda. Just wasting

time. You?"

"First opportunity to check the sale. Hey, how's Stormy doing? Haven't seen her in a while."

A weight settled in his gut. They'd told no one about their separation. Actually, he had no clue what story Stormy was sharing. He merely dodged the questions the best he could. But Glenda was a coworker and given how the rumor mill churned, she probably had an idea. "She's helping her sisters. They've started a new business."

"She left her classroom to do that? I thought she loved teaching." The Chatty Cathy probed too close. He suddenly envisioned her holding tweezers over him while he was trapped on the Operation game board waiting for the life-ending buzzer.

"It was a timing thing." He hoped that was vague enough and moved her off the subject. "Well, I better be going. I'll see you later, Glenda."

"Sure, Rob. But hey, you're okay, aren't you?"

What did he say? That he was among the walking wounded? "I'm fine. We're fine." That was an out and out lie. The alternative was emotionally bleeding all over Ward's patterned flooring. He waved and hustled toward the land of power tools in hopes that would discourage Glenda from following.

Once upon a time, he enjoyed working with his hands to build things. There was a coffee table in their living room and matching nightstands in their bedroom that he'd made for Stormy. But since his promotion, there'd been no chance. At first, he'd wondered if that'd been the problem—his days and evenings filled with meetings and paperwork. It kept him and Stormy from seeing each other like they used to. Maybe she'd been lonely. Another reason to start a family, so she'd not be sitting there alone waiting dinner on him.

Apparently, that wasn't the case.

He found advertisements for a new saw that pictured a finished cabinet. That looked intriguing. Should he? Get back to woodworking? It'd be something to keep his mind occupied. He could make it for Stormy. Just to prove he remembered. After whipping out his wallet, he pulled his credit card free, handing it to the clerk.

The high school kid industriously working this Saturday night smiled so that his braces gleamed and rang up the purchase. Probably got paid on commission and it was his first sale all evening. He punched in the numbers on his department phone and awaited the approval code. His gaze flicked up at Rob and the smile disappeared. "I'm sorry, sir. Your card's been declined."

"That can't be..." Right. Stormy took half the checking account and he had to decide what bills to pay. His Wards card was on the lower end of the priority list. He shook his head. "I'll go take care of it. Thanks anyway."

Rob hustled from the department before the kid offered to hold the table-saw until he found cash.

Like he needed a new saw. Could this evening get any worse?

"Glad to see you again, Rob." Glenda.

He paused and knew it was a mistake.

"How about a cup of coffee at the Burger King? Bet you've got time to kill and maybe we could talk." Her smile bordered on eager.

Rob shook his head. Perhaps too vehemently. He wasn't into confiding, and he certainly wouldn't pick Glenda as his confidant. Besides, whether Stormy was in Greentown or Kokomo, he was still a married man. "Thanks anyway. I'm heading home. Don't want to be late." Let her wonder what he meant by that.

"Sure, okay. But if you change your mind, call me. Bet it gets lonely."

How did she know? Did Stormy tell anyone? Was it a lucky guess? Denials would appear as too much protesting.

"Bye, Glenda." He made a beeline for his exit.

An hour later he was in his garage. He'd changed into his grubbies and discovered plans for a different cabinet he'd wanted to make, yet never carved the time. With his tools and wood all laid out, he started. The effort soothed his mind. He let go of the pain of being without Sunny while WLS played over his radio. Bill Bailey kept the music coming, mostly the top forty hits—"ABC" by the *Jackson Five* and "Everything is Beautiful" by Ray Stevens. But "American Woman/ No Sugar Tonight" by the *Guess Who* stung. He should've switched the dumb thing off. Instead, he wallowed. "Turn Back the Hands of Time" stabbed a little harder, but he kept working, trying to ignore the words. Then the DJ cued a blast from the past. Out of the blue.

The opening strains to "Stormy" sounded, and Rob's vision glazed with moisture. He ran his forearm over his eyes and blinked to clear them before lining up his cut. The board rested against the brace and he lowered the blade.

The shock hit him before the pain. Blood spattered and he held up his hand to see he'd nipped the tips of his left index and middle fingers.

Rob searched for a clean cloth to stanch the flow while holding his left hand with his right. Nothing.

He fumbled with the doorknob, finally getting to the kitchen where he grabbed the first towel he found before swiping his keys from the hook and stumbling to the car.

Driving would be a challenge, but he knew he'd better get some stitches. Howard County Community Hospital would be closest. He just hoped he could hold it together until he arrived. If Stormy were here, she'd be taking care of him. But if she were here, he wouldn't have gotten careless when her song played.

After he parked in the lot, he wasn't sure he'd make it to the entrance. The shock had eased. Now his hand throbbed, and the sight of his blood oozing through the towel made him wobble.

At the emergency front desk, the night nurse met him coming in and helped him to a wheelchair. He started to protest but getting off his feet wasn't a bad idea. She rolled him straight back and called for the doctor.

When they unwrapped his hand, Rob noticed their faces relax. They must have imagined worse, which made him feel better.

"So, Mr. Crawford, what happened?"

"I was working with my saw. Didn't move my fingers out of the way. Should've had my guard in place but got distracted. Stupid, I know." No need to divulge just how stupid.

"Agreed. When was your last tetanus shot?"

Rob hadn't a clue. He shrugged.

"We'll add that to the list. You'll need stitches." This doctor was all business. Which was fine. Rob wasn't in the mood for chitchat. He was too busy berating himself as it was.

Doctor Mendelssohn left his nurse to wash the wound before he returned to sew the fingers. "You'll probably lose your nails on those digits, but they'll grow back."

"Great."

"Is there anyone we can call for you?" The nurse had her sympathetic expression down to a T.

Rob shook his head. "No, thanks."

"Then we'll need you rest here until we're sure you won't faint on the way to your car. I'll grab you some juice and crackers." Miss Nurse strode from the room.

"You'll want to go straight home. Keep your hand elevated. It'll help. The shot will wear off before morning.

Here's a prescription for pain medication. You're going to need it. I'll get you enough pills to get you through until you can send someone to get it filled." Dr. Mendelssohn put in the last stitch as the nurse reappeared with her snack tray. They traded places and she wrapped up his injury until his hand appeared mummified.

The doctor scribbled out the prescription and handed it to Rob before heading out. He turned at the door.

"Be careful driving."

Rob saluted with his good hand, and the doctor left for the next patient.

"Make sure you drink all the juice. I'll take your insurance card now and get your bill written up. Be right back." She flashed her big-teeth smile and bounced from the room.

Rob lay against the exam bed pillow. Great. Another expense he hadn't planned on, and not enough cash in his wallet to cover. How would he take care of this?

Click here to order your copy of Stormy. https://www.amazon.com/dp/B09BKMGXGK

Or scan here.

Made in the USA
Monee, IL
29 December 2025

36827634R00152